CRITICS RAVE ABOUT [illegible]

DIVINE F[illegible]

[Jackson] "has a wonderful [illegible] guage. There are some great connections with previous books and a surprise at the end." —*RT Book Reviews*

A CURIOUS AFFAIR

"For a very different type of murder mystery and some very quirky characters and a twist at the end you won't see coming . . . in this tale, curiosity does not kill the cat!"

—Romance Reviews Today

DIVINE NIGHT

"Not to be read quickly, Jackson's latest is closely connected to the two previous Divine stories. . . . This is an excellent addition to this series." —*RT Book Reviews*

WRIT ON WATER

"An intriguing mix of mystery and romance, with shadings of the paranormal, this is a story that pulls you in."

—*RT Book Reviews*

DIVINE MADNESS

"This tale isn't your everyday, lighthearted romance . . . . Melanie Jackson takes an interesting approach to this tale, using historical figures with mysterious lives."

—Romance Reviews Today

DIVINE FIRE

"Jackson pens a sumptuous modern gothic. . . . Fans of solid love stories like those of Laurell K. Hamilton will enjoy Jackson's tale, which readers will devour in one sitting, then wait hungrily for the next installment."

—*Booklist*

THE SAINT

"This visit to the 'wild side' is wonderfully imaginative and action-packed. . . . [A] fascinating tale."

—*RT Book Reviews*

MORE PRAISE FOR MELANIE JACKSON!

THE MASTER

"Readers . . . will not be disappointed. Her ability to create a complicated world is astounding with this installment, which includes heartwarming moments, suspense and mystery sprinkled with humor. An excellent read."

—*RT Book Reviews*

STILL LIFE

"The latest walk on the 'Wildside' is a wonderful romantic fantasy that adds new elements that brilliantly fit and enhance the existing Jackson mythos. . . . Action-packed."

—*Midwest Book Review*

THE COURIER

"The author's imagination and untouchable world-building continue to shine. . . . [An] outstanding and involved novel."

—*RT Book Reviews*

OUTSIDERS

"Melanie Jackson is a talent to watch. She deftly combines romance with fantasy and paranormal elements to create a spellbinding adventure."

—WritersWrite.com

TRAVELER

"Jackson often pushes the boundaries of paranormal romance, and this . . . is no exception."

—*Booklist*

THE SELKIE

"Part fantasy, part dream and wholly bewitching, *The Selkie* . . . [blends] whimsy and folklore into a sensual tale of love and magic."

—*RT Book Reviews*

THE ARRIVAL

"*Bonjour*!" called a softer, sweeter version of the voice that had hailed him earlier.

Dark hair had slipped its modest arisaid and now whipped about in the wind. The lady skidded to a halt only a handsbreadth from Colin's outstretched arms. Delightful eyes, the color of Highland whisky, moved over his face. Colin noted that though the woman wore a traditional leine, the delicately pleated garment was fashioned of silk rather than linen or wool, and it draped most gracefully over her bosom. Her embroidered kirtle was long, but not so great a length as to drag upon the ground—a sensible precaution as the rough terrain would quickly shred the delicate material.

She said breathlessly: "We did not expect you so soon."

"We've had favorable winds," Colin answered. "Colin Mortlock, at your service, Mistress Balfour—your new master of the gowff." And so much more.

Other books by Melanie Jackson:

DIVINE FANTASY
A CURIOUS AFFAIR
DIVINE NIGHT
WRIT ON WATER
DIVINE MADNESS
THE SAINT
THE MASTER
DIVINE FIRE
STILL LIFE
THE COURIER
OUTSIDERS
TRAVELER
THE SELKIE
DOMINION
BELLE
AMARANTHA
NIGHT VISITOR
MANON
IONA

The Night Side

Melanie Jackson

LOVE SPELL NEW YORK CITY

For my cousin, Sarah—what a lovely person she has grown to be.

LOVE SPELL®

August 2009

Published by

Dorchester Publishing Co., Inc.
200 Madison Avenue
New York, NY 10016

ISBN 10: 0-505-52804-5
ISBN 13: 978-0-505-52804-9
E-ISBN: 978-1-4285-0719-7

Printed in the United States of America.

10 9 8 7 6 5 4 3 2 1

The Night Side

The king sits in Dumfermline town.
Drinking the blude-red wine: O
'O whare will I get a skeely skipper,
To sail this new ship of mine?

—*"The Ballad of Sir Patrick Spens"*

PROLOGUE

Colin Mortlock sat at his table in his private study in York and read the messenger's missive a second time, trying in vain to make some sense of it. It was not that the letter's words weren't straightforward enough. The sentences were all simple statements and arranged logically, though penned in a very ill fist by someone obviously not often given to scrivacious pastimes.

The difficulty came with comprehending the context in which the message was written, and in certain absences of comment when some remark would have been normal.

Colin shook his head. He did not for one instant suppose that the brief interregnum in the north isles had made the new laird of Skye any less intelligent or capable of looking after the clan's demesnes than his ruthless and half-insane father and uncle had been before him. But Colin was still uncertain of precisely what the MacLeods wanted of *him* in this instance, and whether he should be wary of answering this intriguing familial summons.

The letter even began interestingly, using both Latin and the Christian calendar. This was certainly a change from the style of the previous laird, who had disowned Colin's mother when she married a Catholic sassun and moved south to the lands of the enemy English—*might the French pox rot them!*

> *To our cousin, Cailean Mortlach, at the season of the mellowing moon, in the year of our Lord 1544*
>
> *Greeting Dear Kinsman!*
>
> *Sorrowful tidings we have had of the death of the fifth king of the Scots called Seumas. Many brave lives and things more precious were lost at the rout of Solway Moss. But such must be expected after the dissolution of the treaty of perpetual peace.*

The Treaty of Perpetual Peace designed by Henry VII and James IV had lasted a mere eleven years and had ended at Flodden Field when the flowers of Scottish nobility—and King Henry's own brother-in-law—were all mowed down in one bloody battle. The Solway Moss debacle was rather more recent. It was an exaggeration to say that there had been heavy casualties at Solway, unless one counted the death of pride among the fatalities. If that were added to the score, then the battle's losses reached tragic proportions—at least among those who hadn't been there.

The facts of the battle were either amusing or horrible, depending on which side you were on. A great many border Scots had been cheerfully captured by the stunned English army, apparently deeming arrest by the sassuns preferable to fighting under a Scottish king whom they believed had persecuted them in their own land.

Colin shook his head again, this time in bemusement. Such a scandal would have been unthinkable under James IV. Colin did not know what had happened to Scottish pride. The Scots, Highland and Low, had always hated the English. The dislike was obligatory, part of the received truth that arrived with baptism in the cold peaty water, and possibly through a mother's milk. So this event at Solway was unique in Scottish history. All Colin could imagine was that this Lowland enthusiasm for the English monarch must have stemmed from what had happened at the battle of Soom Moss that previous year.

At Soom Moss, King Henry—sometimes called Harry—had taken twenty-one Scottish nobles as prisoners, fed them a Christmas feast and then let them go again. It was one of the eighth Henry's splendid gestures—less excessive than his Cloth of Gold feast with the French monarch, but still quite memorable to the Scots. There had not been such a fete between the two opponents since the Yuletide wedding of Alexander to Margaret, when Henry III had put on a resplendent Christmas feast and the guests drank three tons of wine in five days. The Archbishop of York had provided 600 oxen, drawn and quartered, some of which had come from Colin's ancestor at Pemberton Fells. Even then, his family had been in faithful service to the crown.

Colin snorted and then allowed himself a small smile. He might sometimes be baffled by the Scot Lowlanders, but he knew the northern Gaels' minds very well. They were very like the Norse mind, and this show of wealth and magnanimity on the part of the

English king, while popular with the Lowland masses, doubtless infuriated the MacLeods and many other Highland lairds. They hated their king for allowing the shameful incident to have come about. They believed that, had James lived among his men, as a good king should—fought side by side with his troops as the lairds did—then his men would not have indulged in such cowardly behavior, and all of Scotland would not have been disgraced and left in the hands of an infant queen and her inept mother.

No, if the new Laird of the Isles was actually sorrowful at James's passing into the afterlife a few weeks after this disgraceful battle, it was the first that Colin or anyone else knew of it. There had been only an uneasy truce between James and the Lairds of the Isles, with the current times leaning more often toward the side of unease than truce. Solway would have been the final stone in the cairn of their faltering relations. James should probably be happy that he was already dead. Things were about to get ugly in the North. Civil war was possible.

Colin most certainly didn't envy Scotland's regent, Mary of Guise, the task of knitting up the unraveled politics of the North and in the Isles for the infant queen. It would take great skill and cleverness to keep the throne for her daughter. Fortunately, this was not his problem anymore.

Colin went back to his letter, squinting at the nearly illegible text.

> *Sir Michael Balfour and his thirty sons were also recently lost to this world. There remains only his daughter and a young nephew at* Noltland Castle *near our kin on* Orkney.

This was where the letter began to get obscure. Everyone had heard the amazing tale of the deaths of Michael Balfour and all of his sons in one battle—leaving only his daughter as heiress to his fortune and a distant kinsman, a lad of twelve, to inherit the title—but Colin had not the slightest notion what it had to do with the MacLeods of Skye. MacLeods were descended from the Vikings who had settled in Orkney, but Noltland was now in the territory of the Keiths and Gunns and MacKays, and it was very unlikely that these others were going to stand aside if the MacLeods made a grab for power.

"Cousin, cousin, what do you intend?" Without indulging in offensive pridefulness, Colin knew that he was accounted as being an astute man. But though he could sense that his cousin was steeped in some purpose in regards to Noltland, what this project might be, Colin could not yet see.

Not truly expecting enlightenment, Colin read on.

> *Reports of a favorable nature have reached us, and we have need of you in Orkney. You must for a time forsake the lands of this King Eachann and return home at once to Dunnvegan.*
>
> *We hope that you have not forgotten your* gowff.
>
> *Yrs with great affection,*
> *Alasdair, MacLeod of the MacLeods*

Now, this was the puzzler, the contradiction that could not be explained. The MacLeods were panophobic of all foreigners—which, sadly, Colin was considered to be, in spite of his mother being sister to the last laird. And this reference to his boyhood training in the game of golf—a sport he actually detested and played most ill—was frankly beyond his comprehension. He could only conclude that one or the other of them was suffering from a distemperature of the mind.

It would be reassuring to know that it was the MacLeod whose humor and reason were so disturbed, but unhappily Colin could not place his oath upon the ailment resting with his Scottish cousin. His own nature had lately been excessively troubled by odd humors, which he suspected had begun affecting his judgment.

Colin had for a long while been vaguely unhappy and restless, and he knew that his night wanderings along the long corridors of the east wing were the cause for some concern among his small entourage at Pemberton Fells, and for restlessness among the ghosts. Even his faithful MacJannet was worried about what these noctambulations might mean.

The reasons for his discontent were not easily explained to his people. Certainly, he led a lonely existence and was often long from home and in the company of hostile strangers. But that had not been his difficulty lately, for he was always at home. He had, in fact, had a surfeit of his beautiful but empty estate. And, left to his own devices, he had lately had begun to see himself as a human failure. He had no real friends, aside from the faithful MacJannet, no lover anymore, not even a wife or thankless child.

By all common measures, he was a success. His father had done well in his chosen calling, as had his father before him, finding favor with both Henry VII and Henry VIII—and being granted extensive tracts of land for information about enemies they had gathered for these monarchs. Colin, too, had served in the capacity of eyes and ears for the crown, and been rewarded for his time in the Netherlands and France.

But this was no longer enough for him. King Harry was growing old, and his political embrace of the Protestant faith had left a country still very uneasy with its religion and monarch. No one had much confidence that the sickly Edward would survive to take his father's place—and that left the Catholic Mary as next in line for the throne. Already there was talk of it. Many in the North actually supported her claim. Colin knew this because he was supposed to be of the True Faith, as his father and grandfather had also been, and he wisely kept abreast of these affairs.

Rencontre seemed inevitable now. Colin did not doubt that he would survive the political machinations of those who struggled for the throne—after all, he knew far too much about everyone in power for any faction to risk touching him—but still, he did not relish the lonely, wasteful fight ahead. Religious struggles were so futile and uninteresting. They lacked subtlety, something that appealed to him when he stooped to indulge in politics of his own.

And now there had come this letter of rapprochement from his kin in Skye. A letter that was full of intriguing references to many strange events and people. Might this not lend purpose to a life that had lately been lacking in stimulation?

Colin drummed his fingers on the arm of his chair. It was madness. He shouldn't even be thinking about accepting the summons. The suggested journey smacked of potential grave danger and certain discomfort as he traveled roads that went from bad to nonexistent. He recalled little of his childhood visit to the Orkneys beyond vast, disagreeable expanses of gray rock, stinging midges and biting ponies. There were no roads. And the region's politics were certainly among the bloodiest and least subtle in Scotland. It was for this reason that his father had never permitted him or his mother to return to the Isles once her homicidal brother had become chief.

Still, was the potential for swift death not better than slow suffocation from boredom? And for an intelligencer, born as well as bred, there really wasn't another choice, was there?

The only thing that might hold him back was the castle itself. One other childhood memory he had done his best to repress was of being terrorized by ghosts, unhappy shadows overseeing the memories of their earthly demise. There were dozens of them from the dank dungeons to the highest room in the tower, all of them hostile and forlorn. His mother, who could also see these apparitions and lived in terror of being named a witch for the affliction, had assured him that the sad perseverations could not harm him, but he had never been convinced that the ghosts agreed. And since most of them had good reason to hate MacLeods, he was not reassured of their benevolent intentions.

Still, he was a man grown and much better able to handle the dead. Had he not learned to use these often-instructive perseverations as tools in his investigations?

"What say you, Brother Stephen?" he asked the sad shadow of a monk sitting in the corner of the library. Colin didn't truly expect an answer. Brother Stephen had no head. The poor wretch was the least informative ghost Colin had ever met. Not that he visited with many. The shades were stupid, as a rule, and interested only in their own downfalls. The best most could do was to replay their violent ends, thus naming their killers.

A decision reached, Colin rose to his feet and went to the door. He pulled it wide and addressed both the messenger who waited and his faithful factotum who lingered conveniently nearby.

"MacJannet, please begin preparations for travel. We will be going to Scotland."

Thomas MacJannet, well used to his master's peculiar fits and starts, did not even blink an eye at the command. He might well consider his master's plan a foolish enterprise, but he would never admit it before strangers. Such words would abort themselves, stillborn treason that would not be permitted spoken life. This was one reason Colin valued MacJannet above rubies.

Colin turned to the tall, blond lad who stood silently by the window. He supposed that they were kin of some sort, but the boy had not offered his genealogy and Colin had not asked for it.

"You may tell our cousin MacLeod that I shall join him as speedily as I am able."

The golden giant cracked a small smile. "The MacLeod will be best pleased tae hear it."

"One would certainly hope so," Colin muttered, as he retreated into his study and closed the door. "I know full well that this journey is going to be bloody uncomfortable."

But it would also be interesting—or so he hoped. And he was willing to suffer a great many inconveniences to his person if it brought some relief to his mind's endless tedium.

Ye Highlands, and ye Lawlands,
Oh where have you been?
They have slain the Earl of Murray,
And they layd him on the green.

—"*The Bonny Earl of Murray*"

Chapter One

"George, *cher*?" Mistress Frances Balfour enquired of her young cousin in the French tongue, which she was endeavoring to teach him. Her voice was raised slightly against the omnipresent wind. "Do you think it very wicked of us to be out playing *jeu de mail* so soon after my father's death?"

"*Jeu de mail*?" young George asked.

"*Gowff*," she translated, as she carefully lined up her shot on the sparse moor. The trick, she had soon learned after beginning play on the harsh heath, was to completely avoid the thistle hedges because the bristling thorns ripped open the leather balls and spilled out the feathers. Then the wind snatched the emptied sacks and whisked them away. Feathers could be replaced, but leather was scarce and expensive on Orkney now that the cattle was gone.

"Oh."

Frances frowned in concentration. "After all, it wasn't just Father who died, but my brothers as well—thirty of them."

"Well," the boy answered, considering, admiring his elder cousin's graceful yet forceful swing, which bunged those stubborn balls high into the air. "Most of them were only your half brothers. And we were barely familiar with any of them. In fact, I am not certain I recall all their names, so unacquainted were we. Anyhow, many were bastards, which you probably should not have known about anyway."

"True." And it was also true that she was secretly content to have not been well acquainted with them. The few siblings she had known were uniformly arrogant and prideful, and dismissive of her feelings and desires. Her father had been much the same. After he had sent her to a French convent against her mother's wishes, it would have been complete pretense to suggest that there had been any love left between father and daughter, or husband and wife—much less between unacquainted siblings.

Still, it seemed vaguely shameful that she felt so little grief at their passing when she had mourned so long the loss of her mother. However, the sad fact was that she felt much closer to this young cousin, who had also been orphaned at an early age and raised away from his home, than she ever had to her own brothers. She and George shared more than a love of games. They had an intimate understanding of loss, as well as an appreciation for the expensive fluctuations of Scottish politics and war.

As penitence for her lack of filial piety, she began listing her brothers' names, but reached a dead end at sibling twenty-four. Disappointed but unsurprised at her lack of recollection, she sighed and said: "King James even outlawed the game, you know, because it distracted men from serious things."

They both knew that she was speaking of the fourth James of Scotland and not the recently deceased king, the father to the infant queen.

"Nice shot," George complimented, preparing to address his own ball. "You are still a good club length from the cliff, too. Mayhap the birds will leave your ball alone this time. They must be very stupid creatures to not know the difference between a ball and an egg."

Frances nodded, watching anxiously as George began his swing. He had a tendency to throw his head up at the last moment and many of his balls went astray. It was her hope that the new Master of the Gowff would be able to cure him of this habit. As a female, it was not her place to correct his form.

Actually, though he needed a great deal of help and guidance, there was only so much that she could do to aid her young cousin in any aspect of life. She had no more experience at leading a clan than he did, and as little inclination for the job. All she had was money—and even that, only so she was told. She had not actually seen any of it. Had George been older they might have married, thus giving him the money needed to hire men to defend the tower. But as it was, he was too young to wed, and he would not take any money from her even if he had been confident of being able to control a band of mercenaries.

Also, it was an unfortunate fact that her dowry might be needed to bribe a suitable husband into defending their home, provided that one could be found. Supposedly they were under the regent's protection, but the seat of power was a long way away, with Mary de Guise probably very busy holding the throne for the infant Mary, and the MacKays, Keiths, Gunns, and MacLeods were very near. As long as the prize of her hand and fortune was still a possibility, Frances's rapacious neighbors seemed content to woo and not war. But that would all change when her time of mourning was up and she still refused them entrance to the castle, or if she were to become betrothed to someone else.

Unfortunately, it would also change if someone got impatient with her excuses. The most likely candidate for this dangerous irritation was the new MacLeod. Alasdair was ruthless and quite anxious to consolidate his power at this time when the new Scottish government was distracted by affairs in the South, and consequently he was pressing her hard.

Her unease had grown daily since the laird's last visit, and she was now often awake in the dark hours pondering their situation, and how she might escape marriage. So often was she awake in the dark hours that she had developed a routine of opening her shutters and watching the moon track across the sky. It was after she had started doing this that she had noticed some poor hound howling in the night, disturbing her lonely vigil at her bedchamber window. It began every night after the moon set and continued until dawn. It was not a comforting sound, bringing to mind as it did the tale of the spectral hound that was supposed to live in the dark hole beneath the main staircase. The Bokey hound, as it was called, always appeared whenever a Balfour was supposed to die. She had never seen the beast, but many of the castle inhabitants swore it had been about the night her father had died.

George brought his club down hard, spraying Frances with sand. As with his previous ball, George's latest efforts lofted it off of the true course and out toward the sea.

"Damnation," he muttered. "I think perhaps we need to play as they do in the Lowlands."

"And how is that?" Frances asked, dusting away sand as George pulled another ball from his bulging sporran and dropped it upon the ground.

"Well, you are supposed to take a nip of whisky at the start of each hole. It keeps you warm and limber when you have to get things out of the water. Nor do you mind as much when you lose your ball." A small dimple appeared in his cheek.

"They don't have cliffs in the Lowlands," Frances said repressively. She did not care for whisky and did not want her cousin to develop a taste for it. Many who came to like the *uisge beatha* at a young age were immoderate in its consumption, and it made them drunken imbeciles in adulthood.

"Fortunate Lowlanders," George grumbled. "They may also play *futbawe*."

Frances began to tell him that football was a vulgar sport for common people. Then, seeing him again taking an improper stance and unable to resist any longer, she added: "Try keeping your head down when you swing and do step a little closer to the ball."

George swung a second time. The club connected with a satisfying *whap* and the ball shot over the thistle hedge.

"There it goes!" he said excitedly.

"*Oui*, into the great sand pile."

George's face fell. "Do you truly think so?"

"*Je regrette*, but yes. Do not worry, though. You may borrow my bunkard club."

"Thank you," George replied, going to pick up their

bag. Frances had devised it out of a pannier and a strap so it was not so burdensome to carry their different clubs about.

Both cousins looked around carefully before leaving the shelter of the castle wall and venturing out to the cliffs. There were three sound reasons for this caution. The first was the stinging midges that rushed inland any time the wind abated. Secondly, there was always the possible danger of kidnap by their neighbors. And the third cause, which was by far the most pressing reason for caution, was to avoid a meeting with Tearlach MacAdam.

Tearlach, the mad broganeer of Noltland, was a castle fixture. He had been around from the beginning of Frances's time here, and there was no apparent hope of convincing him to go elsewhere to live. He had been a boon companion of the last Balfour and was, the castle staff assumed, basically well-intentioned in his infliction of company upon the new laird and heiress.

But the two cousins did not care for him. George disliked him because of his bagpipes, and Frances because she found Tearlach's often-obscene abstrusities impossible to tolerate. Frances called him *homo absurdian* when others could not hear, a bit of ill-natured name-calling that she did not direct at any other residents, however annoying their habits.

Possibly this malice was reserved for the broganeer because Tearlach also had the infuriating habit of stripping down to a dirk and boots and then wandering about so that he might "air his pores." He would then take up his bagpipes—which he played so very ill that others referred to him as *Agonybags*—and join George and Frances out on the heath as they attempted to play golf.

His nakedness and awful playing were equally hard to endure.

And of course, though no one else realized it, Frances knew his talk of the healthful benefits of airing the pores was all a lie. She had seen the wicked glint in his eye when he watched her. Like most Scots, he probably thought her a woman of low morals because she wore the forbidden silk of France and played a man's sport—and played it well. She thought it stupid to equate female competence with immorality, but the church had proclaimed it truth, so truth it now was.

Tearlach claimed, when pressed by an angry George, that he followed Frances about so that he would be at hand to protect her if any enemy tried to seize upon her while they were outside the castle walls. Frances did not believe this, either. A naked man armed with only a dirk would be of no assistance in a battle—unless, of course, the glimpse of his bony shanks had the effect of a Medusa upon a raider. Frances's first glimpse had very nearly paralyzed *her*. The thought of facing such male ugliness on her wedding night was enough to end all aspirations of marriage. She could only hope that other men were less repulsive.

No, Tearlach had other reasons for following her and George, and she had soon discovered that they were not polite.

Though some effort had been made to preserve her innocence when she returned from the convent, Noltland was a small castle and its occupants not immune to the sin of gossip. Frances soon discovered Tearlach's unsavory history. He had, in his youth, been a rather dissolute person and a great fancier of those of lower classes who wore the kirtle. Doubtless that was why he had been such fast friends with her father.

There was no sin of the flesh to which he had not turned a hand—or worse body part.

Now that Tearlach was old and unable to "dance a mattress jig," as he so colorfully phrased it, he was in the habit of following young people about in the hope of catching them in the act. He believed it would reanimate his "hanging Jimmie." His organ had been useless since the old laird's death. Guilt at his own survival, when all others had died at Flodden, had appeared in the form of a grievous ghost, a specter that no one except Tearlach could see. The vengeful spirit had removed his ability to copulate. He was desperate to try anything that would again make him able to enjoy a sexual connection with a woman.

Unfortunately, when he could not find anyone to watch, he liked to ask personal questions. The coarse people who lived at Noltland thought this amusing and did not understand Frances's distaste for the man. They excused his behavior because he was one of the few men left near the castle and a piper. They asked: Was he not as impotent as a capon? Why should she fear him and try to escape his watchful eye? She did not have a lover who she wished to keep secret, did she?

He might well be a human capon, but impotent or not, she did not like the man. And now that she had relearned more of her native tongue and comprehended the true meaning of his words, the thought of some of Tearlach's impudent inquiries caused a flush to mantle her cheeks. So angry and embarrassed had they made her that she had, in a fit of rage, accepted the visiting MacLeod's offer to supply her with a young—*and strong*—Master of the Gowff who might serve as her guard and protector when she and George went out to play.

She had also finally told Tearlach that if he again raised the subject of bollocks, pillicocks or membrum virile in her presence she would have him whipped. Further, she had told him that his air-bathing must be done away from her or she would see that his hanging Jimmie was castrated from his body, making him a capon in fact and not metaphor. She would have said more, but the man was fouler than the limitations of the English language would allow her to express. All of her available insults were agricultural, and one could not very well ask what sheep had spawned him without being insulting to perfectly innocent animals that provided them with much-needed wool.

Unfortunately, these threats to his person had only increased Tearlach's interest in her, and until the new Master of Gowff arrived, she did not know whom she could get to beat or castrate the privy-mouthed broganeer. George was too young, and the other castle inhabitants regarded him as some sort of combination of buffoon and lucky talisman—and Frances was not yet prepared to welcome any of her suitors into Noltland's affairs, though she did not doubt that any one of them would be only too pleased to commit acts of violence on her behalf. That was the sort of men they were.

"Are you quite well, Frances?" George asked solicitously, seeing the heat that flushed his cousin's cheeks. "The sun is not too warm for you? If you are feeling *howish* we may retire."

"*Non.* I am well, *mon cousin.* Let us play on through before we are discovered. Then you must go to practice archery and I must go to my loom."

George grimaced and they exchanged a sympathetic look. Neither of the cousins cared for these assigned chores, but in the present circumstances they were necessary and one could only shirk so much of one's duty in one day.

"Do you know, Frances, I truly wish that my father or grandfather was still alive."

"Why, *petit*? Other than the obvious reasons, of course."

"Because then I needn't become a laird, and practice archery, and live in this drafty old castle. I could have remained in the South and attended university."

Frances sighed in sympathy. "I understand, *mon cousin*. I understand. I do not like living in a drafty castle either. But be of good cheer. Our new Master of the Gowff shall be here soon. That will be pleasant, *oui*?"

In behint yon auld fail dyke,
I wot there lies a new slain knight;
And naebody kens that he lies there,
But his hawk, his hound, and lady fair.

—*"The Twa Corbies"*

Chapter Two

Colin entered Dunnvegan through the sea gate that waited silently at the end of the deep fosse where the lightly-crewed galley was moored. Given a torch by one of the sailors, he was sent up alone to the castle gate, a matter he and the silent MacJannet found most curious and even a bit alarming. But ever a slave to curiosity, he waved his concerned servant away and took the long, dark climb up the curving, rough-hewn stairs at a brisk pace without checking to see that his sword and dirk were still in place beneath his cloak. An angry ghost with a cloven head and a bloody hollow in his chest where a heart once resided followed him closely. Barely ashore and already the ghosts were gathering.

It struck Colin as more than odd that he was not to receive the welcome of the prodigal son, Highland hospitality being what it was. But except for a lone man with a lantern at the top of the stairs, there was no one living to greet him as he stepped into the castle.

So, his visit was clandestine. This added another layer to the mystery of his summons.

His nocturnal welcomer—if such was the man—was elderly and seemed to understand only Norwegian. Fortunately, Colin had a facility for language and still retained his native tongues of Gaelic and Norse, so he was able to answer the garbled greeting politely. This earned him a certain level of approval, though not so much approbation as to cause the oldster to actually smile upon him.

They traveled down a deserted corridor, which felt especially cold and dark in its loneliness, though the evening was not at all chill and the torch shed adequate heat and light about them as they walked. Perhaps it was the unhappy ghost that cast a pall over the passage.

The old man knocked once upon a heavy, iron-strapped door, and then opened it without a word. He jerked his head, indicating that Colin should enter, and then backed away, taking his lantern and the ghost with him.

Colin wondered if perhaps the man's tongue had been torn out. If so, by whom? Probably not Alasdair. His cousin was capable of cruelty, but he tended to simply kill people who annoyed him. He hadn't the patience for torture that his father had possessed.

The room beyond was well lit by a large fire burning on the deep flags and several torches set in sconces in the wall. There were two large wooden chairs pulled up near the hearth, neither presently occupied. Above the hearth was a stone carving, a bull's head embedded into the rock of the wall. As art, it was not appealing. As a reminder of the MacLeod's absolute power within the castle walls, it was most effective.

Heavy footsteps approached, and Colin turned to greet his cousin. He had only a dim memory of his time with Alasdair, but the memorable features of a prematurely stern face and the scar at the corner of his left eye were easily recalled.

"Greetings, cousin," Colin said softly, watching as the big man closed the heavy door behind him and set a bolt in place. It was confirmation of the MacLeod's desire for privacy, had Colin truly possessed any doubts about the nature of his visit.

"Health upon you, cousin," Alasdair responded, finally smiling. "You had a good journey?"

"Favorable winds all the way." Colin shed his cloak, partly because the room was warm. Partly to be better able to reach his sword.

"That is a good omen. Freya is with us."

The two men approached one another and embraced cautiously. Both were armed with swords and dirks and had *sgian dubhs* tucked into their boots. Thanks to their other silver ornamentation, they clanked when they took one another's arms.

"I am glad that life among the sassuns did not stunt your growth overmuch," Alasdair said.

Colin found himself glad of his extra inches. Though he did not expect to be molested, and was counted a deadly swordsman thanks to his ambidexterity, he had come as a near-stranger to a land of giants, and it would not do to be the only dwarf among these chesty, arrogant leviathans.

"Let me pour you a glass of the Lowland wine they tell me you favor, and tell you why I have brought you here when winter is approaching."

"Certainly," Colin said with a smile, but inside he was lifting a brow. Such haste and lack of pretense—

even with a stranger—was unseemly, and a violation of all manners and protocol. To use it with a family member only just returned home was unheard of. The situation had to be most urgent and secretive.

That usually meant that someone—typically the laird—was in circumstances inimical to his health and or power. Someone or something had to be threatening the new MacLeod. And whatever it was, it couldn't be removed with a battle-axe or broadsword, or else Colin felt sure it would have been dealt with already.

This knowledge, rather than providing a sensible notice of alarm, only served to further whet Colin's curiosity.

"We are the sons of Frey," Alasdair began, handing Colin a goblet and waving him toward a chair. The chalice was made of silver, not gold, but beautifully crafted. Most MacLeods favored silver because of their connection to—and fear of—the faeries. "All MacLeods have a blood tie that cannot be broken. There are neither mountains so hard, nor seas so vast that these bonds will ever be sundered. I reckon my kin to the hundredth degree."

He drank. The MacLeod managed not to shudder at the wine, but plainly he did not care for it. He probably considered it an effete, womanly drink.

Colin sipped politely to acknowledge the toast, enjoying the fine Madeira his cousin despised. He waited while Alasdair took his seat. He tactfully did not mention his mother being cast out of the bosom of her family for marrying a foreigner and also for having The Sight. Perhaps the ties of blood "to the hundredth degree" did not extend to the females of the line, especially if they were suspected of being witches.

"You have heard of the fate of Michael Balfour,"

Alasdair said abruptly, either abandoning his appeal for clan loyalty or else feeling he had said enough on the subject. MacLeods were not sentimentalists.

"Indeed. The story is already legend. There are Balfours in the South and they can speak of little else."

"Thanks to this stupid war, this Balfour is survived by only two relatives. The lad's name is *Seoras*."

Colin mentally translated: the boy was named George.

"The other is the daughter of Michael, one Frances Balfour. She is the heiress of Noltland Castle and all its lands and monies. She's a comely wench, too, even though she has the look and manner of the French about her."

Colin stared carefully at his cousin's face, wishing that he could see it without the tricky wavering of the firelight. Alasdair's tone and the use of the girl's sassun name suggested that he was either very wary, very respectful, or very interested in this heiress. The fact that he had commented on her attractiveness was interesting. Heiresses could be missing limbs and teeth, as ugly as a Highland sheep with mange, and still be considered desirable. Consequently, their appearance was not often dwelled upon.

"Aye?" he prompted, wishing more detail.

"At present she is well enough protected by her father's remaining men. Thank goodness the braggart was not so stupid as to leave the castle completely unguarded or the wolves would be upon her." Alasdair shrugged, looking more annoyed than gratified in the dead laird's foresight, in spite of his grudging words of praise. "However, if she does not choose a suitor soon, I fear that come winter some of her neighbors may attempt to take the castle and force her into marriage."

"Are any of them likely to gain her cousin's consent to wed? Or the regent's?" Colin asked carefully.

"*Seoras* is but a boy. 'Twould be an easy matter to get rid of him. And the regent . . ." Alasdair shrugged. "Well, Mary of Guise is very far from here. Busy as she is in the Lowlands defending herself from the sassuns, all could be accomplished before she was even aware of events."

"True. The regent is presently much occupied with things in the South." Colin's own tone was bland. He didn't mention John Knox and the troublesome reformers who had begun to spread their militant religion over the land. It was not just witches who were burning.

"Aye, she's getting a rough wooing from the English and their cursed religion—a pox on them all!"

Colin took another sip of sweet wine. "So, being that the regent is elsewhere occupied, out of the goodness of your heart you wish to offer the Balfours some protection?" he suggested.

"Aye—protection." Alasdair smiled happily at this tactful, though mostly untrue, summation. "The only thing that will make Noltland safe is for the girl to marry someone strong enough to hold the keep."

"And to keep *Seoras* safe until he is grown and can look after the keep himself?" Colin suggested.

Alsdair shrugged again, but said, "Well, aye. Of course, if she wanted him kept. And if the Bokey hound does not claim him."

Colin blinked at the implied ruthlessness and then asked: "Bokey hound?"

"Aye, a fiend, a hound of Hell that howls when the laird is to die. They say the beast has been lately seen abroad." Alsdair actually looked a bit uneasy. He was a Christian, but only nominally, and his Viking roots were still firmly grounded in the world of vicious monsters and fearful alchemies.

"And this hound is going to kill the boy?" Colin found this tale of a hound to be rather convenient, and suspected it was an invention designed to terrorize either the MacLeod or the youngest Balfour. If the former, he had to wonder who at Noltland Castle had invented the tale. If the latter . . . well, that matter needed further cogitation. And though suspicious, Colin himself did not dismiss this wild tale out of hand. He had yet to see an actual hellhound, but he had seen enough other things that he did not rule out the possibility of one's existence.

"Well, perhaps it shall. Who knows what devilish beasties may do? But what of it? The lass will have no need of him once she is married. He would only be in the way of her own children," Alasdair pointed out with the ruthless logic for which he was famous.

Colin blinked again, and wondered if Frances Balfour could be anywhere near as cold-blooded as Alasdair seemed to think her. "And you have approached the girl with your offer of protection?"

"Aye—and the stubborn lass won't have me! She says she is still mourning her father and brothers and isn't prepared to wed anyone until the year is out."

"That is not unreasonable, surely," Colin suggested. "She did lose thirty-one of her family after all."

"Aye—aye! But they were Balfours—just bags of prideful wind. How sad could she be?"

Deciding to be direct, Colin asked: "And my role in this affair is to be what? An emissary to plead your case to Mistress Balfour?"

"Nay. 'Twould do no good. I've had emissaries aplenty there and gone myself. I even offered her the choice of my kinsmen who would take her to wife—though why she would want another when I am willing to wed her is beyond all kenning."

Colin, noted for his tact and delicate diplomacies, did not comment.

"What I need, cousin," the MacLeod went on. "Well, I need someone inside the castle. Someone who can earn her trust—someone to persuade her that the MacLeods are not greedy and cruel, and that she should trust me."

The irony of this request did not seem to present itself to the MacLeod, who doubtless considered himself to be only normally ambitious and merely firm in his dealings rather than merciless.

"I see. And I am to be that person?" Colin asked. "But why? Surely there is some other who could do this."

Alasdair shook his head. "You are dark like her father and a Lowlander as well. Mayhap that will lead to some liking. She does not seem to care for blond men." Alasdair did not appear concerned with the fact that his proposed bride did not favor his golden looks. "Also, you have skills as an intelligencer. You Mortlocks have always been subtle and sneaky."

That was true, though Colin rather thought of himself as being less devious than perceptive. "And MacLeods were always as stubborn and unbending as steel," he muttered in the English tongue. He found that he was beginning to feel very sorry for this unknown Frances Balfour. A determined MacLeod was a pitiless thing indeed.

"How do you suggest inserting me into the household?" he finally asked. "Or is this for me to plan?"

"Well, cousin, there is the beauty of it. The girl has spent much of her time in the Lowlands and France, and she has acquired a taste for gowff. You are a Lowlander, too. It will serve in this instance."

Somehow this sounded vaguely insulting, but Colin let the matter pass. All Highlanders and islanders had low opinions of those who dwelt in the Borders and the sassun lands beyond.

The rest of the plan, however, was too ridiculous to let go without comment. "Alasdair, this is a preposterous and unsensible notion. And dishonest," Colin added scrupulously, though he knew the argument would fall on deaf ears. "What will she care about my being a sassun Lowlander? There are better ways to go about this wooing. Send her some tributes. Or let her go to the MacKays."

"Now, laddie, don't say that! She is likely to be my future bride—if I can get rid of that MacDonnell wench my father plighted me to. I must keep her safe until she comes to her senses. I could lay siege to Noltland, but she would not like it—and the bloody MacKays would likely be there, too. And if there are MacKays, then there will soon be Gunns. This is a much better plan—much less wasteful. You will soon come to be friends with the girl, convince her that she and the boy need my protection. And later, if she remains stubborn about marriage, you can open the gates for me and let my men in." The treacherous betrayal of his hostess was suggested casually.

Colin reminded himself that, while he had been raised with the chivalric tales of love, the Norse had no such romantic notions to hamper them. Expediency was the order of the day.

For a moment he made no comment, choosing to

sip his wine and reflect carefully. Finally he asked: "Are the MacKays and the Gunns still at war?"

"Are the MacDonalds still the stinking spawn of the devil?" Alasdair asked rhetorically. "Of course the MacKays and Gunns are at war!"

"And the Keiths?" Colin asked.

"Still murderous bastards, every one of them," his cousin declared with a touch of pride, reminding Colin of the fact that he was related to Keiths on his mother's side.

"Hm . . . You know that this may prove a tricky undertaking. Noltland, that is a tower fortress, yes? The most northerly one in Scotland, if I recall, and right upon the sea. It is also completely surrounded on land by MacKays and Gunns and Keiths. And the Bishop of Orkney also has an interest there, has he not? Besides that, you know it will be cold and boring—and worse come winter."

"Aye—but 'tis not so ill a place for all that it is on the sea. I hear that they have wrights, carpenters, smiths, one damned clever armourer—even a magicked *seannachie* who plays strange songs upon the pipes. And there must be some fighting men left as well, as their pikes are seen up on the battlements, changing at regular hours. And there is also sport to be had—good otter-hunting—and there are some cattle to bleed in the cold season so none shall go hungry."

"Aye, and they also have constant war with their neighbors, and perishing damp and cold, and apparently a spectral hound—not to mention disease in the winter, for they have *only* cow blood to eat."

Alasdair waved a dismissive hand.

"You fuss over nowt. There has been no real plague on Orkney for a goodish while." Apparently war and cold were so commonplace as to not require comment.

Colin wondered if he might actually like eating otter and blood pudding.

A moment of reflection convinced him that he would rather not take the culinary risk. He was not *that* inured to hardship. If he went to Noltland, it would be with food.

"You've not actually been in the castle then?" he asked absently.

"Nay, she'll have no one in while they are in mourning. Smart lass," he added grudgingly. "If she allowed me inside, she'd have no way to rebuff the MacKays and Keiths and Gunns."

"I see." Colin frowned a little. "It's good that she is at least that sensible."

"In any event, you needn't worry about an overland journey through MacKay country, for I shall send you by sea in the galley," Alasdair coaxed, then added as inspiration struck: "'Tis the fastest route. The safest, too. And I may send some tributes with you, since they would actually arrive. Some woolens, belike, to keep you warm. And if you are quick about it, you could be well away again before winter anyway."

"Tributes are good. And if we are taking the ship then you may also send some wine, some sheep, and a few more cattle as well."

"What! Cattle?" Alasdair glared while he ruminated. Apparently his desire for the heiress was stronger than his parsimony. "Very well, you may have a score of sheep and four head of cattle. And I'll send *all* my wine along."

"Thank you. Your generosity will doubtless impress Mistress Balfour." Colin gave his cousin a moment to think about this, and then said, "Now, about this idea of a game of gowff—"

"Ah! I have anticipated you. I've had my bowmaker craft twoscore clubs of yew for you—bunkered clubs, butting clubs—and also fourscore boiled feather balls. Frances prefers them to wood or dung."

"I see." Colin hunted for something complimentary to say before dashing his cousin's hopes for this mad plan. "That was most farsighted of you. However, there is still a slight problem with this arrangement."

"You do play, don't you?" Alasdair looked suddenly dismayed. "It is said that even the sassun king likes to play this Lowland game."

"Yes, I can play. But I do not think that my arriving at Noltland Castle in a galley requesting a game of gowff is perhaps the most likely method of gaining entrance," he said patiently. "They have different manners in the Lowlands, it is true, but as she has already refused you entrance—"

"But it *is* the best way! It is all arranged."

"It's all arranged? Truly? But how?" Colin was more than slightly taken aback. The girl's desire for golf must have reached a stage of mania if she was willing to risk the precarious balance that held her many unwanted suitors at bay.

"Aye. You are Noltland's new Master of the Gowff. And no one can object, as you are a sassun foreigner—and therefore likely to be stupid about the ways of the North."

"Master of the Gowff?" he repeated.

"Aye. I told Frances that I would find her one, since it was the only thing she would have of me. I have taken care of your clothing and everything you shall need."

"My clothing?" Colin asked evenly.

"Aye, laddie. We still wear the plaids up here." He glanced at Colin's attire and shuddered. Then he jerked a thumb at the corner of the room. Folded neatly on the end of the table were a length of garish red wool and a saffron-colored sark.

Colin looked down at his handsome doublet and trunk hose. He did not see any cause for distress in his attire. He had deliberately avoided wearing the more bombastic codpieces presently favored at court and chosen to bring only those that posed the most modest and probable of erections.

"I am more than happy to wear the tartan," he lied. "But what is that thing?" He eyed askance the vivid fabric pile.

"It's your own tartan, laddie! The girl specified the design herself. Her Master of the Gowff is to have the proper uniform of office."

It was Colin's turn to shudder. He would look an idiot—a popinjay! No one wore cloth tinctured red with blackthorn and deadly nightshade anymore. And as for the yellow shirt . . . it was hideous.

"Why so strong a shade of red?" he asked plaintively. "It looks like battlefield gore."

"Well, it is that way so you might be plainly seen out upon the greensward, she said." Alasdair tried to sound encouraging, but fell rather short of total approval. As a soldier and hunter, he would never wear any plaid that made him so conspicuous.

Colin, also a hunter—though in a very different world—for once agreed completely.

"Is there a greensward?" he asked hopefully. Greenswards and uniforms—however ugly—suggested pleasant amenities like herb gardens, music, and a propensity among the castle dwellers toward civilized activities like bathing and general castle cleanliness.

"Well, not exactly a greensward. There is a goodly stretch of green thistle though, and a bit of heath and a tiny wood. And a great many rocks where there are hares. Among the boulders, they are a better chase than red deer." Seeing Colin's dubious expression Alasdair added: "Be reasonable. After all, lad, this is the coast they are living on, not the damned Borders."

Colin sighed. "I didn't really expect that there would be shorn meadow to play on, but one does like to hope for something more than thistles and boulders. They shall shred the leather balls in a trice."

He rose and walked to the table. He fingered the vivid plaid. It was actually very finely made, if one overlooked the color. Mistress Balfour had even arranged that he should have a brooch with his own badge, a pair of sticks crossed over a gowff ball. The pin's design lacked a little in inspiration and stature, having no fearsome beasts in its crest, and also looked to have been fashioned by an apprentice smith, but it was still a kindly thought.

"Tell me: why all the secrecy here at the castle about this plan, cousin? It is surely more than mere shame at my clothing that has kept you from welcoming me home in the usual manner."

"Nay!" Alasdair denied. "I welcome you. 'Tis just that I do not want anyone to know of my plans for you yet. Some might think that I was being too soft with the Balfours. Those idiot MacKays, for example. They have no appreciation for subtlety. They would see this plan as the act of a weak man. Anyway, I do not want them to know that you are my cousin."

That was probably true; this plan *was* rather weak.

It was also true that they would probably act immediately if they thought the MacLeod was preparing to take the castle by stealth, so for his own safety it was best that Colin's identity remain hidden.

"Why, my own stepbrother dared taunt me for not besieging Noltland immediately," Alasdair complained aggrievedly. "And he threatened to go to the MacDonnells and tell them I was ready to beak my troth with the Glengarry's daughter."

Colin turned and stared. "Torquil did this? And did you banish him?"

"Aye. Banished him straight to Hell with an axe in his head. *I had to*," Alasdair added pettishly. "I can't have people carrying tales to the MacDonnells and questioning my judgment. Anyway, it wasn't as if he was my true blood kin. Mother's dead now, so there was no one to be bothered by his loss. Anyhow, I did the decent thing and cut out his heart to put in her grave before I gave him up to the sea."

"I see." So it was Torquil's ghost he'd met on the stairs. Colin tried to feel bad for him, but failed.

"Four and twenty years is plenty long enough to have learned some sense," Alasdair continued. "He should have been less stupid if he wanted to live."

"One would think so," Colin agreed, both fascinated and horrified by this person who shared his blood. He wisely did not ask about how Alasdair intended to break his betrothal with Glengarry's daughter. It would have to be something violent and beyond the usual degree of horribleness, he was sure, for Glengarry very much wanted this match.

"So you'll do it, cousin? You'll go to Noltland and get the heiress for me?"

Colin looked down at the ugly wool and found

himself smiling. *A master of the golf*—forsooth! He had counterfeited many roles in his career, but never this one. It was a vastly amusing notion, given his rather poor style of play. Falconry and archery had received more diligent attention in recent years, and always there was the sword, but golf had been avoided like the Dutch plague. He would be lucky to recall which end of the club was used to hit the ball.

Of course, the whole situation was farcical madness, and his cousin the most insane one of them all. Any reasonable man would refuse the task and return to his hearth in York before the winter set in.

"Cousin, you'll do it?" Alasdair asked again.

"Aye," Colin heard himself say. "At least I shall go to Noltland and meet this heiress and see what may reasonably be done to keep the castle from falling to your enemies."

He picked up the plaid and draped it about himself, fastening it with his brooch. Then he selected one of the newly made clubs and, after addressing an imaginary ball, affected a brisk swing.

The MacLeod made an effort to look solemn but ended up hiding his face in his sark's broad sleeve and pretending to cough. Colin doubted that Alasdair would be so amused when he discovered the alternative plans for the heiress of Noltland that were taking shape in his sassun cousin's sneaky mind, but Colin saw no need to inform him of them just yet.

O forty miles off Aberdour
'Tis fifty fathoms deep,
And there lies gude Sir Patrick Spens,
Wi' the Scots lords at his feet.

—*"The Ballad of Sir Patrick Spens"*

Chapter Three

Colin took in the ragged coastline as he was rowed toward the shore in a tiny boat crowded with golf clubs, a large number of traps, four people, and two unhappy sheep. His nose was wrinkled clear to his forehead and he wished for a handkerchief so that he might cover his offended nostrils. The unpleasant briny smell of sea-damp ovine combined with the up-and-down motion of the boat was upsetting his liver.

Noltland's gray zed-plan tower looked right at home among the other sea-swept boulders that littered that far northern coast. Much of the cliff face was red sandstone, which had split into giant fissures along its bedding plane and was now being invaded by sea wrack and destructive salt. He had no doubt that the tower, from its cellars to its attics, had been impregnated with the smell of the sea, which, on a good day, was bracing. And on a bad day—or any occasion when a shark was being butchered in the flensing shed—rather more pungent. It made him grateful that he resided inland at York.

As they drew closer, he could see that it was not a true wood that ringed the keep, but rather heaps of thistles that besieged the tower's lower walls.

Colin frowned. Doubtless the vicious weeds helped secure the fortress against intrusion, a prudent precaution given the area and the circumstances under which the tower had devolved upon the heiress and new laird of the Balfours. However, as an emblem of warmth and hominess, the thorny wild flowers were sadly lacking in welcome. In fact, the entire precipitous slope where the tower sat failed to suggest any vestige of tranquility or bonhomie on the part of the builder. Frankly, he'd seen castle dungeons more agreeably appointed.

To be fair, there was little cause for optimism among the keep's inheritors, and the builders may well have sensed its fate from inception. Noltland's owners had all come to bad ends. There had been the Tullochs who built the place one-hundred-odd years ago, and then the Sinclairs who died out to a single female, and now the Balfours, whose northern branch was also becoming extinct with amazing rapidity. And if the MacLeod had his way, the tower would shortly be changing hands again. There were MacLeods in Harris and Lewis—and of course in Skye—why not the Orkney's Noltland Castle as well?

It would, Colin knew, take a great deal to discourage his cousin from pursuing his chosen course of acquiring this keep; the only hint of unease he had shown was at the preposterous tale of a spectral hound that haunted the Balfours.

Colin exhaled slowly. It was not that he was entirely decided against the plan of seeing someone installed at Noltland—so much would depend upon what he found at the fortress. Mayhap it would be better to establish someone strong within the keep rather than permit a bloody massacre of defenseless innocents by the ravaging wolves who lived nearby. But whatever was eventually done with the heiress and young laird, he did not see himself playing the Trojan horse for the MacLeod. Murder and rape of the infantry was not his favorite method of securing political appointments, and he would not assist in that particular project even to win favor with blood kin.

A flash of now-familiar red caught his eye. A female and a lad were up on the cliff's ragged edge, both clad in gay colors, which were an insult to the gray of sea and stone. A telltale plume of sand shot into the air, explaining their presence outdoors on such a blustery day. Obviously, they were taking exercise. At a guess, the boy was either beating a badger to death with a stick or else he was trying to get a golf ball out of a deep bunker.

Colin watched the boy's wild swings with a critical but sympathetic eye. The lad had a bad habit of throwing up his head just before he struck. He would have to be cured of that or he would never be able to control his ball. Colin knew this from painful experience. He had finally broken himself of the habit by tying a stone about his neck. The weight of the rock, and a few blows to the chin and nose from the heavy pendulum, had finally convinced him that he needed to stop jerking his head up when he took his shot.

Colin's brows drew together. The two youngsters stood perilously near the ocean, a most insalubrious locale, and with the wind as strong as it was—

Even as the thought was conceived, a wad of brown leather, hurled by a furious hand, shot over the cliff and headed for the rowboat. Colin leaned out quickly and snagged the sack before it hit the choppy water, but his rescue lowered the gunwales sufficiently that he was splashed with freezing brine for his troubles. Neither of the other human occupants uttered a word of reproach, but the two sheep bleated pathetically and began to mill about in their tight quarters.

"Oh, hullo!" a young voice called down from the cliffs. Arms waved violently. "Did you get it?"

"Aye! And right sorry I am, too," Colin shouted back, as he wrung out his plaid, which he had draped carelessly around himself. The boatman, another giant MacLeod, and MacJannet—both of whom had only had their boots wetted—grinned at him. Colin ignored them. "You're throwing your head up before the shot and pulling to the left."

The lad laughed. "So Frances says. You must be the new Master of the Gowff. Frances! Come meet your new—" The boy turned his head away and the words were lost to the wind.

At that moment the boat pulled up against the only bit of available sand, and Colin quickly alighted, leaving the snickering MacJannet to cope with their traps, and Olaf MacLeod to deal with the transfer of livestock. The other sheep, he had been told, would be brought in from the larger vessel a few at a time by rowboat, the cattle lowered into the ocean and forced to swim for the shore. It seemed a certain way to lose the valuable animals, but he had to assume that his seagoing cousins knew what they were doing. Ponies could swim, perhaps cattle could, too, and to be fair, he could not see how they would convince a large bovine to stand still in a rowboat with the sea heaving up and down.

Colin looked up from his wet knees to see two spots of bright red hurrying down the gray cliff face, and he moved swiftly to intercept the children. The scree looked treacherous and such haste did not suggest a mature degree of caution.

"*Bonjour*!" called a softer, sweeter version of the voice that had hailed him earlier.

Dark hair had slipped its modest arisaid and whipped about in the wind. The lady skidded to a halt only a handsbreadth from Colin's outstretched arms. Her clothing, accent, and very air declared her as French, whoever her father might have been.

The lady was also not a child.

She said breathlessly: "We did not expect you so soon."

"We've had favorable winds," Colin answered in French, returning the ball to the lad and then making his obeisance to the lady. "Colin Mortlock, at your service, Mistress Balfour."

Delightful eyes, the color of Highland whisky, moved over his face. Colin noted that though she wore a traditional leine, the delicately pleated garment was fashioned of silk rather than linen or wool, and it draped most gracefully over her bosom. Her embroidered kirtle was long, but not so great a length as to drag upon the ground—a sensible precaution as the rough terrain would quickly shred the delicate material.

She also had small pearls for teeth and a lovely smile to accompany that softly accented voice, which he wished to hear speaking his name in tones of solicitude. But before she could address him a second time, the first of the sea-traumatized sheep ran bleating past them, distracting her from more pleasant conversation.

"What is that?" Mistress Balfour demanded, startled and dismayed, as she pulled her skirts aside before they were wetted by the sopping animal.

"That is a sea-sickened sheep."

The seaweed-draped creature ran straight up the hill and into the recently vacated sand pit. It complained mournfully and began to roll about, kicking up the sand and sending gritty showers down upon them.

"But it is an unfair hazard," Frances objected, stepping away from the granular rain. A second ewe ran past, apparently no happier than the first and every bit as determined to cover herself in sand. "I was preparing to take my shot. How shall I manage with these creatures milling about?"

"Now, be not so downcast. That, mistress," Colin said with amusement, "is no hazard. That is our dinner. Speak kindly to them, for they are not long for this world. In any event, they add sport to the game."

"*Vraiment*? They are dinner? I suppose they are another bribe from the laird of the MacLeods?" Her pretty lips curled disdainfully.

"Aye, they are. One I absolutely insisted on. There's wine, too," Colin said unrepentantly.

"How generous." A dimple appeared briefly in one cheek. Frances's eyes held his for a moment and then shifted, looking past his shoulders at the beach. The lovely lids widened. "And what are those?"

Colin turned. The first of the unhappy cattle were being lowered into the water over the side of the galley.

"That, mistress, is a Highland cow."

"I do not refer to the beast, sir. What are those clubs in that basket?"

Colin hadn't the first inkling. The MacLeod, not knowing anything of golf or the type of club required, had made several in varying styles and heights. There were enough clubs for a score of men and a great many of them looked like farming implements.

However, it would not do to appear ignorant of his tools, so he lied glibly: "Different angles of head of the club allow varying degrees of loft in the ball. Not knowing what sorts of terrain we should be facing, I brought them all."

"Truly?" George breathed. "I did not know there were so many kinds of clubs. I have never seen half so many in one place."

The young laird of the Balfours sounded impressed. But a look at Frances's countenance showed that she was still skeptical.

"It is the same principle as is applied to shooting a cannon," Colin went on bravely, hoping that this would prove true. It seemed that the principles of trajectory should relate equally to both things, and there was a very good chance that Mistress Balfour would not be able to contradict him on this subject.

"And that ridiculous thing with leather wrapped about its head?" Frances demanded as MacJannet and the overstuffed pannier drew abreast of them.

"That is for use in sand," Colin explained, removing the club and inventing an explanation spontaneously. "The hood is removable, as you see, but it has been found that when playing with a leather ball that leather will cling to leather and it assists the ball out of deep dunes."

"That does not sound entirely fair play," Frances said slowly, stepping closer to inspect the ungloved head.

No, it didn't sound entirely honest, Colin had to admit. But there was no way to take back the statement, so he added mendaciously: "King Henry himself uses just such a club."

"You have played gowff with the English king?" Finally, Mistress Balfour sounded impressed.

"Indeed," he said, feeling virtuous at finally telling some truth. He had in fact played with the king. Twice. The first time, he had been greatly reviled for his play. It had been his initial attempt at the game since leaving Scotland as a boy, and he had suffered the misfortune to twice hit Bishop Moore's broad arse with wooden balls. Doubtless he would have been asked to desist from play, or arrested for assault, but the king had been vastly amused at the bishop's rough treatment and insisted that Colin remain with them.

Fortunately—since Colin did not enjoy appearing the butt of jokes, nor the bishop the butt-as-target—the king's gout had flared up soon after crossing the stream into which he so improvidently waded, and they abandoned play before Colin committed the unforgivable sin of striking his monarch with either club or sphere.

The second time he had played with the king, he had put in some practice in anticipation of the event, and his game was greatly improved. He had not once struck another player.

Of course, he had split three balls by cannoning them off the castle wall, and lost any number of them in filthy water hazards—for which he had been penalized at double the usual fine, privy streams being so devastating to the pages' velvet livery. But for all the destruction of clothing, and the king's disappointment at his improvement in the sport, Colin still considered the match to have been a success.

"Well, shall we play on?" Colin asked of his new

mistress. For himself, he would have preferred a few hours' rest to regain his land legs and some dry clothing. However, such an inclination was probably not what was expected of a true Master of the Gowff.

"*Oui!* But perhaps you are fatigued? I would not have you exhaust yourself while travel-tainted," the beauty suggested politely, clearly hoping that he would not claim weariness.

"Not at all. If you will overlook my ceremonial nudity, I should be happy to begin at once," Colin replied with a deprecating gesture. He was not wearing the scarlet brat Mistress Balfour had provided, but rather one of the MacLeod's hunting tartans. He did not plan on wearing the violently red cloth a great deal unless the lady insisted. "Let us proceed. MacJannet will bring the clubs."

Colin turned to the young laird and smiled. "We shall have to work on your form before all our balls end up in the sea. I brought a great many with me, but the supply is not endless."

"I think the matter is hopeless," George confided shyly. "We are between the hawk and buzzard here at Noltland, and I cannot seem to make the ball fly straight."

"You shall," Colin promised. "To begin with, I suspect that you are standing somewhat behind the ball. And it may be that your club is of an improper length." This was a fairly universal bromide and he felt safe offering it.

"*Oui*, he is behind the ball," Frances agreed. "And there is—"

A sudden hideous wailing split the air, making Mistress Balfour break off abruptly and assume a ferocious scowl.

"That sounds almost like pipes," Colin commented, squinting up at the battlements from whence the ghastly noise came. "Are you slaughtering pigs today?"

Frances and George both grimaced.

"That is Agonybags," George explained. "He likes to play the pipes when we are out gowffing."

"*Agonybags?*"

"The creature's name is Tearlach MacAdam—and if he approaches us with his man-staff I wish you to beat and castrate him," Frances said.

"I beg your pardon?" Colin asked, exchanging a puzzled look with MacJannet, who was playing respectful ghillie and standing a pace back with the pannier of clubs. Surely *man-staff* could not be a vulgar name for a club?

"If he comes down from the wall without his clothing I wish you to beat and castrate him," Frances repeated. "The MacLeod said that you would assist me in every possible manner to improve my game. This would assist me. Who can play well with that monster about?"

"Is he apt to come down without his clothing?" Colin asked, a frown forming between his brows. He did not relish having to inform Mistress Balfour that his assistance with her game would likely stop short of perpetrating grievous bodily harm upon anyone—especially not the insane.

"*Oui*. It is most annoying. How am I to play with that filthy man about, torturing the dead skin of an animal? And he is not a fit sight for my cousin, who is still most young and innocent."

"Have you considered taking away his pipes?" Colin suggested. "That would be less drastic than actually destroying them or him. Pipes are quite expensive, you know."

"That is a most clever idea," Frances agreed. "And perhaps we should remove his tongue as well. He could not speak without a tongue."

"His tongue?"

"*Oui!* His tongue and man-staff and pipes. I want them gone from my presence."

Colin stared, quite dumbfounded. The woman, he was certain, was not jesting. But surely she could only suggest such a spleenful thing because she had never seen someone tortured.

Disturbing as her speech was, it did partially explain the MacLeod's attraction to this female. Her expressed sentiments were very much after his own heart.

"It is on account of his handstaff not working anymore that he bothers Frances," George innocently explained.

"His . . . handstaff?" Colin echoed again, feeling foolish but still hopelessly adrift. The only meaning he had ever heard applied to handstaff was one that a lady would never speak about, nor a gentleman in her presence.

"Aye," George explained. "His pillicock, the bald-headed hermit, his—"

MacJannet coughed. "If I may? To be delicate, I believe the lad is speaking of Polyphemus, the one-eyed Cyclops of Greek legend."

"George!" Frances scolded. "I do not wish to hear of this again. Tearlach speaks enough about such things!"

"Quite!" Colin agreed, frankly shocked at the conversation. "But I am still rather puzzled. What has this creature's, er, impotence to do with you?"

"Nothing! Have I not said so repeatedly?" Frances asked, stomping up the narrow cliff trail, her tiny feet sinking deeply into the loose shale. "If a ghost took away his manhood then he must ask the ghost to bring it back!"

"Ghost?" Colin knew he sounded startled.

"The matter is a little unusual," George explained, breathing heavily as he toiled upward after his cousin. "Now that Tearlach cannot be with a woman anymore, he likes to talk about . . . things. This kind of speech used to aid him in . . . well . . . *things*. He thinks that maybe speaking with Frances will help him to become himself again and then he can lie with a woman."

"I see." Colin had to admit that if anything could reanimate wilted flesh it would be Frances Balfour. "But the ghost—"

"But Frances does not care for it, as it is disrespectful," George went on. "And *I* do not care for his music. It hurts my ears until I cannot think. That is probably what chased the ghost away."

"What ghost?" Colin demanded for a third time.

"Oh, the one that appeared after my father died. It blamed Tearlach for being alive when my father was dead. Since then he hasn't been able to um . . . do things."

"What idiocy!" But was it? The pipes squealed again, causing a shooting pain in Colin's skull. "Why has no one thrashed this creature and taken his pipes away?" Colin demanded.

"It's bad luck to hurt a piper," George explained as

they topped the rise. "And we have no other to replace him. Ranald used to be our piper, but he is dead. And frankly, no one wants to risk any more bad luck. Besides, I don't know who *could* kill him, as all the men are—"

"Ah, merciful Virgin!" Frances swore, a hand laid against the shapely bosom that jutted beneath her silken leine. "He comes!"

"Aye, but he has his plaid on," George reminded her. "And he has not said anything to you. Yet."

"If he speaks to me of pudendum, notches, ruts, heaping, coiting—"

"Quite!" Colin interrupted, horrified at the list of indelicate words tripping off Mistress Balfour's delicate tongue.

"You are to beat him," Frances instructed. "I insist upon it."

"Certainly." And he would, too. It occurred to Colin that his original thought that this poor creature might be suffering from more than lameness of staff could be correct, for this belief in impotence-causing ghosts sounded like an extreme weakness of the mind. Still, even the stupidest of creatures could be taught to avoid certain things if the right techniques were applied.

MacJannet coughed again, warning them that Tearlach was upon them.

"Leave us," Frances said imperiously. Her tiny foot tapped impatiently. "I do not want you here."

"Now, mistress! Ye ken that a cannae leave ye alone wi' strange men."

"I am not alone. My cousin is here, and these are not strange men. This is Monsieur Colin Mortlock, my Master of the Gowff, and his servant, MacJannet."

"A sassun! Clasped at yer bosom?" Tearlach gasped. "Well, most surely I cannae leave ye now. We know wha manner o' people these sassuns are."

"No one is clasped at my bosom. Nor shall they be," Frances Balfour said stonily. "My bosom is quite alone and contentedly so."

"And what manner of person is that, ancient one?" Colin asked, more amused than offended. While the old man searched his memory for more insulting words, he hurried on, "Any road, I am only part sassun. I am of clan MacLeod on my mother's side."

"And mair the shame for it! A MacLeod! As well to hae a starving wolf in our midst."

Colin was inclined to agree but could hardly say so with Frances and George standing about. "Be that as it may, if you are to remain with us, I must insist upon silence while I instruct my students. If you cause them to miss a shot I shall have to throw you into the sea to collect their balls," he explained pleasantly, earning a look of approval from his new mistress.

"Aye! You and wha' army, ye fiery pimpled pillico—*Ack!*" The old man got no further before Colin picked him up and hove him over the side of the short cliff.

It was not a long drop and there were no boulders below; still, Colin watched attentively to see that the oldster did in fact emerge from the surf with limbs unbroken. His present goal was to instruct, not maim.

"He fell in the water," Frances said on a note of disappointment, watching as the bedraggled man toiled back up the cliff face.

"Aye, but it is very cold water," Colin answered consolingly. "And now he shall have to go and find dry clothing. So we will be left in peace."

However, Tearlach did not follow this sensible

course. It took him a few moments to regain the cliff top, but when he did, he turned immediately in their direction. His expression was dogged.

"So, it is as I feared. The man is daft," Colin said softly to MacJannet.

"So it would appear."

"This may prove fatiguing." Colin selected a club at random and handed it to Frances Balfour. "I should like to see your form with my stick in hand," he said blandly.

She did not react to his leading remark, suggesting to Colin that in spite of her horrifying vocabulary she truly was an innocent.

"As you wish." Frances's face and voice were both dubious, but she calmly set about addressing the ball. Her swing was clean and forceful, and it sent the leather pouch straight into the air, where it fell to earth only a few feet away.

"*Mon Dieu*!" she breathed, dismayed.

"Not at all, mistress," Colin said quickly. "That is the design of this club. I thought we should see how they all performed before resuming the game."

"Ah! That is sensible," she said, relaxing. "George, you must try this one. It will be good for sand."

The dripping Tearlach rejoined them. "You must be one for coo-kissing," he said, squinting at Colin through dripping gray locks.

"He means that you are rough, sir," MacJannet translated, sotto voce. He added, before Colin could react violently: "Coo-kissing is a mild vulgarism but not actually indecent speech."

"I shall be rougher still if you use impolite language in front of your mistress again," Colin said sternly, handing the club to George. He instructed the lad: "Move up a wee bit and try to keep your head down."

Tearlach searched Colin's expression, and finding strict purpose there, wisely waited to speak until George had finished his swing and the ball landed back in the same place it began.

"How should I ken yer intentions tae the mistress? There were a sassun here once what went after a lass, and before he went away she was left in full disgrace and broken-kneed."

"What? He broke her knees?" Colin asked, distracted in spite of himself. "Try again, George."

"The saying is actually 'she hath broken her leg above the knee,'" MacJannet explained.

"Aye—and so she had been! Hit on master vein, she was by this sassun fancier of the kirtles! And he didnae do right by her."

"He means that this unfortunate maid had a child filiated upon her by a dissolute person from England who fled before a marriage could be arranged," MacJannet reported, clearly warming to his role as Tearlach's interpreter.

"Thank you, MacJannet, I followed that much. Hush now, both of you. George, try that swing again. You are still throwing your head up. I may have to tie a heavy stone to your neck to help you recall the need to keep your head still."

"Does that work?" the boy asked hopefully.

"Aye, but it is best used only as a last resort. 'Tis too easy to lose one's teeth when the stone flies up."

"Oh."

George looked down with determination. This time

the ball managed to travel a couple of feet. Deciding not to press his luck, Colin urged them to move on.

Below he could hear the bellowing cattle coming up onto land. They sounded no happier than the sheep, but at least they were alive.

Tearlach followed them determinedly, though he was plainly interested in the cows milling upon the beach. "They're aboot as restful as a nose full o' wasps," he observed. "They took tae that ocean wi' as much pleasure as the Devil takes tae holy water."

Colin handed Frances a different club and stood back smartly. It took her only a moment to let fly with a mighty swing. The leather ball sailed into the sky and seemed to disappear into the clouds.

"*Bien Dieu!*" she breathed happily if irreverently. Her smile was ecstatic.

"That one's away wi' the angles." Tearlach exhaled through his teeth in veneration. "Who'd have thought that some wee lassie could hit a baw sae far?"

"Frances, that was amazing!" George congratulated. "You've never hit one so long."

Colin was astounded, too, but did not permit himself to gasp.

"Very nice," he said cautiously. "We shall have to see where it landed, of course, but excellently done."

Frances smiled at him, eyes shining. "Ah! Splendid! I wish that we might play all the day and on every day. It is of much good fortune that you have come to us, Monsieur Mortlock. It seems that I shall actually have to say sincere thanks to the laird of the MacLeods for his suggestion of a Master of Gowff."

Colin returned her smile but thought: *Play golf all the day and on every day?* He prayed that this would not be the case, or he, too, would have something to say to his cousin, and it would not be words of thanks.

He made a mental note to instruct MacJannet to pray nightly for rain. He would do it himself, but he and the Lord had not been on the best of terms in recent years.

The twelvemonth and a day being up,
The dead began to speak:
'Oh who sits weeping on my grave,
And will not let me sleep?'

—"The Unquiet Grave"

Chapter Four

Eventually the game came to an end and Colin was finally allowed to enter the keep. It was a good thing that things had gone smoothly with his introduction to his employer, because the MacLeod's ship had not waited for him. He was stranded with the Balfours until his cousin chose to rescue him.

Noltland Castle came as rather a surprise. The first interesting feature was an iron yett that might be used to close upon hostile visitors. It had not the strength of some of the Norman fortifications, lacking a moat and bridge that might be drawn up, yet it was certainly something for which King James II should have been petitioned when it was installed in the last century. The castle was clearly a defensive fortification and could be used against the crown if taken by hostile forces.

Also of interest were a conspicuous number of shot holes built into the walls, a feature rarer in castles built in the last century, when the perpendicular style had been waning. In all, the keep had been designed with one purpose, and that was to hinder intruders. It was not a pleasure palace where lords might play in between their hunts and carouses.

Given that he liked his hosts, Colin tried to put aside his years as an intelligencer and to look at the castle and its inhabitants with the eye of a guest. But it was in his nature to evaluate every new situation for its potential danger to both his person and the crown. Seen with these experienced eyes, the second unwelcome thing that intruded upon his notice was the extreme stillness within the keep's walls.

Of course it was not completely noiseless. There was the eddying wind, which carried the familiar odors of fiery peat and sea. And there were the noises from fowl, which hunted grain in the courtyard while doing their best to avoid a group of children intent on playing some game that involved tossing pebbles at the birds and ominous chants of "Pullet gullet." There were also the ripples of hushed female conversations that echoed softly off of the stone walls that sided the small yard.

In the distance was the slow clanging of a smith at work, though the blows he struck sounded as lazy and weak as a child's. All about Colin was the hushed quietude of a churchyard.

A churchyard. Colin nodded at this description. It fit well. There were no horses about, and of the cattle and sheep that had come from the MacLeod, there was no sign. Colin assumed them to be grazing out on the heath—he hoped that they found something to eat out there. Belatedly it occurred to him that bringing animals to Noltland had been a mistake. If there was not enough grazing for them, they would have to be slaughtered immediately and that would be a waste.

Colin frowned and exchanged a long look with MacJannet, who nodded slowly.

It reassured Colin that MacJannet felt the strangeness as well. His bored brain was not imagining things. It *was* too calm. There was a sense of silence beyond the stillness of observation that followed the arrival of a stranger into a small and isolated community. Something was amiss at Noltland.

Mayhap the silence was partly mourning for the dead laird and his sons, but still it seemed to him that there should have been the sound of men practicing their swordplay or shooting at butts, and there should have been laughter as they teased each other about their mistakes or praised one another's prowess. However, the courtyard was bereft of any males save those who had been in Mistress Balfour's retinue.

Colin paused, watching and listening intently. There were a few small buildings standing against the walls, which might serve as stables, but they were stout and shallow, thatched with bracken and pegged with hazel sticks. They would shelter no beast larger than a pig or sheep.

This was not the sort of place where men would spend their time. It belonged to the women and children. Yet, where could the men be if not in the vacant yard? There were no fields to tend and no sign of nearby crofts.

Colin looked next at the battlements where he expected to see guards posted, and exhaled in shock. There were no men on the ramparts, only some pikes leaned against the wall and a woman seated on a three-legged stool, winding yarn into balls. Occasionally she would look up from her work and cast an eye over the landscape, but she seemed to be the only lookout facing south.

Colin turned about slowly. There was another woman seated on the wall that overlooked the sea, but she was occupied with dipping stripped rushes into fat and not paying attention to the MacLeod's retreating galley.

To the east and west, the battlements were bare of all but pikes.

"'Tis a shame," Tearlach commented, and for one moment Colin wondered if the man had actually perceived his thoughts. But then the oldster went on with an apparent non sequitur: "The master and the Keith were brother starlings. She were a MacKay—and a faithless notch. She betrayed them both wi' a buckface cuckholder in clan Gunn. She said she were seduced by the master, but I say that nae woman but a halfwit is ever seduced against her will."

For the moment, Colin was too distracted to reprimand Tearlach for his conversation, and MacJannet too busy to translate the more unsavory parts.

Emboldened by Colin's silence, Tearlach went on. "Master and I used tae gae holing. Had meself a fair horn-colic in them days. The master did envy me that when it came tae wenching. Mayhap he envies me still and that's why he haunts me."

MacJannet finally turned to stare. It was plain to Colin that he understood what the old man said, and equally apparent that MacJannet had no wish to render the words in an understandable vernacular. Colin prayed that the oldster's conversation was equally incomprehensible to Mistress Balfour, or she would likely renew her demand that the obscene creature be beaten and castrated. That would be a pity, as he seemed the only remaining adult male in the castle, and his information—however garbled—could be of use. Unless it truly was the *fallacia consequentis* it first appeared to be.

"Now there is just the laddie." Tearlach went to clap a hand on George's back, but the boy skittered away with an expression of distaste. "And how am I tae teach him the proper way fer a man tae drain his juices? We've nae agreeable ruts of life aen this castle, saving the mistress. But she'll nae be coited until after marriage. Though I offered her an herbal pessarie an she wished to lay wi' a man and not get herself wi' child."

Colin stared in disbelief. "Good God!"

"Wha?" the old man asked.

Colin decided that he was unprepared to comment on Tearlach's offer of birth control, though he was feeling hourly more sympathetic to Frances's expressed desire to have the old man's tongue removed. This castle was no place for a lady—and apparently it never had been. The dead Balfour had obviously been diligent about practicing his seigneurial rights among the female inhabitants. How else would he have come to have thirty sons under one roof? Colin found himself moved to pity for the former mistress of Noltland and prayed that he would not meet her ghost.

"George will learn about these things in the fullness of time—and without your assistance!" Colin said adamantly.

At least he hoped this was so. This old satyr was not a proper person to see to the morals and education of a youth. There *had* to be someone else more fitting of guardianship. "Now, we will have no more talk about this. And, if I were you, I would never speak of these things to the lady again. Your mistress is quite capable of knocking your head across the heath any time she chooses. She has already mentioned that you need castrating."

Tearlach turned and eyed Mistress Balfour with new caution. Her swing with these newer, heavier clubs was indeed formidable, and there could be no denying that she—most inexplicably—did not care for his presence. At the moment she was engaged in conversation with an elderly woman who was busy drying fish on polished Ballachulish slates, and not paying him any heed, yet she retained her hold on one of the thicker clubs from MacJannet's basket and was only a few paces distant. That club could do great damage to either his head or his other, more valued, organ.

"And another word of advice," Colin added. "Do not play those pipes before dawn or I will hunt you down and throw them into the sea."

"Ach! That willnae hurt them. Many a time it is that they have fallen in the brine."

Colin could well believe it. He had never heard pipes sound so ill. They were some horrid degeneration of sound that was closer to screaming than music. Nevertheless, he felt he had to make his threat formidable.

"Perhaps not, but there is every chance that they will be carried out to sea if the tide is on the turn. You'd have to swim to Norway to see them again."

"Hmph! Lowland heathen!" Tearlach snorted and stomped away from his unappreciative audience. A nearby gander hissed at him, perhaps also offended by the noise he produced.

"May I offer you something to drink?" George

Balfour asked, rejoining Colin and MacJannet now that Tearlach was gone. "We haven't any proper whisky. 'Tis a brew made with new heather and only a little malt, but it is still rather good."

"Thank you," Colin answered with a polite smile that concealed his thoughts.

"Frances would conduct you about, but she will be engaged for a while yet," George said with slight awkwardness. "She is always very busy. It was lucky we could play today. Come inside and I shall show you over the place. It is not a difficult castle to learn, being quite modest and mostly a tower."

"Of course."

They entered first into a great hall whose ceiling was made with only a moderate vault, which had but one fireplace built on a wall opposite the circular staircase that led up and down to other levels. It was not an unusual design for castles built in this era. Colin knew that directly below them would be the lower vault where the servants, and sometimes animals, would be quartered in winter or in times of war. Beyond that would be the dungeons.

Being a young keep, the latter would not be so sullied with blood as many older prisons, but still, all dungeons were dreadful. The air was invariably foul and dank, and only dark deeds were done there, the kind that made angry ghosts. At the moment, it seemed unlikely that anyone living was in residence below, but Colin made a note to himself to explore after everyone had retired to bed. He was curious about this Bokey hole where the spectral hound was supposed to live. It sounded like an excellent place for a secret passage. If there was any danger to be had from that quarter, he preferred to know about it in advance.

Colin let his eyes wander upward and pause at the entresol. The room was more functional than ornamental, as was the narrow winding stairs, which could be easily defended by men with pikes or swords. And one ghost. The apparition first announced itself with an auditory herald, and Colin was able to school his face into calm before it appeared. The apparition was vague in the daylight, but he could plainly see that the haunt was a young man, dark and cruel of face, and he was dragging a body down the stairs by its heel. The only sound was the wet clunk of the victim's battered skull thumping down the treads. As usual, no one else seemed aware of its gruesome presence. If they felt anything, it was probably an instinctive avoidance of a cold spot in the room. The spirit would be stronger and clearer at night, and Colin made a note to himself to avoid the stairs after dark unless it was an emergency. He had yet to meet a ghost that had hurt him physically, but some were very adept at inspiring terror and could be obnoxious once they realized that he could see them.

"You like it?" George asked.

"Indeed. It is a most sensible design." It said a great deal about the thoughts of the builder that even the interior of the castle was assembled around the possibility of war. This certainly was no rich man's toy.

The only surprise in the great room was a grand baldaquin of silk and gold canopied over a heavily carved cross-framed chair of state, which was more suited to an earl—or even a king—than a mere knight. Colin doubted that the present regent knew of this display of power, and that if she did that she would be pleased by it. Monarchs, and especially regents, tended to be sensitive to these things because of their many wars with the rebellious lairds of the Isles, and were apt to react with opprobrium when they met with such usurpations of state. It might be wisest if the chair were taken down before they petitioned for royal help, if that were the path to be taken in defense of the keep.

There came a stir in a narrow passage, and then a serving wench arrived with a tray upon which rested a silver ewer and four goblets fashioned in the intricate design of the Gaels.

Refreshments were quickly but silently poured. Colin accepted his cup with a word of thanks that seemed to fluster the serving woman, and then raised his goblet in salute to the young Balfour. He was pleasantly surprised to find that it contained the sweet wine sent by the MacLeod rather than the offered brew made from heather. He wondered how the women had managed to move the heavy casks that had arrived on the ship, for he was quite certain that the MacLeod's men had not been allowed inside.

MacJannet had also been served with a silver goblet of fine wine, though he was supposedly only a servant. Colin wondered if it was because he was a man. Those seemed so scarce at Noltland that mayhap every one was valued. Too, there seemed a lack of the formality among the servants that usually dominated such households. Perhaps a siege mentality had set in and they had dispensed with class roles. And perhaps they had all lost so much that mourning united them.

George tossed back his wine, wearing an expression of delighted surprise, and then, wearing a new flush in his cheeks, suggested that they continue their tour of the keep. His young tongue quickly relaxed in the genial company and he grew expansive. He pointed the way to the privies and solar and even the kitchens, and then offered to conduct the men to their chambers. All the way up the stairs he regaled them with gruesome stories of haunts and portents. Obviously, he didn't believe in any of the ghosts that supposedly haunted Noltland. This was simply the grisly appetite of an eleven-year-old boy finding an outlet in a male audience who might appreciate the sorts of things his female cousin doubtless abhorred.

Colin murmured appreciatively, discounting most of what the boy said, thinking all the while of Noltland's household oddities and what they might mean. Obviously the boy did not care for his inheritance, which was in itself odd. And again, it was telling that both Colin and MacJannet were given the grandest rooms upstairs, where George and Frances also slept. They were either there so they could be observed by the castle's mistress, or they were placed there to offer some protection from unknown dangers. Whichever the cause, it proved that something was definitely amiss in Noltland Castle.

Colin's chamber was a far cry from his spacious rooms at home, but it was also less mean than many a bedchamber in a battle fortification. From his room he had a view of the ocean, which, at the greater height and on so pleasant a day, seemed a less fearsome thing. The tide had turned and was back on the rise, and the surf was shying about like a nervous animal as it came in contact with the upthrusts of coastal stone. It even seemed to murmur sweetly as it briefly withdrew from the rough shore, leaving only a line of thin white foam scalloped on the rocks. It was a transient pleasure. The honeyed voice would only last until the next storm. With the wind driving it, the sea would scream as it was split open by the knife-edged rocks.

Colin had already seen entirely too much of Tearlach MacAdam but was not all that surprised when the newly dressed piper sought out him and MacJannet in chambers for further conversation.

"See that smirch'd floor?" Tearlach demanded abruptly, pointing at a darkened patch of stone beneath a carved chest. "That's where the first master of Noltland got rid of his wife."

MacJannet blinked.

"Leastwise, that's where he put the top half of her. Done her to death with a reaping hook. But who could blame him, so shrewish was she. Balfours were always marryin' witches and poisoners."

"Perhaps the *wives* were driven to it," MacJannet muttered.

Knowing that it was probably a mistake, nevertheless Colin asked: "And the lower half?"

"Tossed out the window intae the sea. Except she didnae go intae the sea as the tide was out and it made a right mess when she hit the rocks. The servants saw everything. Well, how could they not when there was bit of her all over the walls and ground?"

MacJannet was as stiff as a poker. Colin hoped it was disapproval and not superstitious fear that had arrested his breath.

"She's still scarin' the servants," Tearlach added. "They say her legs gae runnin' aboot on stormy nights. But I've seen 'em sometimes just floppin' about on the stones." He *tsk*ed and looked up to see how this story was being taken.

"And the rest of her?" MacJannet asked in a faint voice.

"Well, she cannae get aboot without legs, can she? Nae, she just knocks on the chest askin' tae be let out. But we never do let her. It's a wicked enough time dealin' wi' her legs."

Colin doubted this story, but if the ghost did disturb his rest, he would have the chest removed.

"And the Bokey hound?" he asked, sounding only mildly interested. This familial fixation with ghosts was getting annoying. So much superstition would impede any efforts at reasonable conversation.

"Aye, poor mutt. He mostly stays below stairs until some puir soul is tae die. He crawled there after the master beat him, and there he died, the miserable beastie. Some reward for knocking the poison cup out of the drunkard's hand. But Balfours are mean."

So! The beast might not be a hellhound. It could be a ghost. Animal spirits were rare, but Colin had once encountered a spectral horse and its ghostly rider in Cornwall.

"How charming. Does any room in the castle not contain some grisly ghost? Perhaps we would be safe in the privies?"

Tearlach's brow furrowed. "Well, there is at times some howling and moaning in the privies."

"That is not entirely supernatural," MacJannet pointed out. "Particularly if the meat has gone bad."

Colin shuddered. Tearlach's vulgar conversation was beginning to affect even the prim MacJannet. The man was a verbal plague.

"Enough. When is the evening meal served?"

"After nightfall. We never eat before full dark,"

Tearlach answered reluctantly, clearly wishing to continue his discussion of ghosts and other horrors.

"Then I shall see you at dusk and not before," Colin said, indicating to MacJannet that he should eject their visitor from the room.

Tearlach, who was finally beginning to read Colin's gestures, hied himself away without further argument, though with a great deal of muttering. MacJannet closed the door gently and then cleared his throat.

"Go ahead and speak your mind," Colin invited. "I know that you are unhappy with what you have seen."

"I believe that we may have barely arrived in time to prevent a disaster. You must see that Mistress Balfour cannot continue to care for the boy and this keep alone. She's sly, but that is not sufficient to keep the local wolves away." He sounded disapproving. MacJannet had very set notions about the roles of the sexes.

Colin grunted. "Aye, I do see it. And I know that clever females can be a nuisance, particularly if their hearts are evil, but do you know, MacJannet, in spite of the current fashion, I have never cared for a total absence of wit in women? And especially not in one who must serve as an ally."

"I do not think that we are seeing any such lack now. And I did not say that she was evil," MacJannet protested mildly. "'Tis simply not a task for a woman alone. And she must be made to see it before disaster befalls this keep."

"No, she's *not* lacking in wits, is she?" Colin smiled widely. "I think Mistress Balfour is a very devious and brave creature. And likely quite willful. This is going to be a most interesting time, and possibly even an arduous one, wresting power from her tiny hands."

"Indeed." MacJannet sounded considerably less happy than his master.

His pessimism with their circumstances was confirmed quickly after Colin said: "I suppose that you made note of the complete lack of pampered paunches in this keep."

"I did. Winter may see the end of some of these people if supplies of meat are not found."

"That is also my belief," Colin replied. "And so . . . we will have to journey back south almost immediately, I fear."

"Aye?"

"The remaining Balfour men must be brought home, of course. I suspect you'll find them somewhere near Blar-na-leine."

"And how shall you arrange their freedom from the queen's service? She'll be reluctant to let any of her men go," MacJannet said. He was not challenging Colin, only seeking enlightenment.

"I believe that the Bishop of Orkney may be of some help. He can probably persuade the regent that the royal child's interests are better served by allowing the men to return north and defend the castle."

MacJannet blinked. "I didn't know that you included the bishop among your many acquaintances. You generally do not involve yourself in religious matters."

Colin smiled. "He doesn't like Beaton, you see. And any enemy of the cardinal can be made good use of." Seeing MacJannet frown, Colin added: "My friend, it is nice to know that I still have some secrets from you."

MacJannet shook his head. Plainly he did not agree. "I cannot say that I care for this plan. There are too many variables to calculate, and any of them may go disastrously awry."

"Nor do I love it," Colin agreed. "But it is the only one that has presented itself, so what choice have we? You can't be suggesting that we leave these innocents to the MacLeod's tender mercies."

MacJannet shook his head.

"At least the castle is sound enough," he said after a moment, trying for something cheerful to say. "I doubt that anything larger than a hare could get in or out of it with the yett in place—and not even that if the gates are barred. They look strong enough to hold back the ocean."

Colin gave his friend a playful look. "I hope that you are wrong, my friend, for I fear that we are going to face some heavy rain and I'd prefer it escape the castle, for I would as soon not get my feet wet when I explore the dungeons this evening."

"You won't like drowning, either," MacJannet said unhappily.

"You think the dungeons may flood when the tide is in?" Colin clarified. "But I shouldn't think the tide would often get that high. And it will not, unfortunately, rain so much until December. I'll likely end up playing gowff every bloody day."

MacJannet shook his head. "I was speaking of the drop-hole down to the sea. It is almost certain that they have one. No Scottish dungeon is truly complete without one," he added without irony.

"You have a point. It has to be examined, though. A sea egress is an improbable choice of entry for a malefactor, but it is something else to investigate in order to say with certainty that the castle is secure." From human enemies, at least.

"It is best examined from a safe distance," MacJannet warned. "And with a torch."

"Of course, my friend. Of course. I'll use every caution."

MacJannet snorted, not at all reassured. "You don't know the meaning of the word."

They had not saild a league, a league,
A league but barely three,
Until she espied his cloven foot,
And she wept right bitterlie.

—*"The Ballad of the Daemon Lover"*

Chapter Five

Frances watched tiredly as one by one the ribbons of dying light were pulled down from the clouding sky and tucked below the horizon. It was night again. At last their daily labors were at an end. Only the cook and sculleries still had heavy work before them; she had ordered that as sumptuous a dinner as the larder could bear was to be prepared that evening in honor of the new arrivals.

All afternoon while Frances had worked at the loom, her thoughts had been dwelling upon her new Master of the Gowff. Silly of her to be so distracted by him. Even though he was obviously of good birth, it was not as though he was a potential suitor, particularly not in her present situation when she already had too many men pursuing her. Still, she dwelled upon his face. She was even annoyingly weak of knee and careless of hand, which twice caused her to miss with the shuttle and snarl her work.

Frances sighed at her wandering wits and consoled herself with reason. She was not to be blamed for her inquisitiveness. It was an inborn trait. And Colin Mortlock was not at all what she had expected. In her experience, sporting-mad gentlemen were not interested in mundane household matters. To their minds, meals appeared by magic. Linens mended themselves. One might completely disarrange the furniture or set new servants to old tasks, and as long as they had a place at the table and a fire in the hearth, most men would not notice any difference. They cared for golf and hawking—and perhaps debauchery—and nothing else.

Yet, from the moment he had entered the castle, she could see that Colin Mortlock was making careful observation of its arrangements, assessing the people who worked there and treating everyone—except Tearlach—with great courtesy and interest. He'd even urged George to confide in him about their alterations to the castle's defenses and dungeons.

Frances bit her lip. Perhaps it had been a mistake allowing anyone into the castle. Colin Mortlock and MacJannet were temporarily isolated at Noltland and could not carry tales back to England, but eventually the world would suspect that there were almost no men left at the keep—only ancients and babes—and then others would come calling, swords in hand. What if Colin said something to these tiresome men when they came to woo her by force? Though probably reticent with her other neighbors, he would likely speak to his cousin . . .

She had hoped to delay the time when their extreme weakness was revealed until George's position had been strengthened by recognition from the new regent, or her father's men had returned home from the war. Could Colin be trusted? Could he be convinced to hold his tongue?

The facts as they stood were grim enough without betrayal from within. She wished that she could simply throw a blanket over the unpleasant truth and smother it forever. But that was not possible now. She would have to tell this Englishman and his manservant something plausible about why there were no men in the castle, or else reveal the truth and throw herself on his mercy and plead that he keep silent if he ever left them, or if his cousin came to call. Unfortunately, trickery wouldn't serve. She had no way of conjuring soldiers even for a day.

Of course, begging for his indulgence didn't appeal to her either, so that left honesty and an appeal to his better nature.

However, the amount of truth she told—and when—was still negotiable. She would likely begin by suggesting that most of the men were away taking cattle to market, which would conveniently explain why there were no cattle at Noltland, or else she could say that they were looking after sheep in faraway crofts. It wasn't a completely preposterous tale to tell a city-dweller from England, especially if everyone told the same story.

Of course, convincing everyone that they must be discreet was going to be a difficult matter. Desperation was mounting with the approach of winter. Hope that the survivors from Noltland Castle would return home had faltered with word of the English invasion at the Borders. The last of the poor crops was being harvested now. If the winter were light, they would be well enough situated—but if it were long and harsh?

Many of the women felt that it was better to surrender to one of the other clans than to risk starvation. Frances did not agree. The local chieftains were apt to go to war upon Noltland the moment control passed into a neighbor's hands, through sheer bloody-mindedness at being denied the castle for themselves. They would then be not only invaded but also besieged. Besides, she was not ready to sacrifice her freedom and George's birthright just yet.

Frances bit her lip. It bothered her to lie to Colin Mortlock. It would be difficult to look into his knowing eyes and utter half-truths—well, *quarter* truths—but it simply had to be done. He was from England, not part of the politics of the North, and therefore might be sympathetic, but until she knew whether his loyalties would lie firmly with Noltland and George, she could take no other chance.

Frances sighed again and turned from her narrow window. It was a bother, but she changed her gown before going in to dine. Part of keeping up the pretense that all was well at the castle was her acting the role of confident mistress. Ladies did not receive guests—even those who would be working members of the household—at their tables with woolen lint clinging to plain homespun.

She chose a dress of dark uncut velvet in deep sanguine red to wear over her willow green chemise. The unboned bodice could be worn with a modest bum-roll, and did not yet show signs of wear. It would also be warm in the drafty hall.

Frances paused near the base of the stairs and surveyed the room before her. The air was more festive than it had been since her arrival from France, but it still seemed oddly uncomfortable and cold. She would never get used to the unpleasant atmosphere of the castle.

It wasn't that there were too many shadows. The dining hall was fitted with dozens of flaring torches and a bright fire in the hearth, so only a few precious candles were needed on the table. Frances tried not to fret that there were a dozen more candles burning than she would have liked to have seen. She knew that they still had a reasonable supply, but they had to be made to last, at least until she found someone to send for supplies. At present, she dared not let any of the castle occupants leave, for once it was known to the outside world that unescorted women were seeing to such tasks, the speculation about Noltland's weakness would begin.

Annoyed, she snatched up the hem of her skirt and started down the stairs. Immediately her foot tangled in the thick velvet, and without a banister nearby to check her fall, she began a headlong tumble down the remaining steps.

But in less than the blinking of an eye, Colin Mortlock was before her, receiving her into his strong arms and restoring her balance with a swift embrace. His hands were firm but gentle as he set her on the floor.

"You look flustered, mistress," he said, taking her gently by the elbow and guiding her toward the table. "Please allow me to see you to your chair."

"Thank you," Frances answered, still a little breathless from her averted tumble. She smiled gratefully, much struck by Colin's grace and swiftness.

She also had to admit that her gallant rescuer looked quite comely by firelight, which flattered his dark hair and brows.

"I am but a little tired by my day out on the moor. Usually I do not play for so long," she added truthfully. "I fear fatigue has made me clumsy."

He hummed sympathetically, studying her face in return. "In that case I shall have to make certain not to tire you out with such long games. I have no desire to see you harmed through my offices."

Colin seated her carefully, his hands touching fleetingly in the middle of her back. It was of course impossible that she could actually feel the temperature of his palm through the thickness of her clothing, but her imagination said that his hands were very warm. She flushed, aware of the eyes upon them.

Confidently, he took a seat at her side and leaned down to greet a pale George, who suddenly looked quite small and thin seated behind the massive board. His all too apparent vulnerability made her heart clutch. How was she going to keep him alive?

Food was brought at once. Frances recognized the oysters en gravey and wondered where the wine for the dish had come from. A quick sniff told her that it was heavy with leeks and missing aromatic spices, but it had some almonds for decoration and would probably pass.

There was bread, too. She knew it would be good if rather heavy. They did still have eggs and flour, and a bit of ale and honey for flavoring.

Next came the chawettys. The pies, made without suet because there was little left, could have anything in them. They were what became of all the kitchen scraps that could be mixed with crabapple cider that had gone to vinegar and stuffed into a coffin crust.

The last dish brought to the table was a pair of chickens. They were not served with pears and grapes for none were to be had, but the chopped parsley, hyssop, and savory smelled nice, stewed and prepared with more wine.

At first there was little conversation, as the women were busy devoting themselves to their meal, but presently they began to speak among themselves and to answer MacJannet, who had set himself the task of putting everyone at ease. She noted carefully that even the servant had the manners of a gentleman. Perhaps it was the English way. If so, she liked it. In her experience, Scottish men were too rude and direct. Some, like her father, were even brutal.

The elder and often sourly disposed Anne Balfour would say that it was typically English, and that it was objectionable. But she had a deep-rooted dislike of all things foreign, Frances's clothes among them. Nor did her dislike stop at the border; she disliked Lowland Scots, too. Many days, it seemed that it was all she could do to tolerate George.

Frances glanced several times at her new companion while they dined, but could not think of any harmless conversational topic to inaugurate with those thoughtful eyes always upon her. Of course, she was also uncomfortable eating while under scrutiny. After her clumsiness on the stairs, she feared she might well upset her plate with her careless hands.

Finally she sighed and turned slightly in her seat so that she faced her Master of Gowff head on. She tried to think of something intelligent to say.

"Mistress Balfour," Colin said quietly, also leaning slightly in her direction. Their cuffs touched and the embroidered threads clung to one another. "If you will forgive me for being forward . . . ?"

Frances blinked and raised her eyes from their hands and entangled linens. "But of course."

"I think it might be a reasonable precaution to invite Sir William Kirkcauldy to visit Noltland," he said unexpectedly.

"The Bishop of Orkney?" she asked with understandable surprise, and even a bit of confusion. "But—I am a devout Catholic, sir. He might not accept."

"True, he does not love Catholics, but the rest of your people are not so devoted. And neither is George." Colin picked up the ewer, which had been left on the table, and poured out a measure of wine for her. His tone was soothing. "The bishop isn't a bad fellow, really. And previous bishops have had ties to Noltland."

"But why would he come to see me? Is he not very busy vilifying the Catholics to the south?"

"Just Beaton, who has plainly begged to be vilified," Colin said with a fleeting smile, which Frances found most appealing in spite of the subject of their conversation. "And he has a new apprentice named John Knox who may carry on the harangue in his absence. As to why he would come to Noltland, as it happens I have had some dealings with this man and believe that he would be willing to visit me and to make the new laird's acquaintance."

Frances shook her head, not in negation but in an effort to shake loose from her jumbled thoughts, which impeded the route of logic through her tired brain. "Again, I must ask why. Even if you have some familiarity with him, why would he come here rather than asking you to visit at his convenience? And why should we ask him? As you know, I am yet in mourning and we invite no one to the castle."

Colin's face grew serious. "It would be a good thing for the Balfours to be seen with strong friends. And there is nothing wrong with turning to a man of God in your hour of need."

"And why should we need strong friends?" Frances asked, assuming an easy pose, though she was rather alarmed by the trend in their tête-à-tête. It was disturbing to think that her new Master of the Gowff could claim intimacy with someone like the Bishop of Orkney. It suggested that he was very aware of the region's politics and even had preformed sentiments. Perhaps she should have expected this, coming as he did from a Protestant nation, but she had hoped that his being English would mean a high degree of ignorance of politics in the North.

"Everyone needs friends, mistress. The Balfours more than most. And I could not, in good conscience, recommend asking any of your neighbors for support, for it would likely embroil you in their old feuds and bring suffering to your home."

Frances was not happy to have her own concerns voiced aloud. And if he was this aware of local dealings, then obviously tales about distant crofts and cattle markets were not going to serve. Her heart began to thud.

"You seem to know a great deal about our affairs for one so newly arrived from the South." She took up her goblet and drank, trying to decide what was best to do. Her impulse was to send this man away immediately. But was that wise when he already knew their weaknesses? And how could she transport him back to Dunnvegan? He would surely demand an escort, and there was none to be had.

"We have politics in England, too," he answered wryly. "I've seen a great deal of political machination in my time. And I must tell you, mistress, that you have done a magnificent job of keeping the wolves at bay. I know of no one who has ever done better at outwitting her foes."

Frances blinked at the praise, pleased at the recognition but again feeling off balance. He was sly, this one!

"What I cannot understand is how you have managed to convince everyone that the castle is still inhabited by men." Colin shook his head. "The MacLeod has no notion of your diminished population."

Frances sucked in her breath, rather alarmed that she was unable to formulate her lie with those intelligent eyes gazing into her own.

"You needn't answer if you prefer not," Colin said kindly. "But the matter is an obvious one. There have been no men here for some time. There is a great deal of work that needs doing . . . Well, I should have to be blind not to see how things are, and though I have many faults, blindness is not among them."

"Is it so obvious then?" she asked hollowly, again picking up her goblet and drinking down the sweet wine. It was far easier to look into the red depths than into Colin's eyes.

"Aye, to anyone who has been inside the castle for any time. Thatching is an art that cannot be well-faked by inexperienced hands."

"I see. And you do not think that I should ask the MacLeod for assistance?" she asked. Her mind was racing with ways to prevent Colin's leaving, now that he knew their secret and was so obviously informed of northern politics. "How odd, as it was he who recommended you. I should think that you would be all admiration of him, even if he does not care to play gowff."

"Alasdair has many fine qualities, though play at

sports that don't involve bloodshed is not one of them," Colin said diplomatically. "And by all means, ask the MacLeod to come to Noltland if you wish an outsider to manage your affairs. But I promise that you shall never be rid of him thereafter."

"He cannot be bargained with?"

"No more than a beast," Colin answered frankly.

"You see no difference between the two?" Frances didn't, either, but was shocked that Colin would speak so bluntly of his kin.

"Aye, of course I do. A beast, though perhaps vicious, will not lie to you. Nor does it covet everything it sees."

"This is very plain speaking." Frances realized that she was whispering, her voice the thinnest of threads.

Colin, all apparent sympathy, poured her another goblet of wine. "Aye, it is." He smiled suddenly. The creases in his cheek held her gaze riveted. "So will you not then be equally plain with me? I am most curious. How have you carried on this ruse? You move the pikes about at regular hours to suggest there are guards, I suppose?"

"Aye, and light watch fires at night." She quickly drank down the deceptively sweet draught. It made her a bit light-headed; she had grown unused to wine. "And we keep watch as well. We are always prepared to lower the yett during the day if someone approaches, and it is down every evening before nightfall."

"But that is not all, surely?" Colin asked, breaking off some bread and setting it on her plate.

"*Non*. Every score of days we take an old cow hide and smear it with the blood of a chicken or a hare and then hang it from the castle wall as though drying the pelt from a freshly slaughtered animal."

"And so everyone outside believes that you are regularly slaughtering cattle. And where there are cattle, one supposes there are men to tend them. And you also use the forge so the smithy seems occupied." Colin shook his head and added mostly to himself: "And that is why Tearlach is tolerated. None but a man with soldiers in his care would order the daily playing of those pipes. Mistress, you have my admiration. And these were all your stratagems?"

"*Oui*. Except Tearlach." Frances frowned at her blunt admittance, and looked at her goblet as though blaming it for her loose tongue. "I have grown unaccustomed to wine. I did not mean to speak of that. You must not either if you value your safety. Your connection to the MacLeods would not save you from the MacKays. It would, in fact, condemn you if you were captured." She turned stern eyes upon him and lifted a brow as she waited for his answer.

"You may be certain that I shall not speak of it to your neighbors," Colin promised as he smiled down at her. "Truly, I've no wish to be invaded either."

"No, you would not, would you?" she said slowly, some nervousness abating.

"Of course not. Now, why don't you tell me who our enemies are? I know what Alasdair thinks, but it is plain that he has been rather misinformed about the situation."

"Enemies?" Frances felt stupid.

"Aye. Why is everyone so fearful about nightfall? Every room is brightly lit with torches. The servants even go about in twos and threes, glancing worriedly at dark corners as though searching for assassins."

"Oh." Frances dropped her eyes. The urge to confide her worries to Colin warred with the church's teachings that Protestants were the tools of Satan and often in league with demons who were sent to corrupt and murder good Catholics. Such Godless men, with their rationalism, would not understand about spirits of evil. They would sneer and possibly even laugh at tales of spectral hounds and evil hauntings.

"Come! Surely it is not so bad a thing that it cannot be named," Colin said.

"But it is," Frances assured him. "For three nights now someone has heard the Bokey hound in his hole beneath the stairs. Always this hound bays when there is to be a death in the house."

Colin sat back in his chair, his mobile face at last arrested. "Have they now? But what unusual timing." The words were said aloud, but Frances knew that he wasn't really speaking to her.

"*Oui*."

"This is most interesting."

"It is more than interesting, monsieur," she said with a touch of indignation. Discretion was abandoned as anger licked through her, though she kept her voice pitched low as she answered. "The hound always appears in the flesh when the master of the castle is to die. I am very afraid for George and do not know how to protect him from this evil."

"*Pshaw!* I shouldn't be too alarmed yet. A hound, or something, has been heard but not seen. It is likely some beast living on the heath, kept by a cruel master, and it howls at night because it is lonely. We shall have to make an effort to find it and see to its liberation. However, in the interest of avoiding panic until we determine which is the shrieking beast, I think you should put aside these stories of the hound and instead set about discovering how many of your human enemies are lurking about the castle environs and spying upon you."

"How are we to discover the spectral hound if he is outside the castle?" she demanded, then, considering Colin's other point, added thoughtfully: "Or an enemy that controls such a one?"

"I doubt we shall have to. I am fairly certain that the hound—spectral or otherwise—shall discover us in the fullness of time," he said calmly.

"*Oui*, and so am I certain of this." Her tone was tart. "It causes me much alarm, this threat of discovery. I do not wish George to die. I have a great fondness for him."

"Have some more wine," Colin said, resuming his soothing air. "You should eat. Have some of this excellent chicken and you shall feel better presently."

"Have you no fear of evil and its minions?" Frances asked, baffled by Colin's attitude of calm.

"Oh, aye, a lively fear. But I do not think it is true evil we are facing here. I have some experience with the supernatural realm in my own country, and so far I have seen nothing to suggest that George is endangered by anything spiritual or demonic."

Colin smiled slightly as he heard Frances mutter something beneath her breath. Her French was growing slurred, but it sounded like: *The sisters were correct. All Englishmen are mad and blind to the true nature of evil.*

"We are agreed then? I shall write to Sir William Kirkcauldy on the morrow, and we will begin seeking out this suspicious rustling beneath the stairs." He knew that he was being a cad, overpersuading Frances to cooperation when she was the worse for wine, but did not desist.

"You may write all the letters you wish," she told him waspishly. "But there is no one to deliver them."

"Of course there is. MacJannet loves to travel in the autumn. He has not ever visited Sir William, and will enjoy himself immensely out in the fresh air."

"*Vraiment?*" Frances leaned over and looked down thc tablc at Colin's faithful factotum. As calm as his master, MacJannet spoke easily with George, illustrating some point with a wave of his hand. All about him, women stared with vaguely worried eyes, but the weight of their gazes seemed not to disturb his conversation or demeanor. Perhaps this phlegmatic obliviousness was part of being English.

She turned back to Colin. "If your man actually wishes to make a perilous journey to go see Sir William, then I fear that your poor MacJannet is *un cretin*."

Colin laughed. "No, mistress, I assure you that MacJannet is not an imbecile."

Perhaps hearing this, MacJannet turned his head and looked up the table.

"*Non?* Then he must also be mad," Frances whispered sorrowfully, making an effort to enunciate her words. She was feeling very tired. "And we have enough madness in Tearlach MacAdams."

Instead of denying the accusation, Colin actually chuckled. Frances thought muzzily that it was a great pity one so handsome should also come from the land of the blind and insane.

You crave one kiss of my clay-cold lips;
But my breath smells earthly strong;
If you have one kiss of my clay-cold lips,
Your time will not be long.

—*"The Unquiet Grave"*

Chapter Six

"Bloody hell," he muttered. Too late to rouse MacJannet and trap their intruder before he escaped, Colin leaned forward and peered through the narrow opening that passed for a window and assessed the heavens and what little he could see of the world below. The sky beyond the niche was sullen, the moon blotted out to a faint halo as the clouds began to release their heavy burden of rain over Noltland. The only other light came from the failing and abandoned watch fires, which would shortly be drowned. He could not see anything more than the shadowy yett below, which was an annoyance, even though he had no real hope of catching their late-night visitor leaving by so obvious an exit.

Frustrated, Colin drew back from the warped and ill-fitting panes and drummed his chilled finger upon the thick stone sill. He stared into the rain as he considered what next to do.

The already inauspicious view of lowering sky was further impeded by ugly iron links that hung from the parapet above. Mist and rain had condensed on the thick chains until it fell in heavy drops, which were blown against the poorly fitted glass. The iron bands swung in a gentle but heavy arc, pushed along by the boisterous eddies, or maybe the ghostly hands of one of the poor wretches who had died in the cages that had once been suspended from them.

George had confided to Colin as they passed this way on their tour that the first order he had given—at Frances's urging—was for the removal of those ghastly cages and the bones of the poor wretches who had perished in them. The dead, regardless of estate or crimes, were interred in the castle's ossuary—which Colin had declined to see, in spite of his young host's enthusiastic invitation. There would be time enough to meet the castle ghosts later. The chains themselves would have been removed as well, but they and the gibbet had been embedded into the walls at the time of construction and no one could decide how to take them down without dismantling the castle itself.

Colin frowned in distaste and wondered at the architect who would have planned such an abysmal prospect for the rare castle windows. Who would want to look at a starving man when there was the ocean to consider? It must have been at the request of someone with a vengeful soul, he decided, turning finally to go down the stairs. Probably someone without a wife. He could not imagine any mistress tolerating such a ghastly view. Of course, he could not picture any wife submitting to the housing of thirty illegitimate sons either, yet that was what the last Balfour had done.

Colin peered down at the deserted and drafty hall where he knew he needed to search for clues to their intruder's identity. As he was debating whether to waken MacJannet, a slightly paler shade of darkness glided up to Colin's right side. He was not alarmed. The shadow smelled faintly of lavender and walked with soft, feminine feet.

"Is it the Bokey hound?" a soft voice whispered, as the shade leaned over the balustrade and peered at the now-empty hall. "I thought I heard a wail."

"No, it was not a spectral hound." Colin answered, also speaking at a hush. It was dark, but he could feel Frances looking at him. He had a momentary and insane urge to explain to her about his ability to see real ghosts.

"Then, there is no danger?"

"I would not say that," Colin answered slowly, then added: "What a bloody nuisance. It is not as if we did not have enough difficulties besetting us. Now we have this jester trying to sow seeds of panic."

"A nuisance?" Frances repeated, tasting the word. Then: "Panic?"

"Aye." Colin flipped open the lantern's door, setting free the caged light, and proceeded down the steep stairs at an unhurried pace. "Come along. It is too late to capture our unwanted prowler, but we had best investigate what was done."

"You wish me to go down there?" Frances asked softly, but no longer whispering since Colin was not using any more silence than one would to be courteous of those sleeping. She hurried after the lantern's comforting light, preferring its protection to that of the small dagger she carried clutched in her fist.

"Let us first have some better illumination," he said, going to the large fireplace and stirring up the peat. It took a bit of coaxing, but embers eventually responded to the fresh fuel he fed it. "There is less chance of having specters visit us with the hearth well lit. Look about while I tend to the fire, but have a care not to stray far."

Reluctantly, Frances complied, though she was uncertain of what to look for and did not wish to drift too far into the wavering shadows.

Light flared up suddenly, illuminating the room. Frances sucked in her breath and murmured a shocked and horrified exclamation at what was lying immediately before her slippered feet.

Colin looked questioningly at her, and she pointed a shaking dagger at the large paw prints revealed by the fire's renewed brightness. "It was the hound! He has come to claim the Balfour!" Her voice shook.

Colin glanced once at the floor and then returned his gaze to Mistress Balfour. The lady's nightwear was elegant and foreign. He could see the embroidered cuffs of a silk chemise peeping out from under a velvet robe of a mulberry shade called Murrey, which was presently popular at court. The chemise itself seemed to be a popinjay green sometimes referred to by the appalling but accurate description of goose-turd green. Whatever it was called, the combination was striking by firelight. He had to put the night rail, and its wearer, firmly out of mind before he was able to speak as a rational man intent on business.

"It was *a* hound," he said finally. "A large one, about the size of a two-year-old heifer." He walked to the marks and knelt down, comparing the print with the palm of his hand. They were a good match. He grunted and then took out his handkerchief and began scrubbing the prints off the floor.

"What are you doing?" Frances asked, clearly appalled.

"Cleaning up the floor. Have you a broom?" he asked. "That would make the task easier."

"But . . ." Frances tried to protest his lack of awe in the face of evil, but couldn't find the proper words while he was so deliberately scrubbing out the hound's markings.

"It is just crushed lime," Colin told her. "Someone covered the beast in powder and sent him in to scare everyone. It was a stupid trick and not likely to terrify anyone who had a good look at the thing. Our villain is not the most intelligent of beings."

"No?" Frances asked, not prepared to admit that the prints scared her, and that the hound that made them doubtlessly would have, too.

Colin looked sharply at her pale face and was moved from annoyance to sympathy. Once, as a young man, he had been confronted by what he thought was a ghost in the company of a spectral hound. In the moments before he realized that it was only a caped and masked figure with a white dog seeking the anonymity of darkness while reporting to his father, it had felt as though his mind was plucked smooth of every thought and emotion save fear. It was as though the strands of reason had been torn out at the roots, and all that was left was blank, terrifying dread that made one gibber and freeze. And once terror took hold there was no reasoning with it. Bolting horses maddened by lightning were more discerning than a panicked human mind. The trick, he had discovered, was to cut off the flower of fear before it ever blossomed in the brain.

"Anyone who is at all acquainted with spectral hounds could tell you that this beast is not one of them. We have a few that haunt where I live. They fall into two varieties. One is thought to be a devil that enjoys making mischief for travelers. The other is a cu-sith, a faerie dog that guards the entrance to fey strongholds. They are protective. This is neither devil nor faerie, but rather *a damned trick*." He spoke with studied scorn, which he knew would serve as a restorative to Frances's nerves. His father had perfected the tone, and Colin knew that such a reasoned, unemotional manner could not help but banish cowardice and send timid ghosts fleeing.

"How can you tell this for a certainty?" she demanded, finally putting down her dagger and then looking about for the hearth broom so that she could assist Colin in his housewifely endeavors. Her hands barely shook.

"As I said, we have a great many spectral beasts and faerie dogs in York—the black Shuck and the Barghest being the most famous of them," he said matter-of-factly. "Anyone could tell you that the hounds after a soul always travel in a straight, purposeful line. Look at this mess! The beast wandered about everywhere."

Frances looked at the multitude of messy criss-crossed prints. "They always travel a straight path?" she asked, feeling more hopeful.

"Always, even if it means passing through walls," Colin averred. "Secondly, the beast howls three times and three times only—and it is clamorous howling, not whining. And lastly, I had a look at our canine in the flesh. It was no spectral hound."

"You actually saw it?" Frances nearly dropped her broom. "And lived?"

"Aye, I did see it, from the top of the stairs."

"What did the beast look like?"

"It looked like a large dog covered in chalky lime," he said. "And I think you should know, only rarely are spectral hounds white. Faerie dogs are pale green. Hellhounds are black. I have heard of only one white hound and it was headless. And none of them leave paw prints."

"Headless? As in, it has had its head removed?" Frances asked, appalled but fascinated.

"Aye. And I shall tell you something more since you are so ignorant of Scotland's ghosts." Colin's lips twitched as though he were suppressing a smile, but Frances found that she did not take umbrage at either the lecture or his amusement. "Spectral hounds come in two varieties. There are those that have no tails and those whose tails curl up over their backs. What they do not have are long tails that wag. And never, under any circumstances, do they turn their leg up upon furniture," Colin said wrinkling his nose and gesturing with a languid hand.

Frances finally grew aware of the smell of urine that flooded the room.

"Ah, *mon Dieu*!" She dragged a chair away from the spoiled table leg. Her housewifely instincts were plainly revolted. "Then it is all a disagreeable trick and George is in no danger?"

"He was quite well when I looked in on him," Colin answered, evading her question for the moment. "However, this must be investigated fully."

"Now? But why? If it is only a dog—"

"Because the castle should be sealed tight, yet somehow the hound—and perhaps his keeper—got inside. I do not believe that it was an accident, either. Someone brought the dusty beast here to try to cause fear among us. If a beast can get in, so may others. We must find where it retreated and close the doors against it."

"Ah! We can follow the tracks, *oui*? And discover this weakness in our safety?" Faint enthusiasm showed in her voice. "That would be most wise."

"Aye. We'll find tomorrow how they got past the perimeter walls," Colin promised. "It is a pity that it has begun to rain, for MacJannet and I might have followed the beast outside this evening and discovered where it is being kept. Now we shall have to content ourselves with making the keep itself safe from further visitations."

"This now seems like a . . ." She hunted for a word. "A stupid jest. A child's game. But you think it is something more than wicked sport?"

"I do not know why it should be anything more than a jest designed to frighten you into the arms of one of your neighbors," Colin told her in a wonderfully frank tone, meeting her eyes as he answered. His father had also taught him how to sound earnest when he lied. "But we should not take chances, should we?"

"*Non.*" Frances was sober. She had grasped the implications in spite of his reticence. "If someone wished to harm George by stealth, they could pretend it was the hound that killed him, could they not? And if I were taken away by my husband, there would be no one to look after him when I was gone."

Colin nodded reluctantly. "Aye, someone could do exactly that. And no one would look too closely at the facts of the matter if the story of the spectral hound were widely believed."

Frances swallowed, but she did not panic at the

news that her cousin might be in danger. Colin's comforting presence and prosaic manner forbade any hysterics.

"Do you know who is doing this?" she asked him.

"Know? Nay. It could be anyone. There are many who might want young George gone." This was truth, as far as it went. Suspecting that his cousin might be behind the clumsy effort was not the same as *knowing* that Alasdair was directing a campaign of misdirection so that he might kill the young heir and have the castle all to himself if Colin failed to soften the heiress. And it was also unfortunately true that the Balfours had other neighbors—many of them—just as determined to win the heiress and the castle for themselves. They made as reasonable suspects as his superstitious cousin, and were closer in proximity.

And there is also Tearlach, Colin realized suddenly. Or someone else within the castle who might want to see Frances removed. That explanation made rather more sense. Some longtime resident could very well know about a secret passage or hidden staircase. And it might be that they did not wish George any mortal harm, but merely wished to drive Frances into marriage with some wealthy, outside party before siege and starvation were brought upon them.

Colin shrugged off his fruitless speculations and returned to the task at hand. They would clean up the hall before the others arose, thus depriving the malefactor of the spectacle of a dawn panic among the servants. Then, after everyone had broken their fasts, he and MacJannet—and Frances, if she were of a mind to join him—would search out the place where the hound had gained entrance to the keep.

With luck they would also discover some clue to the mischief-maker's identity. Anyone desperate enough to employ such means to force Frances into seeking outside protection might also be willing to act as spy or traitor in other ways to an outside clan when this plot failed. Treason happened in small steps and often ended in bloody murder, even when it wasn't the perpetrator's first intention.

"Shall we follow the trail now and clean as we proceed?" Frances suggested, peering at the pale prints, which dwindled as they headed back for the stairs. Stripped of their supernatural horror, which blinded the mind to reason, she now found it a simple matter to track the beast's comings and goings.

"Aye. Though I have a fair notion where these shall lead us."

"*Oui?*" Frances swallowed and then guessed: "The dungeon?"

"It seems inevitable," Colin answered. "'Tis that or the privies. Those would be the only places where one might come and go completely unobserved."

Frances shuddered. "I do not know which I prefer less to see by night. There are rats in both places."

"I certainly know which I would rather avoid while it's dark," Colin said as he wrinkled his nose. "You may trust me on this as I have had some little experience with privies. Velvet and cesses are not a happy union, particularly when working in the dark where one cannot be certain of one's footing. I simply cannot imagine why anyone would have them when there are so many tidier ways of handling the necessity. But that's the barbaric North for you."

Frances stared. The remark suggested that her new Master of the Gowff was completely devoid of the nice spiritual sensibilities of a true gentleman, which should have quailed more at the thought of entering a place where so many unhappy souls had perished instead of worrying about possible feculence in the ground-floor privies. On the other hand, in this circumstance she found herself grateful that she was with someone devoid of such nerves: Such obvious calm and lack of imagination did not permit her own thoughts to run away from much needed reason and courage.

Frances straightened her spine and retrieved her dagger from the table. "Then let us be off," she said, thrusting the hindering broom at Colin.

The Master of the Gowff smiled slightly and nodded, either in agreement with the assigned task or in approval of her plan to seek out the place of egress. As he accepted the broom without complaint and said nothing about the weapon she clutched in her hand, she supposed it could be both.

Frances waited for him to suggest that he lead the way in her stead, but when he did not she nodded back, picked up the lantern and started for the door, weapon poised to strike at anyone who might leap out at her.

Colin did not laugh at her alarmed posture. Frances decided that there were most certainly previously unconsidered benefits to being with a man who did not react in a typical overbearing manner when surprised by new circumstances. Her father would most certainly have taken the dagger from her and then selfishly turned out the exhausted household to search for the beast while he ordered her back to bed. He would never have understood the pride that demanded she personally confront the danger that threatened the people in her care. He thought pride and courage were things known only to men. Women were for rutting, nothing more.

There were, however, limits to her courage, and she was not sorry to hear Colin lifting a mace down from the wall before he joined her. Of course the intruder had departed, but a little caution was never a bad thing. A mace would be better suited to stopping an attacking dog than her tiny dagger. She wished she had thought to bring a gowff club with her. With that she might defeat the devil himself.

"*Mon Dieu*," she muttered. "Your wits were surely gone."

"What is wrong?" Colin asked, stepping up swiftly beside her. His eyes scanned the room.

"It is only that I should have brought my gowff club instead of this dagger."

He smiled a little. "Here. You'll feel better with this." He offered her the mace.

After a moment of silent surprise, Frances again nodded and they exchanged weapons. The mace was unfamiliar and very heavy, but she felt more confident having a stick in her hand. She did not doubt that she could accurately strike anything she wished with the longer-handled weapon and loft its evil head out the door.

"Something has been gnawing at the door frame," Colin said, as he bent at the waist.

"The hound?"

"Nay, I suspect a rat. There is no slobber here, and marks are quite low."

"Oh." Frances swallowed. She did not like rats, but a mace would take care of any impudent rodents as well as hellhounds. "Well then, let us take the broom and depart. If it does not clean well enough we may return and fetch some water."

Colin merely nodded.

For he suddenly smote the door, even
Louder, and lifted his head:
"—Tell them I came, and no one answered,
That I kept my word," he said.

—Walter de la Mare, "The Listeners"

Chapter Seven

Though she knew it was foolhardy bravado on her part, inspired by shame at her initial credulity the night before, a just-awakened Frances nevertheless took up her favorite gowff club and a lantern, and started off on her own for a morning exploration of the dungeons of Noltland.

It was highly unlikely, she told herself, that her enemy would come into the castle during the day when he might be easily seen and his hound would look like the earthly creature it was. And if Colin were correct in his assumptions of the previous evening, then the animal could well have gained entrance through the privies, whose outer wall was not far off the ground and had deteriorated over the years of corrosive onslaught. She was therefore in no real peril. After all, who would send a spectral hound to the old dungeon where no one resided or even visited? There was also the matter of passing through a heavy, barred door to enter the castle proper.

Unless, of course, it was a *real* spectral hound and

it lived there as the legend said. Then doors of any weight would be no obstacle for an infernal beast.

Frances shook herself. This was no time for foolishness—at least not imaginative foolishness. Going to the dungeons was another matter. She had a responsibility to her people, and she would feel redeemed for her cowardice if she explored on her own all possibilities of where the beast might have gained admittance to the keep. She could then go to Colin and announce that he needn't spend his days exploring the dungeons because she had already done so, and they would then repair the privy wall and everyone would be safe, and her self-regard would be intact.

Frances paused in the corridor while her eyes grew accustomed to the dim light. Temporary courage and lantern light eventually carried her forward, but she found that it did nothing to ward off the chill of the lower floors, which smelled strongly of the cold sea and something rather sour. Slowly but certainly, the miasma of old death seemed to creep beneath her tucked-up skirts and crawl over her legs, making her long for a hot bath by a blazing hearth.

Underfoot, brittle things crunched and snapped as she walked, causing echoes to flee up the passage and then return, an unpleasant noise which sounded a great deal like a stealthy pursuer creeping up on her from behind. Frances did not look down into the shadows or over her shoulder more than once. She scolded herself for her fanciful thoughts that drained her resolve, and decided that if it were bits of bone instead of the husks of insects she trod upon with her thin-soled shoes, she did not want to know.

She paused again outside the door that led from the basements into the dungeons proper and took a few deep breaths. Of course she had never been in the dungeons before. Her mother would never have allowed it when she was a child. But when they last had been cleaned out, in the year of her fourth birthday, there had been stories about the bits and pieces left carelessly behind in the room used for questioning prisoners.

There was also something worse down here than the cast-off bones of the tortured and imprisoned. The sea hole was one of them. It was a natural shaft carved by the sea when it had made its inland cave, over which the keep had been built. The castle's occupants used to drop prisoners down into it and then leave them to whatever fate the sea chose. Those poor moaning wretches with their broken bodies were completely ignored. No food, no water—except the sea at high tide lapping at them—they must have died screaming, maddened by pain from their injuries and by fear of the dark and drowning in the encroaching waves.

Frances shuddered, this time shaking so hard that the lantern light wavered. She didn't believe that her father had ever used the sea hole to punish prisoners, and therefore any lingering ghosts should not hold her responsible for their demise. But even with this rationalization, it still took all her will to draw back the door's heavy, grimed bolt and push against the warped panel.

The stubborn old door held fast against her. For an awful moment, Frances wondered if there was something leaning against the far side of the heavy panel—something large and hostile to the notion of invasion! Perhaps the hound itself!

But, *non*! She was allowing herself to be influenced by the bad air below stairs. She had to remain calm and think. It might be that a hinge had broken. Or, so near to the sea, it could be that the door had deformed. Old wood in the castle always warped. Every few years, doors had to be taken down and their bottoms planed smooth so they would open without dragging. That was all this was. More force was needed.

Reassured, Frances set down her lantern and club and returned to the obstinate blockage. The thought of placing her hands upon the filthy panel was not a pleasant one, but she had not thought to wear gloves or even a mantle on this expedition, so it would have to be done if she were to prove her mettle and complete her quest.

The door was cold, shockingly so. It made the tips of her fingers tingle when she touched it. She pushed, but naked fingers and palms could not move the chilled door more than a few groaning inches, and she feared she was driving splinters into her hands.

Growing ever more assured by the grinding noise of disuse that no intruder had actually taken this route into the castle, Frances happily laid her shoulder to the door and pushed with all her might.

The panel gave suddenly, loosing a wooden shriek that was probably heard throughout the castle. Frances lost her balance and stumbled a step into the room. Before she was able to right herself, something rushed through the dark behind her and hit her in the middle back. The blow shoved her into the black beyond. She screamed once on her way down the shallow steps—only three of them by the grace of God—but one of the treads caught her sharply beneath the ribs where she heard a sharp crack, and she found that she had no air with which to cry out a second time.

Above her, the door was pulled, protesting, back into place and the bolt shot home. She found herself sealed inside the dungeon without her lantern or her club.

It took a moment for Frances to regain her breath and reassure herself that she was undamaged. The only bones broken had been in her stays, and her bumroll had saved her hips from great harm. Loathing for the cold, filthy floor helped her regain her feet, though she found it necessary to lean against a chill stone wall while she waited for her cartwheeling senses to stop.

Equilibrium eventually restored, she felt her way along the wall, carefully climbing the shallow stairs until she had returned to the door. Of course it was closed and there was no handle on her side. Ignoring the fact that she had heard the bolt shut, Frances tried to find purchase around the edge to pull it back open. But of course there was none. She found only deep grooves, which might have been caused by a dirk or some other tool applied by an ancient prisoner who had managed to smuggle a weapon into his jail.

Frances let her hands fall away from the door. She was suddenly very calm. Tiny sparks of anger were igniting inside her. It was too cold, and the atmosphere too frightening, for them to blaze into a full rage, but the small lights of anger served as an internal lantern of reason and kept the panic at bay.

Her circumstances were not as horrible as they might have seemed. True, she was locked in a dungeon, which no one frequented. But Colin would note her missing presence by the noontime meal, or certainly by the time they gathered for dinner, and it would occur to him just where she was. He and MacJannet would mount a search for her and would effect her rescue immediately. He might even come sooner if he explored here before the privies.

All she had to do was remain calm and not wander away from the door. The sounds of the sea were audible now that the thundering of her heart had subsided. She could smell the brine in the air. Probably there was some sort of grate over the sea hole, but it might have been left open, or rusted away over the years. She had to be cautious about wandering in the dark.

Trembling with cold, Frances closed her eyes against the terrible, pressing darkness, pretending it was only her closed eyelids that prevented her from seeing her surroundings.

For a while she counted the splashing waves, noting that every seventh crash was louder than the previous ones had been. And then she let her fingers take a second inventory of the stone around the door.

Eventually, she grew numb to the cold and even a little bored. It was then that she began to speculate about whose hand she had felt on her back. She did not for one moment doubt that it had been a human agent who had shoved her into the dungeon and then barred the door. A spectral hound would have no need to use doors to restrain her.

It took an act of will to not let the idea that it had been Colin himself who locked her in the dungeon do more than flit briefly across her mind. Colin was a stranger, but not a cruel or evil one. Of course it was someone else who had done this—most likely the inept person who had tried to frighten them with the fake hellhound. And this person had come in through the damaged privy wall, not the dungeon! Therefore there would be no cause for him to return to the basements. And no danger of her being closed in with the chalky hound. She was quite safe, if a bit cold and hungry. All would be well.

Frances began to hum, swaying to her own music as she rubbed her hands up and down her freezing arms.

Colin exhaled in partial relief when he spotted the lantern and the golf club near the dungeon door. He and MacJannet had been searching the castle since breaking their fast, delaying his friend's departure. One of the women had approached them at the table and told him that her mistress seemed to have gone missing.

"I should have guessed that this would be her destination," he muttered, hurrying to the door, where he stared unhappily at the thrown bolt.

"Frances!" he called, forgetting formality as he drew back the bar and shoved on the ancient door.

A voice, heard only faintly over the grinding of the door, answered. Reassured, he put his back into the effort, slamming the door into the wall with a clamorous bang.

Before he had even straightened himself, a freezing bundle of dirty woolens came hurtling out of the dark and into his arms. A strangling vise encircled his waist and he found his nose buried in dark hair.

"I knew you would come!" she declared in French.

Overcoming his surprise, Colin closed his own arms about the tiny body and returned the embrace, though with slightly less force than Frances was using.

"I was pushed down the stairs," she said indignantly, her words muffled by the folds of his cape. "Some vile person crept upon me and shoved me when I was opening the door."

"Bloody hell!" Involuntarily his arms contracted further, drawing a squeak from the dirty bundle as something cracked beneath her clothes. Colin immediately loosened his hold and stared at her in consternation. "Are you injured from the fall?"

"I am cold and filthy and have a great bruise upon my ribs, but 'tis only my stays which are broken instead of me." Frances turned her grimy face up toward his. Her eyes were filled with pooling tears, which leaked upon her pale cheeks. Tiny, smudged hands clasped the front of his cape. "I want you to find the person who did this and punish them. I want them castrated and beheaded and thrown into the sea. I want them burned and strangled and torn apart by horses and lions."

Colin didn't even smile at her extremes of passion. Feeling the broken corset stays grind beneath his hands was a demonstration of what serious consequences the prank could have had.

"Be assured that I will find whoever did this, and they will be punished. But come along now. We need to get you to a fire. You are very chilled."

Her hands tightened momentarily, speaking of her lingering fear and desire for comfort. Knowing they were vulnerable to a second attack in the near dark, it still took an effort of extreme will for Colin to set Frances from him when she was so upset and needing reassurance.

"My dear, we need to leave at once. I did not even bring a sword." Muttering imprecations at his own carelessness, Colin leaned over and took up the abandoned golf club, putting it into her dirty hands. He noticed that they immediately stilled their trembling. Her posture also straightened. It seemed that golf did indeed have some uses as a calmative.

Some men would have found this action alarming,

to be honest, but he was not one of them. Many males preferred their women purely sweet and decorative, but he had always liked some salt to go with the treacle. Frances's strength and courage were assets, not something to be deplored. He would never want her spirit broken by fear.

Frances retreated another step, allowing him access to the dungeon door. Colin closed the panel into the dungeon and put the bolt back in place. He picked up her lantern and then his own. His movements were unhurried, allowing Frances plenty of time to recover herself before they went back upstairs.

"Are you ready to see everyone?" he asked.

She wiped a sleeve defiantly over her cheeks and nodded regally. "*Oui*. I am again calm. But let us depart immediately. Tomorrow I am going to send the scullery maids to clean down here. The floors are a disgrace."

Finally Colin had the urge to smile, but he was careful to do no more than nod. "I think it might be a very good thing to have these basements thoroughly inspected."

"And then I shall order the door to be bricked up. George will never need to use such a beastly place. I will not permit it. We are not barbarians."

Colin nodded again, not pointing out the inconsistency of cleaning a floor that would soon be closed off from the rest of the castle.

"But first we shall repair the privy wall so there are no more evil persons sneaking about the castle and pushing people into dungeons. Tearlach shall do it. That should keep him occupied so he does not complain all day of cobwebs growing on his useless unmentionables," Frances remarked with satisfaction as she brushed past Colin, collecting one of the lanterns on the way.

"A most sound strategy," Colin replied, following Frances closely, though she clearly was in no danger of fainting or hurling herself into his arms now that she had regained her poise.

Colin carefully didn't mention his belief that it hadn't been an intruder who had pushed her down the stairs and closed the dungeon door upon her. There had been no chance of anyone slipping into the castle with MacJannet and his unshakeable companion, George, keeping watch at the privies. Brave as she was, Frances needed a while to fully recover her calm before discovering that they likely had a traitor living in their midst. And that this someone was willing to commit acts of malicious mischief, and perhaps worse, to force the keep's mistress into surrendering her castle to the wrong man—or keeping it for herself. It was rare that females turned to violent crime, but when they did, it was Colin's experience that they were proficient. He had to wonder which of Frances's relatives was trying to hurt her.

Go fetch me water from the desert,
And blood from out the stone;
Go fetch me milk from a fair maid's breast
That a young man hath never known.

—"The Unquiet Grave"

CHAPTER EIGHT

Frances found it difficult to concentrate on her weaving. Her continuing absentmindedness at the loom was understandable to the other ladies, given her recent ordeal in the dungeon. They did not have the entire story, Colin having only relayed that she'd had a tumble down the stairs while searching for a whisky cache her father was thought to have hidden somewhere in the castle. However, it was not her aborted search for the spectral hound, nor even her bruised ribs rubbing against the uncomfortable oak straw chair, that plagued her thoughts that afternoon. Rather it was the lingering, strange sensations that being held in Colin's arms had provoked.

Admittedly, her sojourn there had been brief, but it was proving highly memorable. No other embrace that she could recall had so affected her.

Of course, this strong reaction to Colin was partly appreciation, as she was naturally grateful for being rescued so promptly from the horrid dungeon. But something about that particular moment of embrace had made her heart a little wild. Before he touched her she had not been tumultuous of mind and disturbed in spirit. But her thudding pulse, even now as she sat at rest in front of her loom, continued to be uneasy. There were fine tremors in her hands, and small yet not unpleasant shivers occasionally traversed the length of her body. She knew what this was symptomatic of, and it shocked her to consider that she might be subject to the traditional female follies and weaknesses when it came to a man. Though strong-willed in many ways, it seemed that she was not, after all, above being seduced by a handsome face. This called for some careful consideration.

When they were again above stairs and the time had come for them to separate so she might bathe her hands and face, it had taken all her will not to beg Colin to stay with her. In that moment, she had not been thinking reasonably, or even modestly. Her dignity and position as lady of the castle were forgotten in her new desire. All she had known was that she wanted Colin by her side. Had he not turned away sharply outside her chamber door, she probably would have spoken her thoughts aloud. And then there might have been calamitous consequences either to her dignity or to her honor. She still could not say which would have been worse.

Frances scowled as the sound of Tearlach's curses floated up from the privy, reminding her of the danger that still stalked them. She had to collect herself and concentrate on serious matters. Not that finding their prankish intruder wasn't important, but it was not her most important task. Her reason had become so tainted that it had led her to do a very careless thing in hopes of winning Colin's regard. It was almost as though she were having a grand passion for this man and trying to prove herself worthy of respect by being heedless and brave so he wouldn't think her milk-livered. This was important to him, she sensed. But why should that matter to her? He was but a stranger: perspicacious, and even handsome, it was true; still, he was a completely unknown entity. He might have any manner of hidden flaws to his nature. Eyes in which one might drown, or smiling lips that might hold wondrous kisses were not sufficient recommendations to a lady in her position.

And if he seemed the answer to the terrible loneliness that had been growing in her?

No, she had to be sensible. He might, beneath his fine clothes, be like her father: an immoral man, one whose words to women were like honey but whose heart was steeped in basest, preternatural lust. It seemed unlikely that Colin was such a one, but how was she to know? Lust could do much mischief. Look at her father and how he had shamed her mother with his lovers!

And what did lust do to women? It made them into sirens, then whores and Furies. It was horrifying to think that such a base emotion might even now be coursing through her body, an unwanted inheritance from her father carried in her blood like disease. Could falling in love with this stranger mean that her integrity was injured or even completely lost?

She closed her eyes on the thought and tried to deny it, but Colin's image haunted her, refusing to be relegated back into his proper place. Frances opened her eyes and sighed. She redoubled her stern lecture and thought moral thoughts.

Yes, Colin was tall and seemed strong, but it could

be that, like her uncle in France, at night he put aside his false hair onto a wigstand, his wooden teeth into a box. His codpiece and padded coat could also be put out of the way and then he would appear shrunken, dismantled, perhaps even smelling like goat cheese covered in perfume.

And it could even be worse. He might be truly—eloquently and elegantly—evil. He was kin to the MacLeod. What if he were polluted by his wicked ways? That thought was frightening. The laird of the MacLeods spoke words of affection without any true sentiment. She had sensed immediately that there was no concurrence between the MacLeod's mind and his heart's true desires and the ones he expressed aloud to her. Dishonesty in amatory dealing might be the standard perversion of this family.

Not that Colin had said or done anything to prove he was cut of this same cloth. That was part of the problem. If he showed himself a heartless knave, it would be easy to forget him.

Her own family was peculiar this way. The men did not generally love one another. Nor did they love humanity, or even God. They seemed not to even love themselves. Yet her father had decided to go to war, so to war and death they all went, blithely leaving the women behind to cope with rapacious neighbors and winter starvation. Men were beyond comprehension.

Frances mulled this point over for a moment or two and then reexamined her new feelings with this caution in mind. Somehow, this argument of the sins of the cousin infecting his kin failed to convince her senses to see Colin as a negligible personage unworthy of trust and respect. He was not like any other man she had known.

Frances clenched her hands against their continued trembling and made an effort to smile at the hovering ladies, Eilidh and Sine, wishing they would be less inquisitive and more like the more aloof Anne Balfour.

She knew what the sisters at the convent would say about this infatuation. They would send for a leech to administer a *salvatella*. He would open her *vena amoris,* which ran down her arm to her ring finger, and let her bleed away her infatuation into a tiny bowl. This thought alone was enough to make her feel ill and swoonish. If she did not cease her worrying, her late breakfast would rejumble, and she loathed being sick to her stomach. If only there were someone to whom she could unbosom herself.

But there was no one. She was, as ever, alone. And to be wise, she must run counter to her new instincts until she could better assess Colin Mortlock and his possible threat to her heart.

She picked up her spindle.

Bah! What a fuss over nothing. She was simply vaporish from her time in the bad air of the dungeon; this was all that ailed her. Her situation was deplorable but no worse than the day before. A meal and some rest and her body and brain would return themselves to their usual state, and she would have no more of these wild and passionate thoughts about giving herself to her new Master of the Gowff.

The important thing for her to recall was that virginity was like an oyster. The pearl could be taken but once, and therefore one had to be cautious. Even to the point of marriage. It was her unfortunate experience, learned from her mother before the sweating sickness or her broken heart had carried her off, that even this most holy of institutions was a precarious place in which to trust one's heart.

"Do you think it wise for me to leave the keep at this juncture?" MacJannet asked in a calm voice, which only partially masked his surprise and agitation at Colin's order that he should leave that night.

"But of course. I'd not suggest it otherwise."

"It seems that someone here has grown determined to gain access to Noltland and may be prepared to work some serious mischief. We might see this morning's event as an omen," MacJannet remarked, though there was no real hope of swaying his stubborn friend once Colin's mind had settled on a course.

"Aye, they have gotten impatient and bold. And I fear it may be our arrival that has caused this event." Colin drizzled some wax from the jack onto the folded parchment and pressed it closed with a seldom-used seal.

"And your first thought when confronted with this danger is that I should leave you?" MacJannet asked.

Colin smiled briefly. "No, that was not my first—or even second—thought. But 'tis my latest one, so you must endure. Now, pay heed to my instructions, for your task is a complicated one and the timing is important. On your way south you will make a visit to the Bishop of Orkney and deliver this message into his hand. Have the bishop dispatch his own messenger to Noltland, for there will be no time for you to return with a reply." Colin indicated the sealed parchment and MacJannet grunted. "After that you will discover where the remaining Balfour troops are billeted. Pay them any wages they are owed and persuade them—at whatever cost—that they must return home. I shouldn't think there would be much protest, as they have left their families behind in the North and will be anxious to see to their welfare when they understand the situation."

"And in the event that I am bringing back people who might also have ambitions regarding the welfare of the mistress and this castle? 'Tis not so unusual a thought for a man after all. In fact, marriage to Mistress Balfour seems a most fashionable one hereabouts."

With the wax seal properly cooled, Colin handed the parchment to MacJannet and met his look of mild inquiry with an equally calm demeanor. "You may tell everyone who enquires that Mistress Balfour has become betrothed and has likely already been married. She requires no other suitors."

MacJannet looked down at the missive in his hand as he digested this bit of news. "I thought the wind had shifted to that quarter. But the Bishop of Orkney?" he asked at last. "Will it serve? And what will the regent say to this marriage? She is a loyal Catholic, you know. And your cousin? For that matter, what of Mistress Balfour? You've not asked the lady to wed yet, have you?"

"Very little will be said by the regent on behalf of the infant queen, I should think. Mary of Guise is busy at present protecting her daughter from larger things than my marriage. My cousin MacLeod will likely be, if not happy, then at least content, that Noltland has not fallen into enemy hands. As for Mistress Balfour . . . No, I have not discussed this with her. There has not been an occasion yet." Colin shrugged a bit helplessly. "One can hardly propose to a woman when she has been locked up in a dungeon and is nursing bruised ribs."

"You're all but shoving your head in a noose doing this in backward order." MacJannet shook his own head at the courtship oversight, causing Colin to smile.

"I've done it before, my friend."

"Not this particular noose. And thenadays it was for the benefit of the crown and for handsome payment. What gain you now?"

"True enough observations. But I suspect that if it becomes necessary, kindly King Henry will intervene with the regent to save me from my brashness. He'd not want his chief intelligencer being put to the question by the Scots. And it is likely that Alasdair would also come to my aid, for reasons of family pride if no other. I shall do well enough." If the lady did not refuse him.

MacJannet snorted as he tucked the parchment safely away. "King Henry would send an envoy right enough—and it would be bloody Blar-na-leine all over again. And you'd still likely be dead before he could do anything about it. As for your precious cousin—I'd be a very surprised man if he did anything for you. Come to think on it, you may have a rough wooing with your bride as well. I don't think the lady is going to receive this news with smiles—even if you fail to mention your career to her. And if you are daft enough to attempt to explain what you do . . . Well, ladies do not generally understand that deception can be a good thing. Even if it prevents war."

"*Tsk!* What a pessimist you've grown to be. Fear not, the bishop shall take good care of Noltland and my sacred person until you return. I know Alasdair better than you think, and he will not interfere. As for Mistress Balfour—what wooing betwixt the Scots and English was ever easy? Or the French and English for that matter?" He smiled fleetingly. "And you forget an important fact. Women know how to shade the truth. They are taught from the cradle that sometimes there is a need to lie. It is how they survive in a world when men are their masters."

MacJannet sighed but did not persist in making futile arguments. "And the hound?"

"I do believe we need a rat-rime, some special incantation to lure that vermin out. But you may leave the matter of playing canine pied piper to me."

"Aye, and gladly. You are the one with a twisty mind and taste for danger." MacJannet shook his head again. "Do I leave at once?"

"After the evening meal will be fine. I am sorry to put you out at night, but I think an unannounced departure under the cover of darkness might be some added protection for you. In any event, it has stopped raining so you shall not be too terribly wetted. And be sure to take your tooth soap. All they will offer you up here is burnt mouse heads flavored with lavender."

MacJannet shuddered. "You are all solicitude of my well-being."

"Nay, that I'm not. And you have been a bloody good friend to me, MacJannet, so I am sorry to do this when you are still travel-tainted with weariness."

The Scotsman blushed at the sudden praise and began to scowl, speaking differently. "Hoots away wi' ye. Worry about your own hide. 'Tis as weary as my own, what with chasing hounds all night, and it's like to be in a deal more danger." MacJannet's misplaced accent returned in an instant and grew suddenly thick with his agitation.

"But I shall not have the long walk you will face. Perhaps you should go and have a nap for an hour or so, my friend. 'Twill make me feel less guilty for abusing your good nature when night falls."

"Ach! Don't be haverin' on about that again. We've helped each other out of tight spots too many a time to be keeping a reckoning now."

"That's true enough, my friend. I simply wished you to know that I am not unmindful of what I owe you," Colin said.

"You owe me? Aye, and where would I be if ye had nae rescued me from that bloody gaol?"

"Still in Crieff, I imagine."

"In Crieff, aye, hanging from the nevergreen tree. Or rotting in a common grave wi' all the other felons," MacJannet muttered.

"You might well have been rotting, man, but never pretend to me that you were a common felon," Colin answered, knowing it would tease his friend. "There is nothing the least bit common about you."

"Maybe aye, maybe nae. It makes little difference to the body, common birth or high, whether it is hanged for wolf or for sheep when the neck is stretching."

"True enough. But it makes every difference to me, for I should not trust you if you were unworthy. And you would be of no use to me if you were only a common man."

Brow beetling, MacJannet retreated from the room, muttering something about Colin's heartless MacLeod blood finally showing itself.

He stopped at the door. "The ghosts will nae trouble ye?"

"Nay. All is well."

MacJannet nodded and left.

Colin's broad smile faded as soon as the door eased shut behind MacJannet. He looked at the woman in the dripping gown who watched him from the corner of the room. There was nothing to worry about, but there were indeed sad spirits here, perseverations of the many unhappy events that had happened at the castle.

Colin turned away, refusing to be drawn in. He had troubles enough with the living. He needed no others beckoning his attention.

His plan was a bold one, perhaps even demented, given his cousin's own campaign for Noltland. But the devil that had prompted him north was still with him, and it seemed to feel that taking Mistress Balfour to wife was actually a sound idea.

It was a great pity he could not be certain that Mistress Balfour would agree with him, for it meant he would have to do something no gentleman should ever contemplate doing with the woman he had chosen to be his wife. It was fortunate that he had learned to be ruthless when the situation dictated.

From their next meeting onward, he would have to become his mistress's seducer. For, once ruined, the convent-reared Frances would have no choice but to agree to become his wife. It was his pleasurable task to see that she was disgraced as speedily as was possible so the Bishop of Orkney could marry them upon his arrival. And that job would be more promptly done with the honorable MacJannet safely away from the castle and not frowning over his employer's transformation into a preternuptualer.

Colin leaned back in his chair and wondered how best to begin his new campaign as a lecher. Certainly explanations of what he did for the crown would have to wait. MacJannet had the right of it—admitting that one lied for a living was not the way to begin a seduction. Such truths were for after the nuptials, if at all.

When shall we meet again, sweetheart?
When shall we meet again?
When the oaken leaves that fall from trees
Are green and spring up again.

—*"The Unquiet Grave"*

Chapter Nine

The chase had begun. The lady was aware of him, but so far, Frances was proof against his attentions, remaining aloof as a princess or goddess to the vulgar lowborn petitioners begging favors at her shrine. But Colin felt certain that with time Diana, the huntress, would be caught in the chase. The slight blush that mantled her cheeks and her odd sidelong look told him that she was not indifferent, for all that she pretended to ignore him.

Colin leaned back in his chair and pondered what lure would best work.

She looked the most delicate piece, presiding over the table in a velvet gown whose vivid color rivaled the primroses of spring. It was cut low on her bosom and framed her long, graceful throat, and had pointed sleeves that showed off her equally narrow wrists to great advantage. She appeared very much the French lady. Past experience told him that no woman would wear such splendid finery if she were truly determined to rebuff an unwanted suitor.

Nor had she bound up her fall of dark hair. Her head was, in fact, completely naked of ornamentation except those glossy tresses. In all other respects she was dressed as a woman of noble birth, but her long, unveiled tresses were a Scottish maiden's badge of availability. And they had not been uncovered the night before. It was an auspicious sign for his campaign that she had chosen to appear thus in public this evening.

Yet he would not have an easy time of things. At the moment, the lady's slim shoulders were turned away from him while she engaged her cousin in animated conversation. As there was now an interested audience watching the castle's mistress and her Master of the Gowff, Colin had to suppose that part of her neglect was due to a mixture of dignity and bashfulness she felt compelled to display before her people. Perhaps her ears had been perturbed by the gossip, which had spread throughout the castle when her supposed adventure and rescue in the dungeon was made known to the populace. Certainly, Tearlach could be counted on to repeat—and embellish—any such tales that were making the rounds.

Her feelings at the moment he could only imagine, but he did not think they included any that were lighthearted or amused. In spite of what the poems and comedies said, being chased in earnest was singularly unamusing—whether it was pursuit by friend or foe. And when one's situation was precarious, and there was an audience, perhaps wagering on the outcome, the attention pricked with a hundred tiny, inquisitive barbs that could penetrate even the thickest skin, never mind flesh as delicate as the lady's. And in this case, she was being hounded by both a friend and at least one foe, and was perhaps—since she was not stupid—asking herself if they were one and the same.

Taking a small sip of wine, he wondered whether it was better to let the lady have her way in rebuffing him or to capitalize on the gossip and demonstrate conclusively to any overly interested parties that his intentions toward the lady were neither innocent nor frivolous.

Down the table, MacJannet met his eye and raised an enquiring eyebrow. Colin nodded. It was time for his friend to depart. Demonstrating his intent toward the castle's mistress would serve to divert attention from MacJannet's disappearance. He chose to believe that it was a sign and did not reprehend himself for being less than a gentleman.

"Mademoiselle," he interrupted her gently.

There was no reply.

"Frances," he said clearly, deciding that he would try speaking to her again before doing anything more overt. He could always take her hand if words failed to move her.

"Monsieur Mortlock?" she answered, at last turning her head his way. For a brief moment their eyes met and then she looked past his shoulder at an empty wall while color infused her cheeks.

"I crave a moment of your time, mistress. Perhaps you might take a turn about the room with me while we settle that fine meal. I desire to have some of these paintings explained to me." It was a blatant lie. There was nothing to explain about the paintings. They were poorly made portraits of her father and grandfather.

Her eyes met his for a second time, this time really seeing him, and then perhaps recalling that there was more afoot than mere jousting between a man and maid, she nodded assent.

Colin rose gracefully and assisted her from her chair. There was a momentary lull in conversation and a hard look from Anne Balfour, who was seated next to Tearlach, but a raised brow from Colin had Frances's kinswoman looking away and swiftly resuming her conversation with the inebriated piper.

Frances's fingers trembled slightly as she laid them on his sleeve, but as the air near the fire was quite warm, Colin did not mistake it for a tremble born of exposure. Though whether it was fear, fury, or passion that shook her, he could not say, for her expression was schooled to blankness. Life in the convent and then in her father's house had taught her well how to disguise her feelings.

True to his word, he did take her on a tour of the room, moving at a measured pace as they stared up at the paintings. He spoke randomly of inconsequential things and Frances answered just as haphazardly. On their second turn through the hall, Colin led them out through a side door and into an empty room. At the moment when all eyes were upon them, he saw MacJannet rise from the table and slip away.

Colin was careful to leave the door ajar so that everyone might see them together in the side room. For the moment, it suited him to have a public tableau of their courtship and for everyone to see that he was behaving honorably.

It was rather colder in the new apartments, and not so brightly lit, but neither of these things could be seen as a detriment, as they would encourage Frances to remain close to his side. He was careful to avoid the one corner where the last fading impressions of a lady in green lingered. The ghost seemed unaware of them and he preferred that it remain that way.

They walked this second dim room as though on promenade. Finally Frances and Colin came to a narrow window that looked out onto the moonlit heath, and there Colin paused. Still apparently shy, Frances confined her gaze to the sill and the silvered landscape beyond the window's distorted panes. Her head was cocked to one side as though listening to the wind, which whispered something secret at the glass, or perhaps the murmur of the sea, which spoke night and day with an enchanting tongue.

"We are making a distraction for MacJannet?" she asked shrewdly, glancing back once at the opened door.

"Partly," he admitted, staring at the lady. She was all cream and ebony, except for the two roses that bloomed in her cheeks. "But it is also a divertissement for me."

"*Vraiment*?" The pulse in her throat grew more pronounced. "How odd. But perhaps this is the way of the English. I have heard you are a rough lot."

Colin smiled wryly, thinking of his earlier conversation with MacJannet. "Do you find it unimaginable that a man might suddenly conceive of a violent passion for a lady and wish to be private with her?" he asked conversationally.

Frances gave a small gasp, and again her gaze fluttered up and then quickly away. "I have heard of this, of course," she admitted, slightly breathless. "But we are discussing a thing much more practical, *oui*?"

"Are we?" he asked. "I think if we were being practical we would be speaking of Paracelsus or Ovid—or perhaps of milking cows."

A dimple appeared in her cheek and her shoulders

relaxed. "That is very English humor, monsieur. What would a lady know of these things?"

"That would depend entirely upon the lady. Not all men like stupid women."

She considered this.

"Do *you* believe then that such a thing is possible? To be smitten with a passion for a total stranger?"

"I must," he answered promptly. "For it has happened to me."

"*Vraiment*," Frances repeated. She did not look at him again, but her small hands clenched the fabric of her skirts. She sounded doubtful when she said: "Usually such things happen to untried youths whose minds are filled with fanciful tales of the romantic. Or to the mad."

"That is so," he agreed. "But apparently it may also happen to men grown, who are not generally so fanciful." He possessed himself of her hand, fetching it from the crushed velvet. The digits were very small, but he reminded himself that they had the strength to grip and swing a heavy club.

Frances turned toward him, eyes wide, cheeks gently flushed. He watched her reddened lips part and wondered if they would speak curses for his impudence, or some form of acknowledgment of the possibility of sharing something passionate, as she put it.

"Where is MacJannet going?" she asked instead, her voice barely a whisper.

Colin blinked at her words and then sighed, banishing romantic thoughts, at least for the moment. He knew how to be patient.

"He has gone to deliver a letter to the Bishop of Orkney," he admitted.

He noted that Frances also had fine brows, which

were, at the moment, drawn together in an expression of displeasure. She looked scorn and anger upon him, not all of it feigned.

"We had not finished discussing the matter," she scolded. "I am most unhappy about this, monsieur."

"There was nothing to discuss," Colin said gently. "I needed to write to the bishop about my affairs and did so. I am of course sorry that you are unhappy."

Frances blinked at the masterful rebuff.

"And when does MacJannet return to Noltland?" she asked, brows relaxing slightly.

"That is difficult to say."

"The bishop will take some time to reply to your letter?"

"I should think that he will reply at once. Doubtless we will receive a message from him before the new moon."

"And MacJannet?" she asked, demonstrating that she could be dogged when a subject interested her. "What shall he be doing while the bishop replies?"

"MacJannet?" Colin replied carefully. "He goes to discover where the remainder of the Balfour men are billeted and to facilitate their immediate return. And then he will see about arranging some better provisions for the castle."

"He can do that? Bring home the men?" she asked, amazed. Those lovely brows again drew together. "But if they are free to return to us, why have they not done so on their own?"

"I imagine they are waiting to be paid. The king died at a most inconvenient moment and the regent has not yet had time to see to such mundane matters." Colin allowed himself to run a finger over her wrist, checking on the state of her pulse. It was not so calm as her expression and voice suggested. What a wonderful little dissimulator he had chosen. He almost smiled.

"And you can arrange for them to be paid and then sent home?"

"Aye." He did not explain that the money would come from his own purse.

"And they do not need to take leave from the regent before returning home?"

"No. That is where the Bishop of Orkney will prove useful. He has many friends and shall doubtless help MacJannet see to the men's immediate and unceremonious discharge."

Frances's sudden smile was dazzling even in the dim room. "And this is why you wrote to the Bishop? *Merci*, Colin," she said, forgiving his earlier impudent transgression and even forgetting their audience as she snatched up his hand and brought it to her face, where she pressed it against her cheek. "That is most kindly done of you. The women here have been most disheartened and fearful of the coming winter."

Colin felt a momentary pang at his duplicity, but did not stop himself from caressing the smooth flesh beneath his hands. "It is very likely that the bishop shall come to call upon us," he warned softly, preparing Frances for the cleric's arrival. "There will be many related matters to discuss."

"And I shall be most happy to receive him," she assured, her eyes shining. "We all shall. I have been in such fear of what would happen this winter, did we not have some of our men return to us."

"I know. This seemed a sound if temporary solution to our difficulties. However, we cannot speak of it in a general way just yet. We do not wish for any gossip to spread beyond the castle until we know who our prankster is and what other mischief he might be planning. He might do something precipitous if he knows his time for action is running short. And we would not want the castle to be besieged, or to fall into unworthy hands because we were careless."

His hair was dark. Deep brown locks rested on a shoulder clad in deep brown velvet; in the gloom it was hard to discern where one ended and the other began. His brows were also dark and straight, and his smile swift and oddly boyish. His eyes, too, were dark, but lit by the fire they gleamed with a purpose and keen wit that could nearly pierce the heart. They skimmed rapidly over her form and seemed to touch as a lover's hands would, should they be allowed.

She should condemn as improper the urge she'd had to make herself attractive for Colin, but she was suddenly glad she had donned this primrose gown and left her hair long, for his eyes told her plainly of his approval.

Suddenly breathless, she brought his hand to her cheek, and then she did not turn away when his long fingers reached out to tilt up her chin and then caress her jaw and throat.

He said something about not revealing MacJannet's purpose in leaving the castle and then in an altered voice: "Forgive me, *ma belle*," he whispered, his words settling over her like a warm cloak as he lowered his lips to hers.

She hadn't realized that so many things could be in a kiss. It was where breaths and hearts met and mingled. Some kisses were shy, even fugitive. These she knew. But now she was aware that in some kisses there was passion that fired emotions and set them ablaze. There could be hope and joy—and desire so strong it took the strength from one's knees and made heat run through the flesh as wild water raced upon the beach at high tide.

She thought she had inured herself to such bodily pleasures, that she had even resigned herself to a life of prayerful sterility that lacked all passion. But Colin awakened all her old, frivolous desires and urged them to voice their longing.

"Ah, Holy Father! May the black vomit seize me!" Tearlach exclaimed, just loud enough to be heard in the room beyond. "You think he means tae take her tae holy deadlock?"

"That is *wedlock*," George corrected sternly and with less volume. "And I certainly hope that he may, for I like him a great deal and Frances must marry someone."

Mortification rushed over Frances, causing her to pull away. How could she have so forgotten herself as to allow this man to kiss her? And before an audience?

"Sorry, *ma belle*," Colin said again softly, also taking a step back and dropping his hand from her face. When he spoke next it was as a gentleman should. "I should offer some sign of remorse for this embarrassment. But I cannot in sincerity do this. I even dare pray you will not shut yourself away from me hereafter. How would I bear the woe if you forbade me from your presence? Say you'll not make it your pious office to stifle my pretensions, for it would be most cruel of you."

Frances stared at him, her mind all abroad and her body still much shaken. Finally she murmured: "I have not forbidden you from my presence, though I probably should. That was not well done. By either of us."

"I cannot help but disagree, as I am sure that it was done just right. I am however greatly relieved that I am not banished." And then he smiled. It was a wonderful thing, magical and distracting.

"But, Colin, I do not wish to be . . ." She hunted for a word.

"Courted? Wooed?"

"*Oui*! I do not wish to be courted before Tearlach and the others. This must not happen again. If I am to have a—*friendship*—it shall not be with the whole of my people looking on. You will recall my dignity—and your own," she ordered. "It is our duty to behave with decorum. To set an example."

"Duty: she is a merciless deity, mistress. Let us render our respects to her but not worship there."

"Monsieur, it is only proper that . . ." she began. Then a sudden thought occurred to her, causing her eyebrows to again draw together. Her voice lowered. "Are you quite certain that you did not do this simply to help MacJannet escape unnoticed?"

Colin's smile widened. "Oh, aye, mistress. I am quite certain that I did not kiss you for MacJannet."

The intelligence probably shouldn't have pleased her, but it did. Of course, she wished to first be considered worthy of participating in intrigue and of being an able guardian for any of his plans or confidences, but one did not want to be kissed for any such dishonest reason. Not when one enjoyed it so very much!

The old hound whimpers crouched in sleep,
The embers smoulder low;
Across the walls the shadows
Come, and go.

—Walter de la Mare, "The Song of Shadows"

Chapter Ten

"Where is Tearlach?" Colin asked sternly of the giggling Frances and George. He reckoned rightly that only something of an evil nature would have the two of them pressing heads together and looking mischievous. "You do know that virilia is a felony in my country, don't you?"

"Virilia?" George asked.

"He is ill," Frances answered promptly and then, with a clear demonstration that she knew at least some things that a lady should not, "No one has emasculated him. The fool flagellated his—his—himself with nettles and then made a . . . what is the word, George? A glister? And now he is probably dying."

"A what?" Colin asked, his turn to be puzzled by a word.

"Actually, it was a feague," George answered. "And it isn't that he's truly dying—just wanting to, you see."

"No, I do not see. I am still, in fact, quite unenlightened," Colin pointed out patiently. "What is a feague?

And why did he flagellate himself with nettles? And did either of you have anything to do with it?"

George colored. "Of course we did not! We could not. I mean, a feague is . . . um . . . it is when someone puts ginger up a horse's fundament."

"And if I were to flagellate him, it would not be with nettles," Frances added.

"And may the good Lord preserve us from this linguistic morass," Colin muttered. "Did you truly just say that a feague was something done to horses?"

Seeing Colin's horrified expression, George hurried on: "It encourages inferior beasts to keep their tails up and be lively in their step when they are being shown to buyers. It isn't strictly honest, of course, and a gentleman wouldn't do it. But in any event, Tearlach gave himself one and it has made a terrible feff. It's worse than if he had taken surfeitwater."

"A feff?" Colin found himself missing MacJannet. He didn't comment upon the late lord's obvious lack of morals in resorting to such trickery when selling livestock, but rather concentrated on the peculiar and possibly dangerous activities of those Balfours closer at hand.

"*Puer.* He had a fleshquake," Frances translated kindly. "Use real words, George. Colin does not understand the silly local language."

"A fleshquake?" Colin asked, turning toward his amused lady and enjoying the way her eyes shone above her belatedly prim mouth.

"*Oui.* And he is now the color of a *feuille mort.* And his flatuosity has cleared the privies and most of the hall. Even the kitchen has complained. We shall be lucky to have any meals prepared today."

"Well, if he has turned the color of a dead leaf, then we must assume that ginger has failed to aid him in—what precisely *was* this supposed to aid him in? You mentioned surfeitwater. Was he suffering from overfullness?"

George glanced at Frances and lowered his voice a notch. It wasn't sufficient to prevent her hearing, but showed an inclination toward discretion that few in the castle possessed. "Nay, it was hippuris."

"He thought this would cure, um . . ." Colin stopped. He was a plainspoken man, but would not speak of this affliction in front of Frances, no matter how much he lowered his voice.

"He says it was from riding a bad horse three years ago, but I have never heard of horseback riding causing . . . this ailment. Personally, I think he used this excuse because no one believes him about the ghost. Besides, everyone knows you shouldn't use ginger insufflation on people. It doesn't cure *that*, even in horses. It just causes friskiness and is always followed by bowelhives."

"I suppose this explains the nettles, too," Colin muttered. The sexually adventuresome in his own country had been known to use nettles as a stimulant. He was tempted to ask about the ghost but decided not to interrupt the present conversation to chase down another point.

"What I find most annoying is that he had ginger root and did not share it with the kitchen," Frances announced. "What a thief and *cochon*!"

"Don't insult the pigs," Colin scolded, but mildly. "Swine are not made the way this creature is. Nor do they steal. Still, that is an interesting point. I wonder where he got the ginger root. That is a bit exotic for this far north, not at all the common stock of a swygman." He, too, could use some local dialect.

"Nay, it did not come from a peddler, I am certain. I believe it was left by my uncle's horse chaunter," George answered. "And as he is dead now, I don't think it was stealing precisely if Tearlach took it."

"That is true, George," Frances conceded. She did not admit to Colin that he was correct about the swine. In fact, she seemed suddenly disinclined to look at Colin at all. Her long lashes were pulled down like a veil and her face was slightly averted. She no longer smiled, perhaps recalling their meeting last night and wondering again where precisely he stood betwixt the boundaries of earnestness and game. She was new to the game of formal dalliance, but still aware that it existed and was played by others.

"I thought I heard a dog fooffing last night and thought maybe it was the Bokey hound," George said, seeming to change conversational direction abruptly. "But I see now that it was only Tearlach haunting the privy."

"That is something to gratulate about," Frances told him, glancing up. Her voice was firm. "You should rejoice that it was not a hound of Hell roaming our castle. Cleaning up after them is most tiring."

"I do congratulate myself," George assured her, but with only half of his heart. "It is just that it would be very different and exciting to see a hellhound. And I can't think that it would hurt me anyway because I *like* dogs. Even ghostly ones." He paused. "Or so I believe."

"You would not want to see one if it meant someone were to die. And hellhounds are *not* dogs." Frances frowned, laying a hand on the curve of his cheek. In another year or two it would firm up, but for now it was still the skin of a child. "George, I know that it has lately been most boring here, *mon cousin*—"

"Nay," he denied instantly, meeting her eyes. "I did not mean to complain. And certainly I don't want anyone here to die—especially us. I was forgetting that part of the legend."

"I know you are not complaining. It is just that . . . *Je regrette*," Frances murmured, spreading her hands wide. "I should not have brought you here until it was safe. I wasn't considering what could happen when I brought you here."

The two young cousins looked at one another, their fondness and concern—and unhappiness—for one another's position clear for anyone to see.

"Perhaps I should send for the myomancer," Frances suggested daringly, proving to Colin that idleness was in fact the mistress of vice. Prophesying was frowned on by priests of both religions. These two needed diversion of a healthier nature.

"Nay, you know what happened last time. We had no sooner started the divination than the mice got free and ran up Sine's skirts, scaring her into hysterics."

Frances's expression grew a shade darker. "Perhaps the tyromancer?"

"Do you really want to spend all day looking for portents in coagulating cheese?" George asked practically. "I should prefer not to."

Frances sighed. "Well . . . then the gyromancer?"

George snorted. "I do not believe that watching people spin until they fall down is a true form of divination." He grinned suddenly. "Of course, it is very amusing to watch, so you may have them up if you will. Perhaps Mr. Mortlock would enjoy it as well."

Colin opened his mouth to reply in the negative, but Frances sighed and spoke before he could answer.

"I don't know what is best to do. Surely there must be something that would put your mind at ease about hellhounds. If sealing up the wall has not reassured you, *mon cousin* . . ." Her delicate brow furrowed.

"It has," George replied. "At least, it has assured me that no one shall steal inside the castle through that old hole. I am just mopish today because Tearlach ruined my sleep. Don't concern yourself anymore. I shall go and . . . and . . . practice archery."

Colin was an observer of his fellow man, not prone to interference, but he suddenly and passionately wished to intervene in this small domestic unhappiness. Both Frances and George struck some hitherto unnoticed string in his heart and it resonated at a compassionate hum, which was hard to ignore.

He knew something about loneliness and loss, and of being a stranger in a foreign land where others assumed you should belong because of your family's blood ties. More than anyone at the castle, he could understand how the solitary situation would weigh down the spirits of two young people used to more genial society and amusements.

But because he had learned long ago to secure his safety by protecting himself from any betraying or weakening emotion, even to friends, he did not make any announcement of this heartfelt revelation of empathy for their plight. Such confidences only came late in friendships, if they ever came at all.

Still, he felt he had to do something. Before Colin

stopped to consider the wisdom of his words, he heard himself saying: "Enough of this superstitious nonsense. Next you'll be calling for a *taghairm* and wrapping yourselves in slaughter bullock pelts and waiting for ghosts to appear. The gloom and bad air is obviously affecting you. Since we can't remain within the castle while Tearlach is ill, we had best go out. I'll fetch the clubs. I think it is time we had another lesson. You'll entirely forget the last one else."

"I should greatly enjoy that. But is this wise?" Frances asked, glancing at the gate. She had not forgotten that danger threatened the boy.

Colin stared at her expressive face, where longing for the outdoors and responsibility for her young cousin were doing battle. "Nay," he answered frankly. "But sometimes we must do what it good for the soul at the risk of the body. King Henry himself said that youth must have some dalliance. We shall be vigilant. I shall bring a sword, and you two must also carry dirks."

The two cousins nodded solemnly, looking a bit like the sad monkey King Henry kept at court. The only time the beast appeared truly happy was when he was allowed to fling food at unwanted guests. His aim was usually quite good.

Colin grinned suddenly. "On second thought, if we are attacked, Lady Frances, you had best use your club on our attacker. Your swing is deadlier than the sharpest blade. Were you a bit stronger I should be tempted to train you in the use of the mace and morning star."

"*Oui? Merci, du compliment*. If you are sure that this is best for George, then I am most happy to comply!" Frances announced, not at all put out by his words. It seemed silly to her that women were not taught to fight with swords and other weapons. She added: "It has just occurred to me that today at least we shall not be followed by the hedge-creep, as he is too busy poisoning the privy with colic to pursue us. And perhaps—with the hole gone—he shall suffocate himself with bad air and even be dead when we return. He already looks like whey."

Colin shook his head at this normal if impetuous speech and wondered if he should even try curing her of her lack of compassion for the piper. It was amusing, but also a bit alarming that the piper's possible demise should cause such unhealthy enthusiasm.

"Monsieur Mortlock, do you wish to dress in your official attire before we depart? You do not seem to enjoy wearing the *coleur de roy* I chose for you."

"Under other circumstances," he lied tactfully, "I should be happy to wear the garments of office that you kindly provided. But I think more subtle clothing is what we need. In fact, it would be best if you left off your crimson cloak for the green one."

Frances met his eyes for a moment and then nodded briskly.

They returned from their uneventful and only slightly imperiling game of gowff, to be met with some interesting, and even alarming, intelligence from inside the lowered gate.

Sine was waiting for them at the yett and signaled immediately that it should be raised to let them all in. Her state of agitation and indignation were obvious as she fluttered up to them.

"That odious Tearlach!" she whispered as they hurried under the heavy iron trap that thudded shut behind them. "I can't believe his inhospitable nature."

"What has he done now?" Colin asked, setting down the pannier of clubs and laying his sword aside. "I thought he was too ill to be making a nuisance of himself."

"We had visitors," Sine began, only to be interrupted by the arrival of a still very pale Tearlach.

Frances and George both frowned at his appearance, and took a step backward from the piper, as though fearing he were still ill and might infect them with his rude smell.

"They were nae visitors. They were rufflers begging charity at the gate."

"They were not rufflers, but rather soldiers lately returned from the war!" Sine objected.

"*Pshaw!* They were naething of the sort. They had the look of fighting men, I'll grant ye. But they were nae returning frae the war. Use yer God-given senses, woman! There is naething here tae return tae—except Noltland. If they were Gunns, MacDonnells, or MacKays, then they wouldnae have been stopping here with their own kin sae nearby. And beyond us there is nowt but sea."

"How many were there?" Colin asked quietly, adding to himself: "They could not have come by boat, for we were near the cliffs and would have seen them."

"Twoscore—that I could see," Tearlach answered. "But more may hae been concealed in the rocks. I was about tae set out after ye."

"Perhaps there were, though we saw no sign of anyone lingering there while we were out. George, come away from the gate," Colin said, his absentminded tone not matching his alarming words. "Don't leave your back exposed that way. I'd hate for an arrow to find you."

Both George and Frances whirled about to look through the iron lath of the yett, and then whisked themselves into the protection of the stone wall. They peered cautiously around the corner, searching out enemies on the moor. There was alarm but also excitement in George's face.

Sine's mouth fell open and her eyes went wide.

"They were assassins sent to kill George?" Frances asked, her face suddenly as pale as the piper's. She didn't find this adventure exciting.

"I doubt it," Colin answered calmly, nipping incipient hysteria in the bud. "But the temptation might prove irresistible if an enemy were granted an opportunity. We'd best not appeal to their worst natures."

Sine's mouth was still slightly agape. "But they said they were hungry," she expostulated. "To refuse them entry was not generous."

"Perhaps not. But it was prudent," Colin said.

"Stop haverin', woman. They had some bannocks and water," Tearlach interjected, looking her over with a haggard eye. "They willnae starve. And the night shall be a fine one, sae they shallnae freeze."

"Colin is correct. I am sorry, Sine, to be so unkind. I know it is not the custom to be inhospitable to strangers, but we must be cautious. This was most wise of you, Tearlach. I had not thought you so shrewd," Frances said, pushing herself away from the wall and coming toward him in a rush of sudden gratitude. Her newly found respect stopped short of allowing herself to touch him, but she managed a smile. "We must all be very vigilant and see to George's protection."

"Aye, that we maun! Or end murdered in our beds," Tearlach agreed, turning about and heading back for the keep. He moved clumsily, as though all his bones were loose in their sockets and uncertain of keeping themselves aligned.

"I was born in England and intend to die there, not in the wilds of Scotland," Colin began.

"Some men hae nae ambition tae better themselves," Tearlach muttered scathingly, proving that though his legs were unstable, his ears were still keen, and his mind reasonably coherent.

"Sine," Frances said to the disturbed older woman, as Tearlach disappeared inside the castle. "Perhaps we should brew Tearlach a posset. We have milk and wine, *oui*? And perhaps there is still some tincture of the moon?"

"Aye, we do have some. Mayhap that would calm his—uh—stomach. And perhaps a bit of rosemary and sage vinegar as well. I'll see to it," she promised, hurrying away, but not before sending a long and very worried look in George's direction.

"Sine," Frances called after her. "Wait! I know you are concerned by events, but do not gossip with the sculleries. We must be discreet and not cause alarm. There is already talk because of the dungeon and suddenly repairing the privies."

Sine's eyes widened as she considered Frances's words, but she nodded reluctantly.

"Those men were truly after me?" George asked, finally finding his tongue. He also pushed away from the cold wall. He said in a small voice: "Having men want to kill me suddenly seems worse than hellhounds. And is especially unfair when I don't even wish to be the heir to this drafty keep."

"They want the keep, of that I am certain," Colin

answered. "It would be most strategically valuable to the clans warring in this region. And being unaware of who is actually in charge here, they may feel that getting rid of you would force Frances and her supposed men into surrendering the castle."

"Only there are no men," George said. He was a trifle pale, but two spots of angry color had bloomed in his cheeks. "Just you and Tearlach. Bloody hell! They could have slaughtered the women, had they been let inside. What if Tearlach had not thought to close the gate against them? And what if they had gotten Frances?"

"They would not have killed the women. And do not forget yourself while counting up men," Colin reminded him, soothing his young wrath with more measured calm. "You've grown proficient with the bow and would be a strong adversary in a fight."

George's thin chest expanded under the praise. "I *have* gotten better," he said. "But you truly think that they would not have harmed the women if they had gotten inside? I have heard some dreadful stories of things happening in the South."

Colin looked into Frances's worried eyes and answered carefully. "They should not have killed them, of that I am fairly certain. In any event, we need not go leaping to the worst conclusion about our visitors. They may have been what they seemed. Still, we can't have them gossiping about affairs at the keep. To have your neighbors learn that there are few men here would be bad. They do not know your cousin's stubborn nature, and, thinking her weak-willed, they would be tempted to besiege the castle and try to force a surrender."

"Bloody bastards," George muttered again, and then, with a guilty start he said to Frances: "Sorry, cousin. I forgot your presence."

"Do not be troubled, cousin. I have been thinking much worse things—only in French. Colin, I believe it is time for us to take George into our confidence," Frances said firmly, laying a hand on George's shoulder. She looked up into Colin's eyes and said persuasively: "It is not right that he should think the danger of the spectral hound is nothing when it is actually quite real."

"I agree, but we cannot discuss this before the others in case there is an intelligencer in the house," Colin answered, picking up the pannier of clubs and his sword. "Tonight, after we dine, we shall retire to chambers and have a council of war. There I will explain my strategy and suspicions, and we shall make a plan that includes George and his talents."

Frances and George both blinked at this announcement.

"In the meantime, you must both go about your day as usual and show no trepidation. It would not do to let anyone suspect that we are in any way fearful of what they might do. Not until we have designed the right trap and want to lure them into the open. I shall see you at table."

"*Incroyable*!" Frances breathed, watching Colin's tall figure depart.

"I've never been part of a council of war," George said, clearly pleased with the idea. His color had returned to normal.

"Nor have I, for it is not at all conventional for females to do this," Frances answered. "But he is a creature of much decision, and I believe we are fortunate to have him for a guide."

"Unless he is the enemy," George added, suddenly thoughtful.

"I do not believe that he is," Frances answered, trying to sound completely sure of herself. She pointed out: "Had he wished you harm he could have killed you already and opened the gates to our enemies."

"That is true," George said cheerfully, prepared to forget his momentary suspicion. "Then we have nothing to worry about from that quarter—which is fortunate, as I quite like him, and I am certain he will be able to teach me to play gowff well. Eventually."

Frances nodded, but did not speak any of the thoughts passing through her mind as they turned toward the keep. It would not be kind to alarm her young cousin by mentioning that Colin was a much more subtle man, and probably quite capable of finding some way other than bloody murder to get rid of the young heir, if that was what he had a mind to do. She did not want to look their gift horse in the mouth, lest suspicion swallow her and send her newfound hope down the long black gullet to despair that always waited these days. But she would still have to keep an eye upon him. It was belatedly occurring to her that Colin Mortlock was too masterful to be a mere instructor of gowff. What had she been thinking? Only a man well born would have such intimate knowledge of the English king.

She sighed softly. It was hard that their problems should be so large. One year ago, all she had worried about was escaping the boredom of the convent. Now she had to agonize over the welfare of all those who lived at Noltland, especially her young cousin. It made for a trilemma, trying to decide which was more dangerous: the hellhound, the possible spy in their midst, or Colin Mortlock trifling with her heart.

O wha is this that has done this deed,
And tauld the king o me,
To send us out at this time of the year
To sail upon the sea?

—"The Ballad of Sir Patrick Spens"

Chapter Eleven

Colin looked at his two small companions and had to smile wryly at the thought of them being his soldiers to command. They were the tiniest, least physically imposing army he had ever seen. Still, he had waged wars of wits with less intelligent allies and carried the day, so he was not concerned overmuch by their intrusion. He actually welcomed their thoughts. The only trick would be to assure their safety while he tracked down the traitor in their midst and dealt with him or her. He had a feeling that both George and Frances would strive for more active participation than he had in mind.

Colin carefully poured out three glasses of wine from the bottle he had brought to Frances's bedchamber and assumed a suitably serious mien. He had already decided to begin their council by explaining the benefits of welcoming William Kirkcauldy, Bishop of Orkney, into their nominally Catholic midst. This would be the tricky part, for the Catholics of Scotland had every reason to fear the reformers massing around them. The Anglicization of Ireland and Scotland had gone further than King Henry had ever envisioned when he had declared himself the head of the Church of England, in order to attain an annulment from his first wife, and had started importing reformers over the border. He hadn't even needed to waste many resources murdering the annoying Catholic Scots, for the Protestant Reformers who embraced Luther's war cry had happily done it for him. The Catholics of Scotland still had the throne behind them, but Colin was certain the Protestants would eventually have their way. The pageantry and corruption that went with the wealth of the Catholic Church had never sat well with the poor but honest Highlanders. And many former Catholic priests, young John Knox among them, had enthusiastically embraced the new faith and its promised reforms.

Personally, Colin found both sides of the religious skirmish to be annoyingly dogmatic, and as dangerous and unreasonable as a pack of rabid dogs. Yet a tool was a tool. He needed a weapon of defense and the Bishop of Orkney was conveniently at hand. The trick would be to not stand up so tall that anyone wanted to lop their heads off when the Protestants came scything for blasphemers. It was Colin's experience that much would be forgiven, but not religious impudence.

"Our greatest weapons are of course our minds and the knowledge accumulated therein," Colin began. "That said, I do not despise cold iron, and suggest that henceforth you both go about armed. At the very least you must carry a *sgian dubh* in your boot. Nor should you venture out alone."

Frances and George nodded solemnly, their eyes very large.

"I know there is some trepidation about bringing the Bishop of Orkney to visit Noltland, but I think I can put your mind at ease about this matter. Though we have passed through an unsettled time, and the religious strife is by no means completely behind us, I can state with near certitude that the reformers are going to have their way politically here in Scotland. There will be holdouts like Cardinal Beaton, who will resist with heroic stupidity until he is assassinated, but they will not prevail, and it is important in the greater picture that Noltland be seen as being friendly to, if not actually aligned with, the forces of change. We are, so to speak, going to walk the crown of the causeway and try not to wet our feet in the spiritual tidewater."

"But—" Frances began, starting to frown.

"However, political consideration is for another day. What is of more immediate importance is that we have some strong ally here at Noltland to hold your greedy neighbors at bay until your men return home. We need someone both powerful and honest to serve as our shield."

"And they say hen's teeth are rare," George muttered. "Where are we to find honest but powerful men?"

"Don't be despairing," Colin answered. "Fate has encompassed us with a tremendous sea of misfortune. But while we are encumbered, we are not completely enclosed, and we can escape this trap as long as we remain vigilant, with a firm hand on the helm until the wind of change comes about."

"The men *will* return then?" Frances asked. "And soon? And the bishop's people shall not need to linger once they are here? I cannot help feeling that we shall attract much unwanted attention if he remains for any time. Our neighbors are not fond of the new religion."

"There shall return as many men as still live and can be found by MacJannet in reasonable time. It is a somewhat tricky task, but in this search he will be aided by William Kirkcauldy, since it is in the bishop's interest to prevent this keep from falling to unfriendly Catholic hands. I believe the terminus, at least of this difficulty, is within sight, so we may be at ease. Stop frowning. These worried looks you wear quite kill my optimistic mood. One would think you had no faith in me," he chided.

Frances and George both exhaled loudly and Colin went on: "The trouble of your neighbors setting about to scare or capture you, George, is another matter entirely. And one not so easily settled. Henceforth, neither of you is to leave the castle grounds unless I am with you. Not for any reason, and not even in the company of the bishop's men. I don't care who summons you. Unless MacJannet or I am with you, you must not leave the safety of the keep. And even within it you must be cautious. It is not beyond all possibility that your neighbors have a confederate within the castle."

"No!" Frances denied swiftly. "It cannot be. Everyone here is Balfour by blood or by marriage."

"I am sorry, but it is a possibility—nay, a probability—we must not ignore. I know the thought is distasteful, and it is not my desire that you feed on the bitter bread of distrust, but you must bear in mind that someone might be playing the part of intelligencer for what they perceive to be an innocent reason. They may even be carrying out tales unaware. Can you be absolutely certain that no one ever has contact with the outside world? What of the beggars who stopped here earlier? What of the widows who might have allegiances with their blood families? Or someone who has a lover? Can you risk your own and George's life on this naïve hope of complete Balfour clan loyalty?"

Frances and George exchanged a glance.

"*Non*, we cannot be certain," she finally said. She turned her troubled gaze upon Colin. "There are probably those who would say I am most foolish to trust you, that *you* might be the intelligencer who wishes us harm."

George gasped softly at her audacity, his eyes going wide and owl-like.

"Very true," Colin agreed affably. "I am, after all, related to the MacLeod. Of course, this hound was heard before my arrival, but it might be a subtle plot concocted by my cousin when he was last here, one to which I am now joined. George, don't look so disturbed. Have some more wine. Your cousin and I are merely fencing."

Frances frowned, trying to imagine the MacLeod being subtle. The image would not form. Nor could she see Colin as being the subordinate Judas to any man. She felt certain that if he intrigued, it would be for his own ends, and she could not see anything he might want that he could not have by easier means.

"Are you an intelligencer for your cousin?" she asked straightly, making George choke on a mouthful of wine.

"Nay, I am not. But he certainly intended for me to be," Colin answered with breathtaking frankness, staring into her pleading gaze and wishing he could kiss the worry away. He tried not to think how close this was to an outright lie. He wasn't intriguing for his cousin, but he was definitely an intelligencer. "And if the MacLeod can plan such a thing, so can others. You are wise to remain wary."

George's seizure of coughing grew worse with Colin's answer, causing Frances to momentarily look away from her Master of the Gowff.

"My cousin, are you well? You are quite red of face." She laid a hand over her bosom, as though to still her own turbulent heart.

"Aye," George whispered, wiping away a tear. "I breathed when I should have swallowed."

Colin took a sip of his own wine before going on. "*My* own cousin, however, forgot the first rule of puppetry. One must be very sure of one's creations before sending them out onto the stage. He did not pause long enough to consider that I might have allegiances elsewhere that superseded the ties of blood. That is a very Scottish mistake, assuming that blood ties are always valued above all other things. It is not always true. Politics and marriage—and greed—can make other bonds just as strong."

"And do you have other allegiances?" Frances asked, looking a bit white about the mouth as she considered this.

"Aye, of course. All men do—particularly men of property. And, before you ask, none have anything to do with a secret marriage to a woman in York. However, I do not care to share the list of these bonds with you at this moment, as they are not relevant to our task and would require some explanation."

Frances glanced swiftly at George, and then wisely held her peace, though Colin suspected she wished to question him about the women in his life who might not live in York.

Colin went on: "What is of import to you is the fact

that your well-being and the preservation of this keep from your neighbors is now my foremost concern."

"But why should this be so? We are strangers to you—not kin, not political allies. I am not your wife."

Colin looked straight into her eyes. "Why? I think you know the answer to that question. As for being related through marriage or politics, give it some time, my dear. I am not *that* impetuous."

Frances flushed a shade of vivid rose. George began to smile. His small body relaxed and his wheezing eased.

"All right. If Frances is satisfied, then so am I. Where and how do we begin?" the boy asked.

"First, we find the hound's lair. If possible, we track the creature and discover our foe, and then lay a trap for both man and beast. If we cannot discover the hound's master, then we settle for the time being for ridding ourselves of the canine nuisance and making it difficult for anyone to steal out of the castle and carry tales to our enemies."

Frances and George both leaned forward. Frances asked, "How do we do this? Have you a notion for where to begin the search?"

"Aye. That I do, and we'll start first thing tomorrow morn." Colin lowered his voice and said impressively: "Here is what we shall do. George, you will provide a distraction while Frances and I begin the hunt . . ."

Frances jumped as the chamber door shut softly behind George and she was left alone with Colin. Earlier, she had been so exhausted that she felt she would drown in sleep the moment the sky went dark. But now she was wakeful, her mind as bright as the noon sun, and whirling like a cyclone with all the plots she and Colin had made.

"You have no final words for me? No questions before I retire?" Colin asked. He added coaxingly: "You were curious enough earlier."

"I think it is for you to speak first," she said softly, staring intently at the yellow handkerchief she wound around her fingers. It had been her mother's, and it was her gesture of continued mourning that she carried the thing with her at all times.

"That is certainly traditional," Colin answered. "Unless the man is a lady's servant. Then he might hesitate before speaking plainly of delicate things."

Frances laughed without humor. "You are not my servant. I have not been so foolish as to think of you as such since . . ." She waved a hand. "For a long time. And you have never hesitated at plain speech—and more."

Colin studied her busy fingers, now completely swathed in linen. "It is true that I would not be content to remain your servant for long. Yet I do plan to be of service." He took her bandaged hand and began unwinding the delicate linen. "And it would greatly relieve me to know that I am not plowing water here. Even the bold sometimes wish for encouragement."

Frances looked up, puzzled by his words.

"Tell me, lady, that I do not sow the seeds of affection in sterile sand when I court you. Your heart does not belong to another?"

Frances swallowed, and thought how best to answer this. Her heart was saying something with great vehemence, but she did not entirely understand. Since Colin's arrival it had been as though she was struck by the brightest light, which dazzled her with emotional lightning. But a part of her knew that after the beautiful lightning, there came a fearful thunder of hindsight and common sense, and it was for this aftermath that she waited, hoping for some determinate sign that would tell her definitively if she should give her devotion to this man.

Her heart said: *follow*. Reason, ever suspicious, bade her flee. She had to favor reason because loneliness could make the heart foolish.

"How can I answer you?" she said at last. "There is no reply that is not either cruel or immodest, and now I have no guardian to answer for me. I do not see at all what we should do."

"Ah! That is true. Unless Tearlach . . ."

"Never!"

"Ah! Yet there is protocol for this situation. We must not despair." His tone was light.

"Indeed?" Frances allowed him to lace their hands together and to turn her to face him. Beneath his fingertips, her pulse raced.

"Aye. One needn't declare oneself forthrightly, but it is customary to give some sign to one's suitor. Now, let me consider . . . You might begin by passing me a rose stripped of thorns."

"We have none," she pointed out. "Only thistles. And their thorns are fixed. It seems to me that this would send an altogether repressive message, *oui*?"

"Sadly, this is true. Well, then, you might begin by saying something like, 'Your face hath taken up residence in my heart.' "

"That is most poetic," she approved, beginning to smile at the foolishness of their conversation. Some of her anxiety departed. "Supposing that it were true, of course, and a woman did not mind being unsubtle."

Colin's teeth gleamed as his lips replied to her smile in kind. He led her toward the fire, seating her on the stool by the hearth. "Yes, always supposing. But if you said this, then I could reply with, 'On my tomb shall your name be fixed fast,'" he went on outrageously. "Which is quite a tribute, for stone masons are rather rare in these parts and marble is expensive."

"Marble?"

"From Italy," he affirmed. "I would insist on the finest."

"That is certainly a commitment," Frances agreed, as he knelt before her on one knee, and raised the hem of her skirt toward his lips. When he paused, she asked a bit breathlessly: "What then would happen?"

"Then I should present you with a sonnet or ode—I shall see to that as soon as we have found our ill-mannered dog and dealt with him. Do you like sonnets?" he asked, kissing her dress before letting it fall.

"But of course."

"Good. Sonnets are shorter. I am not at all certain that I could compose an entire ode," he confessed.

"Not even with my face in residence in your heart?" she asked.

"Hmm—perhaps. But you would have to accept that it wouldn't be a first-rate ode, not on an initial try. You might actually have to sit through many readings of a great deal of ill-sounding poetry before an ode of sufficient skill and passion came from my quill." Colin leaned forward, still taller than she, even when seated. He lowered his face to hers, pausing a breath away.

"Let us begin with a sonnet and see what transpires," Frances whispered.

"Nay. Let us begin with a kiss. 'Tis a traditional form of inspiration," Colin murmured, bringing his lips to hers. "*Lasseir les aler*," he whispered.

Let them go! But what did he mean? Her feelings? Her doubts?

"*Oui*," she sighed, not certain what she was agreeing to, and in that instant, not particularly caring.

Frances exhaled and allowed herself to relax into the kiss's soft temptation. Colin's hands traveled from her hands up the length of her arms and throat until they reached her face. There he made a frame for her chin and rested his fingers against her warmed cheeks.

His lips coaxed, asking gently to be let near her so he could taste. His scent filled up her head and made her dizzy. Her spine melted, her limbs growing weak as her body pressed itself against Colin's greater strength and warmth. Her good sense swooned into insensibility and left her body to its own devices.

Colin gathered her in, burying his face in her hair and murmuring some endearment that she could not hear above the drumming of her heart. Heat washed through her body with the force of a tidal current.

There came a brisk rap on her chamber door, loud enough to interrupt her heart's thunder and intrude on her benumbed brain's dazzlement. Colin rose to his feet and, putting her from him, spun to face the intruder.

As he turned half away, Frances noticed the dirk he clutched at his side. The blade was plain and serviceable, not the sort worn by court fops. It disturbed her to see that even when he made love he was armed and prepared for battle. Some of the delightful, mind-numbing heat drained away from her, stilling her tumultuous pulse and causing the tide of desire to recede precipitously.

She rose to her feet and found that she was able to face Anne Balfour with an assumption of calm that matched Colin's own.

"M'lady, George said you were ready to retire. I am here to assist you. Immediately, if it is quite convenient." Anne's voice was as cool as her gaze.

Frances stared at the widow in consternation. Never had the other woman sounded so cold and disapproving. Her eyes, when they rested on Colin, were as hard as pebbles.

"I shall bid you both good night then," Colin said. Putting up his knife, he added: "Do not forget what we discussed, my dear."

"I shan't forget anything," Frances answered.

Colin nodded once to the rigid Anne and then bowed himself out.

Walking down the empty corridor, Colin considered the small tableau that had just been enacted. He wasn't certain if it was the circumstances of being caught in midseduction, or some natural and unexplainable antipathy, but he decided he did not care for this particular Balfour. He'd seen eyes like hers staring out from under an executioner's hood.

It might be that her moral outrage at their intimacy in Frances's bedchamber had made her speak coldly to Frances. It could also be that for some reason she was less than fond of her niece by marriage and did not wish for her to become aligned with a man who might one day be master. Either way, Colin decided that

Anne Balfour would bear watching. Perhaps Tearlach should be given the honor.

This last thought caused a not entirely pleasant smile to curve his lips.

The last, the dreaded hour is come,
That bears my love from me:
I hear the dead note of the drum,
I mark the fatal tree.

—"The Ballad of Gilderoy"

Chapter Twelve

The weather the next day treated them kindly. George, believing that he was aiding their search by serving as a decoy, was left to his archery practice while Frances accompanied Colin on his explorations.

Admittedly, neither of them was as attentive to the task as they might have been on another occasion, but the sun was making a rare and unseasonable appearance. The golden light demanded appreciation. Too, it was not always so easy to think logically when the object of one's dreams—both waking and sleeping—was so near and one was entirely unchaperoned.

Frances found herself caught in a delightful emotional quagmire made half of rare and heady freedom, and half of desire, and it seemed to her that Colin was secretly smiling about her new irresponsibility. Indeed, he seemed bent on encouraging lightheartedness in both her and George.

And to good account, she assured herself. She had not been raised to approve of a life of delights and diversions, but some recreation was necessary—especially to a boy. Already George's spirits had lifted, and he no longer minded practicing his archery and seeing to the tedious task of mounting a watch on the keep's walls. She had heard Colin suggest that George watch for malefactors to shoot, and this was what had wrought this change of attitude. And George's new interests in turn allowed her to leave him for short periods of time, and ramble through the countryside with Colin, where it happened—most reasonably—that he often had need to assist her through the rough terrain by holding her hand or arm, and they were able to speak freely while no one was about to hear them and turn disapproving eyes their way.

Nor did his encouragement end there. He seemed bent on nurturing a mobility of mind that was foreign to her experience. Perhaps it was some outpost of maturity or experience that she had not yet reached that allowed him to question tradition and, if found wanting, to easily break with it. This was indeed antithetical to everything she had been taught about duty and her role in the universe, but she found the possibilities it offered to be something headier than wine. Her rebellions had all been of the mind and spirit. Colin Mortlock rebelled in fact. Without fanfare or declarations, he simply went his own way.

Frances studied Colin as he slowly scanned the nearby countryside, looking either for enemies or clues. Or perhaps just looking. Who could know what went on in such a free mind? What she did know was that his face, even in profile, made her heart trip along on stumbling feet as it rushed her toward some decision.

Her mother had wanted a match for her daughter

with the son of an old friend. Had her mother lived, it was possible that she would be a *comtessa* by now. And had her father not died so suddenly, it was probable that he would have arranged a marriage for her to someone else—perhaps even the MacLeod, if there were enough to gain politically or financially from the match. In neither case were her wishes or happiness of much concern.

But her parents were gone, and she was left to arrange her own life. She had to choose wisely, for there was no one to avenge her if she were played false by her husband. This had been her dilemma from the moment her father had died.

She had been convinced that a period of reflection was in order before deciding whether she should encourage Colin. But now, it seemed that her heart and body had made the decision her mind could not. It was ready to reap the benefit of the increased liberty granted by her circumstances. What was the point of having the means to pleasure, if she did not use them?

And from this thought, she had somehow in the last days arrived at the point where she was prepared to deliver herself into Colin's care—even with the emotional uncertainty that lingered when she considered the paradoxes of this rather mysterious man.

"Colin?" she called softly, glad she had chosen an attractive gown to wear, glad that she had allowed art to assist nature so she would be pretty for him.

"Aye, love?" he asked, his tone absentminded.

Her heart rolled over anyway.

"*Cher*, look at me." She touched his arm.

Obedient, he turned toward her, his eyes focusing

on her face, his expression softening. "I look," he answered softly, smiling slightly. "What am I to see?"

"Only the one you called *love.*" She was unable to maintain her gaze and released herself from the visual embrace even as she asked, "Do you wish me to be your love? In truth, not just name?"

"What a foolish and utterly dangerous question." Colin reached out and laced their fingers together. "My shy violet, your words are bold, but you look quite alarmed. Are you certain you wish to speak of this now?"

"Need we actually speak of it?" she asked. "Could you not . . . write me a poem?"

Colin laughed softly, but she could not imagine why. "I think these are deep waters that had best be tested before you wade in too far. You have yet to discover what is fashionable modesty and what is true reserve. Only experimentation can tell you this about your nature."

"*Oui*?" She did not entirely understand what he meant, but admittedly she did sometimes look into Colin's eyes and sense that she was drowning. Still, recalling her wonderful feeling of the night before, she wanted to press on into this ocean and see where the tide took them.

"Still, a little adventure would not hurt on so fine a day. And I do mean to have you to wife," Colin explained, perhaps to her or perhaps to himself. "I should be clear about that, if you have any doubts about my intentions."

"But of course." Frances's face lifted to his. Then after a moment she colored as she lied: "I had not thought that you meant otherwise. You are an honorable man."

Colin touched a finger to her crimson cheek and then smiled again. "No rose on earth has such color," he murmured. Then: "What is an honorable man to do? I think there might be divergence of thought on this matter. I have to think what will best keep you safe." He stared at her intently.

Frances could not think what to say. Once again, he was alluding to something she did not understand.

"But then why not? It was always my plan," he murmured, brushing a kiss over her lips. When she did not pull back, Colin turned and urged her away from the cliffs. To her relief, he said: "Come. Let's find a bit of shelter."

They passed behind a small hedge of trees, bent nearly double from years of the sea's furious storms and the constant wind. They were misshapen but balked the worst of the ocean's moaning tempests as they sucked what life they could from the rainwater that accumulated in the shattered rocks where they grew.

In the hollow behind them, nature had laid down a convenient bed of thick moss, not yet tinged with the melancholy colors of autumn that painted the rest of seaside flora. Colin took Frances's hand and led her into the rough bower. He shed his cloak onto the moss and then knelt down, bringing her with him. Frances looked into his eyes, so close, so deep, and thought fleetingly of the puppets Colin had mentioned some night earlier. She felt every bit as bereft of will, a doll to be guided and bent to his resolve. Was this normal? Was it right?

A small inner voice protested. But the voice sounded very much like one of the sisters at the convent, and she chose to ignore it. Frances did not yet know every aspect of her own mind and heart, but she had realized the thoughts that sprang from her religious training had an insidious power over natural inclination. This was power she no longer wished to surrender to some phantom teacher. She didn't know yet if the ethics she lived by were her own, or those of her parents and teachers, but she knew she did not want to evade responsibility for her decision to be with Colin by hiding behind foreign religious training. Truth could not keep company with mindlessness. It would only be her truth when she had embraced it on her own.

Above them, the sky was hard and clear and filled with silver light that pierced the eyes, and she closed her lids against it, preferring the softer fires that glowed within. They were simple and pure. With them to warm her, she was able to unlock the door that had been held fast against desire, and push aside the cold skeletons of parental morals and mistakes, which guarded her against knowing her own true feelings.

A gentle hand caressed her face and then tugged at her cloak's ties. The heavy velvet slid from her shoulders with a sigh barely heard above the sound of the distant waves that paced restlessly, like some soft-footed insomniac, marching up and down the beach as he waited for the night hours to pass.

"Be at ease, my love," he murmured. "It is not your death you go to."

His love. They were just sweet words, but the shackles of responsibility, like stones sewn into the seams of her cloak, were somehow shed as Colin put the drape from her. She felt wonderfully weightless and free.

She sighed, allowing him to lower her to the ground.

If this was the moment he had chosen, then she was ready to render up the virtue that the nuns had labored so diligently to protect. A part of her mind might protest, but only incoherently, for cold, logical thought melted under the twin fires of hope and longing. Reason reeled as it lost solid form and its icy foundation melted into gleaming pools of amorous thought. The moment for cerebration was past. It was the hour when emotion held sway. This was the moment when she would find her truth.

She heard him set his scabbard aside.

Then Colin's lips found hers, and this time they were familiar as well as warm. They called to something inside her that was at once wonderful but also nearly unbearable. Something that craved to be set free along with her mind.

A clever hand loosed the neck of her chemise and it slid from her shoulder. Warm lips touched her collarbone.

"I have always wanted to kiss a woman wearing the wind and sun and nothing more," he murmured, turning his head and kissing the fingers clenched in his hair. "It is how the creator made us. Why should we be so shy with the one we trust?"

"Colin," she sighed, slipping her arms about him and urging him closer. He might want her to wear only the sun and wind, but she wanted to pull him about her, too. To wear his body, if not his love.

It was not what her parents would have wanted, she knew. This passion had come to them before acquaintance—or even complete trust. But she and Colin could begin with this, she told herself, and in time she would come to know Colin's heart, his past, and then comprehend the mystery that surrounded him. There would be time enough for all—

Lucid thought was snuffed out by the desire rising within her. It was an animal, wild, seeking escape, seeking nourishment for all the years it had been denied. It rode with a companion, loneliness, and it, too, was hungry. She had never known that one could tremble so violently from anything except fear. She curved herself into his body, wrapping herself about him and praying he could soothe the beasts that seemed to gnaw at her heart and make her blood rage.

The sun disappeared into a bank of fast-moving clouds, and Colin could feel Frances shiver violently, as the wind that pushed the clouds along ran over them in a long and icy exhalation that carried the scent of freshly wounded plants. Awoken from adoring reverie, Colin looked past the passionate tangle of his lover's hair and immediately spotted the hart's-tongue fern, which had been trampled under a heavy paw. Beyond it lay a patch of bronze lichen raked to ominous furrows by giant claws.

He closed his eyes in exasperation, wishing to postpone thoughts of murder and mayhem and give himself to the sweetness of the moment, but it would be shameful, distasteful, perhaps even suicidal to consider making love in a place frequented by the giant hound. Bad enough that he had even once considered taking her without first explaining who and what he was, and what her life would be with him when she became his wife. In his desire, he had forgotten to be a gentleman—and more importantly, an honest one.

And it was turning cold and stormy. Autumn storms

could be furious and cold. He couldn't risk her health to the inclement weather, however wondrous and unexpected the passion between them.

"I hadn't thought that I was issuing an invitation to danger when I said to come lie with me," he murmured, raising himself slightly. His body didn't like the separation and protested vehemently.

"What is it you see?" Frances asked, her eyes open now and beginning to show fear as her ardor drained away. The sight cooled his fervor more thoroughly than the storm-carrying wind.

Colin, exasperated with Fate and physically much disinclined to rise, nevertheless managed to give Frances a last sweet kiss and then roll to his feet. "We've found our hound's trail."

"*Mon Dieu*!" Frances exclaimed, also coming to her feet, and snatching at her cloak where she kept a slim dagger. It took her a moment to secure the knife, as her gown was prone to slipping with its sleeve and neck untied. "Where is the beast?"

"The remains of his dinner are over there," Colin answered reluctantly. He had just noticed the cracked yellow bone half hidden under the disturbed fern and rucked moss.

Clearly appalled, Frances nevertheless started for the protruding bone.

"Don't!" Colin said, picking up a stick and turning over the yellowed relic. As he had feared, it was human rather than bovine.

"Can we be sure it is the work of the hound?" Frances asked, though she did not truly doubt that it was the hound's leavings. There were no wolves near Noltland, no predators large enough to gnaw bones in half.

"Aye. Look at the bite marks. The width of them is suggestive of something with a large jaw."

"You do not touch it," Frances said softly, shivering in spite of her cloak being replaced. "That is because it is cursed? Or mayhap haunted?"

Not haunted. No spirit remained with the shattered relic.

"Cursed? Not per se." Colin turned and helped her secure her garment. He caught a last glimpse of her delicately flushed skin, and frowned. "Unless my own curses count. Then they and the beast are certainly damned for interrupting us."

"Then you hesitate because it is not from an animal?" she guessed shrewdly. "That is a *man's* arm, is it not?"

"It is not from a well-dressed cow or sheep or deer," Colin admitted, knowing he couldn't keep the truth from her, yet still feeling reluctant to reveal his suspicions. Human bones were bad enough. To confront the gnawed bones of one's own ancestor was gruesome in the extreme.

"Frances . . ."

She ducked her head and said: "Do what you must."

Colin nodded once and then propped back the fern with a stick. He searched swiftly for the proof he suspected might linger nearby. He turned over the pathetic remnant of clothing, which had been a cuff.

"Whose is it?" Frances asked faintly. "Perhaps someone who drowned?"

Colin pulled aside the branches of a leafy shrub and found a narrow tunnel. It pointed toward the keep's south wall, where the cemetery was located. It wasn't likely that individual graves had been disturbed, but there was the ill-constructed mass vault that sat over a burial pit. It backed up against the castle wall.

"I believe the hound has been using its master's secret castle access and has found Noltland's ossuary. I fear he has been helping himself to the bones." Colin let the bush fall back over the opening.

"*Mon Dieu*!" Her lovely flush was fading as her skin turned a shade as translucent as a single layer of oyster shell. "Can we not return it to the grave?"

Colin shook his head. "It is probably just needless worry on my part, but too many of the old graves contain the bodies of plague victims. People who have contact with old bones sometimes fall ill. I do not want you touched by anything so dangerous."

Shivering, Frances fell back a step, grateful to be received into Colin's arms when she stumbled. "Then there is still another way into the castle that we have not found?"

Colin shook his head. "Perhaps not. It may be that this tunnel leads only to the dungeons, and those are now secure. But we must find the opening to the outside and arrange for it to be sealed regardless. We can't have the beast dining on the dead."

"*Oui*. The living must be protected from this dead menace, or we may all fall ill. Winters are a cruel time here." Her answer was again briskly practical and almost made him smile, in spite of having his seduction interrupted.

"And the dead seem to likewise need protection from the living's nasty pets."

Frances shrugged, her color beginning to return to normal. "*Oui*. That, too. But we cannot concern ourselves too much with dead people, Colin. There are too many living ones whose needs are greater."

"Very sensible, my love," he answered, picking up his sword and buckling it around his waist.

"We are going after the hound?" Frances asked. "We could explore the tunnel."

"Nay. We are going back to the keep."

"But—" she protested, tugging on her still-loose chemise beneath her cloak.

"It is more important that we secure the castle," he said flatly, not adding that he wasn't about to go after the hound while she was with him. But that wasn't an answer a valiant—and venturesome—female would find acceptable. "It isn't likely he'd be in the tunnel now anyway."

"*Oui*?"

"*Absolutement. Je crois que oui*," he answered firmly in her own tongue. "And on the way back, we shall look for some dogsbane."

"Dogsbane?"

"Aye, periwinkle it is also called. We shall leave some about the ossuary for our canine intruder."

"*Ca va pas, non*?"

"I may be insane, but not about this. Periwinkle is an effective poison."

Her delightful eyes studied him, their expression very serious.

"What are you thinking, love?" he asked. "I can tell there is something in your mind."

She spread her hands wide in a gesture that might have meant anything. "I am thinking it is strange but fortunate that you know about poison."

"The benefits of travel," he said, a touch grimly. "Come! We must get back to the keep. Tearlach and I will have to seal this tunnel, if we cannot destroy it completely. Damnation! These castles are always riddled with bolt-holes and secret passages!" And ghosts. Though he was reluctant, perhaps it was time to engage with one of the castle's lost spirits.

All down the church in midst of fire,
The hellish monster flew,
And passing onward to the choir,
He many people slew.

—*The Reverend Abraham Fleming,*
A Straunge and Terrible Wunder *(1577)*

CHAPTER THIRTEEN

"Frances! Colin!" George called excitedly, waving to them as he scurried down from the wall.

"What is it?" Frances asked, hurrying to meet her cousin, who wore an engaging grin that alarmed her mightily. "George, have a care on those stairs. They are very narrow and steep!"

"You needn't go searching for the hound today after all," George announced, skidding to a stop at the base of the stairs. "He is here."

"Here?" Colin demanded.

"Aye, outside the gate."

A loud *woo-woo*ing filled the air, underscoring the boy's assertion.

"*Mon Dieu*!" Frances clapped her hands over her ears, and they turned in unison and headed for the yett.

Outside, the view of the barren landscape beyond was suddenly full of a clamorous hound of indeterminate breed, which, at the sight or perhaps scent of

George, began dancing happily up and down and demanding to be let inside.

"I think he likes me," George said loudly, raising his childishly thin arm to point, while looking at them with a not-so-childish face. His eyes were somber when he said: "He's been tied up somewhere. Look, he has a rope around his neck. And that nasty powder is so thick, he must be choking. No wonder he's been baying."

The frayed cord was barely visible under the ruff that ringed the beast's throat. George stepped closer to the gate and said, "Hush, dog! You are upsetting Frances."

The intelligent hound promptly ceased its paean and contented himself with a low whine and turning his worried brown eyes upon the boy. A huge paw was laid on the horizontal bar in clear supplication. The chalky cloud about the hound began to subside.

Colin drew his sword. "George, step back."

"But"—the boy argued, turning large and worried eyes upon Colin—"you *can't* kill him. He doesn't mean any harm. You can see for yourself that he isn't a hound from Hell. It was all just a misunderstanding. He's someone's pet."

"I can see that he is not a hellhound, and I shan't kill him unless he attacks someone," Colin assured the boy. "But you must know that I cannot allow any possible danger near Frances. Step back now. Give me some room. Tearlach, are you ready?"

Reminded of his duty to the frailer sex, the boy reluctantly backed away from the gate. His retreat caused the beast to whine piteously.

Frances, not looking particularly frail, glanced about

quickly to see that no cats were foolishly lingering nearby. Satisfied that they were bereft of feline company, she turned to Tearlach, who waited by the giant wheel that controlled the gate. He was muttering something about *muckle black tykes* beneath his breath.

At Frances's nod, an unhappy Tearlach raised the yett enough for the beast to pass through. The delighted animal, not seeing Colin's sword, or perhaps not understanding what it meant, immediately launched his chalked body at the object of his long, diligent search. He was upon George in one bound, and rising onto his hind legs he dropped heavily onto the boy's thin shoulders, forcing George to the ground beneath him. There he began administering an enthusiastic tongue bath to his human prize.

"Colin! The plague from the bones!" Frances said urgently. "Remove him from George."

Colin sheathed his blade and then grabbed the hound's trailing rope. He reeled in the frayed cord and then began extricating George from the hairy embrace. The boy scrambled to his feet, flushed but clearly unoffended by the canine intimacy.

"Go wash at once, George," Frances instructed, her voice a bit shrill. "Clean every part that beast has touched. The dog has been eating . . . disgusting things."

"But, Frances!" George swiped a hand over his face. He left a trail of white chalk behind.

"At once! You are filthy!" Her tone was imperious and George wisely obeyed, though he looked back with worried eyes and traveled with laggard steps toward the keep.

"You won't hurt him, will you?"

"The beast shall be safe with Colin, *mon cher*," she

assured him. "But go! It is urgent. Trust me. I will explain matters later."

Frances waited until George was gone and then turned. The hound was sitting subdued beside Colin, finally appearing a bit chastened for his behavior, yet still optimistic that he would be let up to play or perhaps offered a meal. She looked the two males over thoroughly. Her voice, when she spoke, was as severe as Colin had ever heard it.

"You, monsieur, are a chalky mess!" Colin opened his mouth to protest, but Frances went on: "You are not at all a spectral hound. You are not any sort of hound. You are simply large. Where is your dignity?"

In reply, a long tongue rolled out of the beast's wide mouth and he rose to his feet. The giant tail began to wag. Clearly he was ready to make friends.

"Do not even conceive of putting that filthy mouth or paws upon me," Frances warned. "I am not George and do not care for slobber. *Il a l'air con*," she added to Colin. "An idiot animal."

"He does not look terribly keen of wit," Colin admitted, glancing down at the lolling tongue, which protruded to an implausible length. "But he has good taste."

"Clearly this is a male hound of Hell," Tearlach observed, coming up behind Colin and the beast. He stooped to peer under the hound's wagging tail. He whistled appreciatively and said with envy: "Aye, this one's a male. I've never heard of a muckle black tyke with such a large—"

"Tearlach!" Colin warned.

"I am aware of the fact that this is a male beast. Sine!" Frances called impatiently. "Do not cower in the doorway. Bring Eilidh. This animal must be washed at once. I do not want this creature in the keep until he has been bathed and—and used the privy."

"Bathed and used the privy?" Sine repeated, leaving the shelter of the keep and coming reluctantly closer at Frances's call. "The dog? Why?"

"Because he has no manners and does not understand where to dine. Perhaps you had best fetch my lavender water. He has—Colin, how do you say *puer le fauve*?"

Unable to help himself, Colin began to laugh. "Aye, he smells a bit like a wild animal. But I do not think dousing him in scent will improve matters."

"Nay. I meant, why bring him into the keep at all?" Sine asked. "Anne has already locked herself in her chamber and refuses to come out while the beastie is here. Couldn't he stay in the stable?"

"*Non*. The young laird wishes to keep him. Anne shall have to overcome her fears," Frances said ruthlessly, causing Sine to blink.

"But, Frances, ye ken how Anne is—"

"*Bien Dieu*! Sine, I do not care for this disfavored mongrel either. He is a filthy creature and uncivilized. But George has been very lonely. He needs a companion and Colin and I may not always be with him. Perhaps this beast shall serve to turn his thoughts from the Bokey hound and his parents' death, *n'est-ce pas*? Anne is a woman grown and she shall have to accommodate him."

Sine's expression softened a shade, but the gaze she turned on the beast was still skeptical. "But the beastie is sae large and fierce-looking. And sae very filthy."

"I'll bathe the beast," Colin volunteered. "And see

that he—uh—takes care of all his ablutions before he comes inside. Sine, what would be helpful is if you would bring a bone for the creature to dine on, and send for George as soon as he has washed. The process will go faster if he is here to keep the hound happy. Tearlach, if you would fetch some water?"

"But, Colin, is that wise? You know what he has been eating. George is young and prone to illness," Frances began. "Many times he has had the fever—"

"I shan't let any harm befall George," Colin promised. "And neither will the beast. I believe we have a new ally in our war."

"Why does he like my cousin so much?" Frances asked, staring at the grinning dog and lowering her voice, even though Sine and Tearlach had left immediately after Colin spoke to them. He had a knack for command.

"Look outside the gate," he said. "Unless I am mistaken, that is one of George's sarks."

Frances went to the yett and looked down at the small saffron-colored shirt, which was barely recognizable, covered as it was in drool and dirt.

"The beast stole it while he was in the castle?"

"Nay. I suspect he was given it by his master. Or, in this case, his mistress. Beasts must be given the scent of their prey before they can hunt."

Frances spun about. "Given it? You mean that he was given the shirt so he would hunt for George? By someone in the castle?"

"Aye, but once again our enemies have misjudged their puppets. This beast is certainly large enough to be a killer. But, fortunately for us, he hasn't the temperament for it. This isn't an angry varden."

"Varden?"

"An animal companion spirit like your Bokey hound. This is simply an oversized pup."

"Oh." Frances looked again at the damaged shirt. She felt a little ill when she imagined the damage happening with George still in it.

"It would have to be one of the women who gave him this shirt, would it not?" she asked unhappily, reaching for a pike. She pushed it through the gate, retrieving the mauled shirt. It hung, sad and empty. "Tearlach is the only man here besides yourself, and though rude and insane, I do not think he means George any harm."

"I'm sorry, Frances," Colin answered. "But I fear it *must* be someone in the castle who is behind this campaign. She may have a confederate outside the walls, but she knew what she did when she stole clothing to give this hound a scent to follow . . . Best if you burn that before anyone else sees it. News of a traitor in our midst might cause panic. It could also drive the traitor into doing something desperate. We don't want her acting prematurely."

Before Frances could reply, George and the other couple children boiled outside in a chattering wave. They rushed over to the calf-sized hound and stared at him admiringly.

"Is he a broonie?" Morag asked. "Or a pooka?"

"Nay, he's just a dog," George answered, stretching out a hand for the beast but stopping short of actually touching him, since it made Frances so angry.

Frances looked at the happy flush in George's too-thin cheeks and the excitement shining in his eyes. She sighed, but relented slightly.

"None of the children are to touch the hound until

he is clean," she told Colin sternly. She added frankly to the children: "He has been eating bones and playing in chalk, which will make you children have hives and be sick in bed for weeks, so you will behave and wait to touch him until he is clean."

The youths turned disbelieving eyes upon her, but nodded obediently.

"May we help bathe the broonie?" Morag asked.

"Stop calling him that! He isn't magical," George insisted. "He is just a large dog."

Frances shook her head at the little girl. "*Non.* You may help dry him, though. I think that Monsieur Mortlock and George shall require much assistance."

"And linen," Sine added, returning with yellowing drying cloths and a sheep bone. The latter was carried with distaste, extended outward so that it would not soil her clothes.

"*Merci*, Sine. You are very kind."

Sine snorted. "I shall stay until I see that Tearlach brings the water," the older woman answered. "Ye'd best go in and speak to Cook. She is not happy about sparing anything for the animal tae eat. And she is saying she won't bring Anne a tray tae her room because if anyone should be having vapors, it is the kitchen staff and not the needle-wielder with pretentions."

Frances sighed and watched Colin and George leading the hound away. The beast would probably eat a great deal and they could spare very little. Still, Colin had said that help was coming. And even if it weren't, she wouldn't take the beast away from George, who clearly wished to keep him. She hadn't the ruthlessness necessary to quash his new happiness. "I shall speak to Cook at once."

Frances turned her mind to persuasive arguments

that would calm Cook, wishing it were possible to tell everyone that the Bishop of Orkney was coming and their men would be returning soon with food and arms, and that all would soon be well.

As she hurried away, she heard Colin ask: "What precisely *is* a broonie?"

"Just another faerie story," George answered, his voice growing faint. "He is supposed to be some sort of imp—a shaggy thing—who helps you find paths in the dark. And sometimes he helps lost fisherman ashore when it is storming."

"Ah, and you don't think that this nameless beast *might* be a broonie?"

"Well . . ." George's tone was considering.

Frances began to smile and paused to listen.

"Do you not think that since I have a hound now, I should have a lymerer's coat?" George asked.

"Ask your cousin. Better yet, you may borrow my plaid of office. It's a splendid shade. You can see it from leagues away. It would be excellent for a hound keeper."

George chuckled, then added confidentially: "I told Frances it was too bright, but you know what women are."

"No man ever really knows what women are," Colin replied wisely. "And the one who thinks he does is a complete suckfist."

Frances nodded in agreement and filed the expression away for future use.

In spite of his promise to Frances, Colin was content to leave the washing of the hound in George's enthusiastic hands. It left his mind free to ponder his two favorite subjects: the perfidious mystery of who had set the hound on George, and the delightful Frances Balfour. Of the two, Frances was the sweeter and more baffling to contemplate.

It came as a surprise, but he realized he was actually falling in love with her. It was not something expected or even sought after, but he supposed that, however surprising, it was natural enough. Even men of wit sometimes succumbed to softer emotions. It was an act of faith and an expression of hope that life had something more to offer than material possessions.

However, the scope of this new feeling was something that could strike terror in the breast, for it was not some pleasant, courtly love he felt. It was something grand, a love that could grow as large as it could ever be known by mortal men. It was love like the music of angels. Love like vastness of the ocean. Love with the warmth and light of the sun.

But what puzzled him more than the emotion itself was, just when had this desire for a wife been born? And what had nurtured the idea unbeknownst to him while his thoughts were preoccupied with other things? For certainly something had nurtured it. Surely such emotions did not spring fully formed from the heart and mind.

Had it happened while he was playing a role as Frances's lover? Had he perhaps finally been taken in by his own simulations? Colin sighed and prudently stepped away from the hound, which was preparing itself for a titanic shake.

It was probably an unanswerable question. He would do as well to take a stance preferred by poets, and blame it all on being hunted by Cupid and hit with his golden arrows feathered with enslaving kisses. Or he could blame it on Frances's magnificent eyes, or the glory of her unbound hair capturing the light of the sun.

Of course, it was not desire alone that moved him. Lust, that fickle jade, lived and died a hundred times a day, a million times in a life. It waxed and waned according to the mood, the hour, and the setting—perhaps even with the moon. Desire, though intense, often survived only as long as what it coveted was in plain sight. Nay, this was something more. It had all the characteristics of a grand passion, a great love. It made no sense, this feeling he had. It could not be quantified, or even completely described. But love her he did. And not even death would change his mind.

Therefore, it behooved him to stop dwelling on sentimental things and to apply himself to discovering the traitor in their midst before someone was harmed. He could not count on Frances remaining valiant but not adventurous when her beloved cousin was threatened, so something had to be done.

He already had a strong suspicion of who had betrayed them, but he would make no accusation without proof. Frances would not accept it. In any event, it was far more important that he discover whom she was collaborating with on the outside, and what she had told them. That there was an outside collaborator, he never doubted.

"We are not calling him Broonie!" George insisted, his annoyed tone breaking in on Colin's reverie. "I think we should call him Harry. Do you not think that a good name, Mr. Mortlock?"

Colin looked at the drying animal. The children's brisk toweling had further aggravated his hair's tendency to curl, and the hound looked very much like an enormous thistle going to seed.

"Well, he is certainly a hairy beast."

"Not *hairy*. Harry! After King Henry. He looks like a lion, doesn't he? And he is big like the king . . . Unless you would like me to name him after you," the boy suggested generously.

"Nay!" Colin said, appalled at the idea, but at George's hurt look he began searching for words of moderation. Inspiration struck. "Too much confusion might ensue. We could never be certain which of us you were calling. I think he does indeed look a good deal like a lion."

That was a lie, but it seemed better than saying the animal looked like the king. It wasn't a comparison the vain monarch would care for.

"Then Harry he shall be," George said happily.

"I like Broonie," Morag insisted.

"I like Tyke," the other boy said, speaking for the first time. "Tearlach said he was a tyke."

George sniffed. "You only think that a good name because you are just six—and you are a girl," he added crushingly, turning to the mutinous-looking female. "You know nothing about giving a noble animal a proper name."

"He's a furry commoner," the wounded six-year-old lashed back, then added something in Gaelic. Colin didn't imagine it was polite.

"You're the commoner! Harry is clearly a very noble animal! He probably escaped from the king's retinue during one of the battles."

The two younger children began to pout, disbelieving of this theory and inclined to say so.

Colin decided it was time to take his charges inside. It wouldn't do to have a second battle of Solway fought in the castle's courtyard while they were entrusted to his care. "Come along. I am certain that Frances is anxious to see our guest now that he is looking so splendid." It was another lie, but the perjury was worth it if it averted battle. "You can tell her all about his name, George, for I am certain that she'll like it."

There were also some things Colin wished to tell her, but he wasn't certain how to go about the task and if she would like his words as well as the hound's name. Could a man ever speak of love on such short acquaintance and not appear irrationally hasty?

And if any gaze on our rushing band,
We come between him and the deed of his hand,
We come between him and the hope of his heart.

—William Butler Yeats,
"The Hosting of the Sidhe"

Chapter Fourteen

It was not a complete surprise, but still a welcome sight when a small band of men in hodden gray plaids and worn capes came riding up to the keep on the afternoon of the following day.

The bishop himself was not among the dun-clad party, but Colin recognized his right-hand man, a Frenchman, Lucien de Talle, the one they rather ironically called *le Corbeau* because he favored priestly black garb. Like Colin, Lucien served as the eyes and ears for others. Unlike Colin, he was an instrument of observation for more than one master, being of service to both the bishop in Scotland and those working for the Protestant Enlightenment of France. Having no liking for servants of more than one master, Colin had nevertheless always found Lucien to be an honorable man, his strong religious views notwithstanding, and he did not hesitate to welcome him into the keep.

Understanding something of the situation at Noltland, the soldiers brought with them a few servants only, and supplies for themselves and their beasts. It took a while for things to be sorted out, but with the help of the very surprised Balfour women—Anne Balfour being excepted, as she had kept to her resolve to remain in her chambers while the hound was allowed to roam at large—they soon had things stowed away and the throng organized into regular watches. For the first time in months, actual guards served as sentries atop the keep's wall, keeping a weathered eye out for malefactors who might fight against what they perceived to be Noltland's struggle for emancipation from the forces of obscurantism.

They had one other man with the company who was not a mere soldier. He was Angus MacBride, a true cleric of the reformed church who, Lucien explained sotto voce, was there in the bishop's stead if Colin was determined to go ahead with his plan to marry Frances Balfour before Noltland's men returned.

Colin could feel the bishop's secondhand glee at the thought of marrying Colin and Frances under the cloak of his religion. Noltland had not firmly committed itself to one side or the other in the religious battle, instead being loyal to Scotland's monarch. He would feel that to perform the marriage of Noltland's heiress was an accomplishment both moral and political.

Frances, unaware of Angus MacBride's calling and Colin's purpose in requesting him, was delighted with Lucien and his soldiers, and was at her most charming. Her tone set the example of how the men were to be received at the castle. George was at his dignified best while expressing a soft thanks for their prompt arrival, and the women were gracious and warm to their somber visitors, though Tearlach was heard to mutter something about *hershippers* and *limmers* overrunning the castle before he disappeared inside the keep.

At first unhappy about their assigned task as guards for this remote keep—and doubtless less than pleased to have the mad piper calling them cattle thieves and rogues when their motives were pure—the bishop's soldiers soon thawed in the warmth of their welcome and promptly fell to work with a will, seeing to the many tasks that had been left undone when the Balfour men went off to war. The good physical work was actually welcomed after the boredom of soldiering in camp when no battle was at hand.

It was several hours before Colin and Lucien were able to find a few moments for private conversation, but after dinner that evening, they were at last able to retire to Colin's chamber, and there had some direct discussions. Colin felt the weight of Frances's gaze as it rested upon his retreating form, but she did not follow.

"*Mon cher*, I thought your plan mad when the bishop first explained it to me. But she is a lovely thing. And most valiant, too. What an intelligencer she would make! Women have a natural gift for this work, and she is intelligent as well," Lucien said with admiration, accepting a glass of wine. He lounged, very much at ease, his crisp black beard thrust belligerently forward onto his chest. His keen eyes scrutinized Colin, veiled though they were by his long dark lashes.

Colin forewent the examination with calm and humor, though he had no intention of discussing his true feelings for Frances Balfour, particularly as he did not yet know if they were truly requited. He was willing to be thought mercenary, but not a sentimental fool.

"Searching for signs of madness?" he enquired, as the visual consideration stretched on.

"Signs of love. But perhaps that is the same ailment. MacJannet is certain that an intense infatuation is upon you and has demolished your wits," Lucien answered.

Colin shot back his cuff and laid a hand upon his wrist. He counted leisurely for a moment, demonstrating the lack of frantic, amorous pulsations. It went counter to his new feeling to disavow his allegiance to Frances Balfour, but it was standard practice in his calling to be duplicitous about amatory dealings. It was no part of true affection to give hostages to Fate, and he did not trust Lucien that much.

"My pulse does not leap, nor is it thready." Next, Colin clapped a hand to his head. "I can feel no fever. My hands do not shake. I have not abandoned civilized dress for the Highland man's drafty plaids and plain blue bonnets. And my senses have not so far abandoned me that I cannot tell that I am in the very north of Scotland in a damp pile of rubble and not in the comfort of my own well-ordered home."

Lucien's white teeth flashed and he laughed softly. "I said 'ailment,' not 'illness.' And it is MacJannet who questions your good senses, not I. I've known you too many years to be concerned that you would lose your head over a pretty face." He waved a languid hand, a delicate gesture that he managed quite well in spite of calluses from his many years of wielding a basket-hilt sword in battle. "It is also quite plain that your taste in effete English clothing has not changed."

"Softly, my popinjay. I've seen you in France; do not forget. I recall a particularly resplendent cloak of crimson velvet. You can easily be a peacock among peacocks when the mood—or the role—suits you."

Lucien smiled benignly, his eyes wide. "But no one else here has seen it. This rough lot would never believe such testimonies. They are boring and unimaginative, if very devout, and would not believe me capable of such sins against convention."

"Convenient, that. I cannot imagine the bishop employing any other sort. One does not want large numbers of men with weapons thinking too much for themselves." Colin watched Lucien's smile widen and then added: "But, if my health and fashion of dress do not interest you, then let us talk of the bishop and his plans. He is still pulling caps with Beaton?"

Lucien stopped smiling. "Aye, they're a fractious lot, these Catholics, encouraged by the Lord of the Isle to every sort of mischief. Either he or the bishop shall end up dead. There's been one punitive foray against them already; a bad business where people went mad with battle lust. No one was spared, not even babes in their mother's wombs." Lucien's tone was suddenly grim and hard as he answered frankly. "They were content before to confine themselves to political stratagems, but are increasingly given to talk of actual battle and the hiring of mercenaries from Ireland and Spain."

Colin shook his head.

"And there will be no help from the throne," Lucien went on. "That is why the bishop could spare a score of men to you and no more. All are needed elsewhere."

"'Twill suffice. If MacJannet is quick at his work," Colin answered, also grim.

"But when was the industrious MacJannet ever anything but efficient?" Lucien asked, lounging back in his chair and resuming a calm tone.

"Never. A fact for which I am most grateful. The situation is perhaps more imperiling than I first thought. I could not put everything into my letter, lest it be intercepted. And certain strange events have arisen since MacJannet's departure."

"*Oui*? But of course they have. Something always arises when it is inconvenient. Confide in me, *mon cher*. I am all attentiveness and anxious to be of service."

Before Colin could speak, there came a distant but ghastly blare, which made the wooden shutters rattle.

"You are slaughtering swine this night?" Lucien asked, sitting forward in his chair.

"Nay, 'tis the piper playing down the sun." Colin fetched the ewer and refilled Lucien's glass.

"Are you certain? The sun was gone some time ago."

"Tearlach is sometimes behind the hour. Ignore it. It will be over soon."

Lucien cocked his head. "The bagpipes are all infernal noise to me, yet this sounds more ill than anything I have yet heard, even from a novice. It sounds like the screaming of the damned being tortured in Hell."

"Well, it might be the baying of the spectral hound," Colin allowed, as nearby, Harry's mournful wail joined Tearlach's ear-splitting disharmony. "Tearlach is sometimes less than affectionately known as the bane of the Balfours."

"A spectral hound? MacJannet spoke some of this

Bokey hound, but he denies that it is of supernatural agency."

"MacJannet is, as always, correct."

"Then you found the beast that stalks your halls and threatens the young laird? You have dispatched him, or do we need to mount a hunt on the morrow?"

"The beast was discovered. He was not however 'dispatched,' as the boy has taken a great liking to him, this extremely unspectral hound, and the monster also apparently likes him. Much to Lady Frances's dismay. She is used to keeping a tidier house."

Lucien laughed softly. "*Alors*! But this is most odd, and a story I must hear at once. Come, tell me the round tale."

Colin took the second seat near the hearth, and with his feet comfortably toasting, he proceeded to tell Lucien of his adventures since setting foot in Scotland, omitting only his cousin's plans of acquiring the keep and Frances for the MacLeods.

"But what a tale!" Lucien exclaimed as Colin drew it to a close. "However, I think perhaps some things have been left unsaid?"

"You are not at all stupid, my friend," Colin answered, sipping his wine. "I think your imagination can supply any deficiencies of detail. They are unimportant matters, after all, as I have no intention of this keep falling into anyone's hands except the Balfours'."

"And the boy? You have plans for him, as well? I rather like him. He is small but quick of wit. In time, he will become a good leader. If he lives."

"George is a difficult matter," Colin conceded. "It is

best if he remains here to see to his inheritance, but I have every intention of removing Frances as soon as may be. And I do not think the two cousins shall wish to be parted."

"Ah."

"There is another matter, as well. Whether we discover the hound's true master or not, I am not certain that I will never be easy in mind leaving George here without a strong guardian who has his welfare at heart."

"Not so long as there is the possibility of a traitor in your midst," Lucien agreed with a short nod. "You have identified who she is?"

Colin stared at Lucien for a full second.

"You did remark that I am not stupid," Lucien reminded him. "It has to be one of the women. And as I said before, they have the gift of scheming."

"Aye, more is the pity. There's no proof, of course, so it makes accusing her difficult."

"*Oui*? But you and I have long experience with knowing things that cannot be easily proved. Treason against one's laird is a dastardly thing. Something must be done, even if it is not done before a royal court."

"Aye, I know this."

"What shall you do then?"

"Nothing, until I find her confederate. She could not be acting alone. And it may be that there is some circumstance that would argue for mitigation."

"I see. But when the other party is discovered, what then?"

"I know not," Colin admitted. "I have no stomach for this new habit of shedding the blood of women."

"Nor do I, *mon ami*," Lucien agreed with a sigh. "But sometimes it must be done. And this creature has conspired at murder of a child, her kin, and her laird."

This quiet dust was gentlemen and ladies
And lads and girls.

—Emily Dickinson, "This Quiet Dust"

CHAPTER FIFTEEN

Frances watched the tenebrous passageway, waiting for Lucien de Talle to leave Colin's chamber. Her own room was dark and growing cold, as the hearth had been allowed to die down to embers. She had known it would be a sacrifice sitting in the dark without a fire and had prepared herself by dragging a stool to the door and supplying herself with a blanket. But the night was proving to be both longer and colder than she had anticipated.

Finally there was a crack in the blackness, and the silhouette of the Frenchman could be plainly seen in the doorway. Frances leaned forward impatiently, stilling her breath lest he somehow hear her as he stood alone in the echoing passage, as though listening for something. She willed him to be gone with thoughts fierce enough to bludgeon, yet Lucien turned back after a single step and said something in parting that gave her pause, even through her single-minded desire to see Colin again.

"You'll remove her as soon as you may, *oui*? Then see about securing the boy's inheritance?"

"Aye, I'll have her away. There are things afoot here of which she is best left in ignorance."

Frances frowned, feeling vaguely troubled.

"That is best. Females, even the finest of them, are not good repositories for men's confidences."

"I've not forgotten my calling, Sir Worry. Be off with you and leave matters in my hands."

Frances quickly eased her door shut as the light of Lucien's candle came wavering down the hall, forerun by the echo of his catlike footsteps.

Could the Frenchman have been speaking of her—saying that she was unworthy of trust? It was rude of him to talk so of her when they were barely acquainted. And worse still that Colin did not defend her virtue to him!

But surely this was not what they meant. It had to be someone else they spoke of.

Frances's brow cleared, and she rubbed a hand over her thudding heart, trying to soothe its alarm. She was being silly. Of course they had to have been speaking of the traitor in the castle. That spiteful person seemed to always be in Colin's thoughts.

As for the talk of Colin's calling and George's inheritance—well, she had not heard what had passed before it. Surely if she had heard the entire conversation she would not be feeling this vague alarm, because certainly all would be explained.

Still, perhaps now was not the time to go and speak with Colin. A calm mind was still far from her command. She should perhaps wait, reflect . . . If she went to him now there was only one way that things would end. And suddenly, she was uncertain if this was what she truly and forever wanted.

Colin frowned at his door. He had been almost certain that Frances would seek him out as soon as Lucien left. She had to be consumed with curiosity about what news he brought. And yet she did not appear.

Either she had fallen asleep while waiting, or she had come creeping down to listen at the door and overheard something that had awakened caution in her breast. Colin thought back to his final exchange with Lucien when his door was ajar and then cursed beneath his breath. If she had heard that, she might very well be suffering from pique. Or perhaps giving birth to new damning and inconvenient distrust.

Lighting his lantern, Colin pulled on his dark cloak and started preparing soothing fictions to pour into his ladylove's troubled ears. Oddly enough, for once in his life he'd have preferred to tell the truth, but couldn't risk the delay that might follow if revelation of his true vocation gave her pause. Let them be wed first. He would make his confessions after.

He scratched at her door and then immediately slipped inside. It seemed wisest to give her no time for denial. Frances looked up from the hearth, where she was stirring the fire to life. Her expression was for one moment startled, but quickly smoothed into polite blankness, except for her eyes, which were unusually large and troubled as they studied him. He was not accustomed to such reserve in her expression and did not like it.

She stood up slowly, her golden gown painted almost red by the fire as it rustled into its proper place. An impatient hand twitched her long dark braid tucked back behind her shoulder. He supposed this was not the moment to mention that her golden skin shamed the sun, nor that he would be unsurprised to discover that she could arouse even inanimate objects to desire simply by touching them, so lovely was she when gilded in firelight.

"So, *cherie*, are you prepared to essay an adventure?" he asked quietly.

The question got a slow blink and then the tight-pressed lips relaxed slightly. "You have news to share with me?"

"Aye, but more importantly, thanks to the bishop I have the means of executing a workable plan. A plan that shall make you and George safe even after the men return home."

The dark eyes blinked again. "You do not believe we shall be safe after the men return?"

"From your neighbors? Perhaps, unless one is still determined to wed you. I suspect that the MacLeod at least will not stop pressing you until you are finally beyond his reach." Colin walked toward her, being careful not to move too quickly or appear at all menacing. Even so, Frances remained unusually stiff and wary. Her posture was a subtle accusation.

"But once the men return, we can defend the keep from the MacLeod!" she protested.

"From danger without. But from within? It would not surprise me if some of the men were of a mind to encompass a marriage with you. There would be a great deal of pressure to have such an event come about to secure your fortune for the upkeep of the castle." He let the words sink in and then added: "And have you forgotten that we have a traitor in our midst? What is to stop this person from opening the gate some night and letting the enemy within these walls?"

"*Mon Dieu*," she sighed, turning from him. She rubbed at her heart as though it pained her. "I have not forgotten. I was simply keeping the memory at a distance as I prepared for bed, for I like it better far from my dreams."

"That is most understandable, if not perhaps wise." Colin stepped closer. He asked whimsically then: "Tell me, *cherie*, will you call out for help if I kiss you?"

Her lips twitched once. "Nay—why cry for help? Unless you need assistance in this endeavor. But is this why you have come? To make love to me?"

"Only in small measure. I have come, first and foremost, to entreat for your heart. And if I cannot have that yet, then for your hand. We can be wed on the morrow."

For a third time, the lady blinked. Any burgeoning playfulness left her as she considered this. "But . . . but how is this possible?"

"The bishop has sent us a minister. Angus MacBride can marry us."

Frances sank onto her stool, a frown between her brows. "He did this at your urging?"

"Aye." Colin knelt beside her and took her hand. "I know it is sudden—and that you have long thought of yourself as Catholic. But consider, Frances. Marry me and there will be no more attempts made on George's life, for our enemies shall doubtless expect me to kill him for them. They will also believe you subdued to my will. This gives us time to discover the entire plot and act against it. It will also prevent anyone else pressuring you into a marriage for reasons of finance."

Frances looked away. "And finance is not a consideration for you?"

"Nay, I've wealth aplenty."

"You speak most sensibly, Colin." Her voice was small and maybe a little hurt.

He snorted. "Good sense be damned. Marry me because you would enjoy it, if you'll not marry me for my money, or to be safe."

"Perhaps it shall be damned. Regardless, I would have some inkling of what is in your heart." She flung out a hand. "Why do you even concern yourself in our affairs? Came you here with this intention to wed me? Is this proposal some plot?"

"A plot? Never."

"Then what?"

Colin hesitated. He did not want to appear irrationally hasty by speaking of the tidal emotion that moved him. Nor did he wish her to think him one of the courtiers who routinely practiced making love to pretty women for the sheer sport of it. That might happen if he answered too poetically.

And there was also the matter of his occupation to consider. He flattered himself that he knew the female mind, at least a little. She might well think later that his omission of information now was a lie. And if he had lied about that, she might believe he had also lied about his feelings for her.

Yet, she waited for an answer, her gaze so solemn and expectant. He had to say something.

He wished he could delay this reply until it might be answered in full, but time was running out for them. There was no time for a courtship. The marriage needed to be encompassed before the Balfours returned home. He had not lied about that. Their traitor would probably assume that he meant to install himself as a master of the keep, and therefore that George Balfour was not long for the earth. It would stay the murder's hand for a while.

"I'd no plans to wed you when I arrived. Nor did my cousin MacLeod suggest it," he added, forestalling her next question. He said lightly but with truth: "As to what is in my heart . . . From the moment I saw you, thought I to myself, this is the loveliest creature I have ever seen. How could I not wish to have you as wife?"

"*Oui*?" The delicate face finally turned his way. She seemed prepared to ponder deeply anything he might say.

It was an effort, but Colin forced himself to continue to speak frivolously and yet with as much truth as he could safely share: "But what is in my heart at this moment I cannot know, for it has gone missing. It seems that you have stolen it away."

"Colin!" she scolded, but dimpled briefly. "This is no time to play the . . . the valet, the fop and flatterer. Can you not understand that I must know what you truly feel before I can give you an answer?"

"I *feel*, *mignonne*. I feel many things, none simple. Answer me true. Is this marriage not what you want, *petite cherie*?" he asked, turning her palm upward and stroking gently toward her wrist. He spoke more seriously. "Aye, it is sudden. But not so unnatural or dangerous for all that. Men and maids have always wed—most often not knowing what was in the other's heart, or even in their own. And thou art surely bold enough to risk this. I have seen your courage many times."

"And thou art bolder still to ask a lady in a night rail to wed!" she answered, retreating a step into formality. "You might have had the decency to let me don my best gown before speaking of such matters."

The complaint was merely a tactic of delay, but Colin answered it anyway.

"Nay, for then you would also don your father's lordly dignity. Though I admire your public display of spirit and courage, I am more interested in the woman than the role you play with such distinction. This woman in her nightdress intrigues me . . . *seduces* me." He pushed her lace cuff aside and pressed a kiss into her palm. Instantly, he felt the pulse beneath his lips hurl itself against the soft skin. Encouraged, he persuaded softly: "Is it not a tiresome responsibility, caring for all in this keep? A heavy one, which you have wished to escape? Then let me take this burden from you, *ma belle*. As my wife, I can protect you and your kin as well."

Frances sighed, but she did not flinch or turn away.

Consent, he urged her silently. *Consent, so that I need not accomplish this marriage willy-nilly. I had thought to seduce you into union with me, but now would have it be otherwise. Let me do this with honor and not trickery or force.*

"Do you not long for the chance to share intimacies without the danger of scandal?" he murmured, tempting her with the hunger he knew she had for the unknown pleasures of the flesh. "For we shall end as lovers if not as man and wife. You know this is so. We have been nearly discovered once already."

She colored, still looking at him with grave eyes that tried to fathom the meaning beyond the words. "You sweep all before you as if it were nothing: my duty, my plans. How can I marry a stranger?"

"It *is* nothing, just . . . just everything. Ah, Frances!

It is well enough to be a courtesan to duty—pay it court and be polite in observation of protocol—but be not its slave. No happiness will ever be found there. Duty is a cold bedfellow." He spread his hands. "Though many would have you believe it is God's will that we be placed where we are—and perhaps it is—we are also gifted with free will and minds that can see the way to other paths. We can take our destiny into our own hands. We can choose another road from the one where our births and parents placed us. Look into your heart. What does it say to you?"

"But my plans—" she began.

"Plans can be remade, even made better. Come, Frances, be not some milk and water maid. Have courage one more time. Say you will enterprise this adventure. We shall make a success of this marriage, I swear. Together we can do anything we can imagine. Come, be my consort."

"A consort . . ." Suddenly she smiled. "Colin! I have doubtless been driven mad, but—"

"But?" He shook her gently. "Speak! If there is some bar, tell me so that I might put it aside. Tell me of this *but*."

She laughed once, a sound closer to hysteria than amusement. "But: I shall wed thee—and make thy life a misery if you be not kind and fair and a gentleman."

"A gentleman, I shall be," he promised fervently. "But in a moment."

Colin pulled her close, allowing himself a single, relieved kiss, which held much passion but not blind lust. Then, his smaller prayer answered, he put her from him and rose to his feet. He'd ask no more of her or fortune that evening.

"I must go now," he said.

"But Colin . . ." Frances also stood, her expression confused. Her small hands fluttered toward him, clasping his sleeve. She protested: "You cannot leave. We . . . we have discussed nothing of Lucien's news, or what we are to do to discover the traitor."

"I believe I know who our traitor inside the castle is." Colin added gently: "And I think you suspect her as well."

"But Colin!" Sadness filled her voice, replacing the brief music of happiness. She pleaded, "We cannot punish her on a suspicion. Even to accuse her would be a terrible disgrace. It might even kill her. And I do not know if I could punish her anyway. She is my cousin. She was also the wife of my brother. She came to me for protection when he died, and I promised to stand a sister to her. How can I forget this?"

"You won't have to punish her, *cherie*. That task is mine now. I know you would make the compassionate decision for as long as you could. I, too, prefer forgiveness and understanding whenever it is possible. But mark me well, *mignonne*. I give no parole to traitors, for with them the sin never ends. I shall not act against anyone without some proof, but if she again attempts to hurt you, or George, then she shall die, woman or no." He added gently: "Get thee to rest now. I'd as soon not have my bride looking as pale as a ghost when she stands at the altar."

He raised her hand to his lips and kissed it fleetingly. He added with feeling: "Dream of me, *cherie*."

Arthur O'Bower has broken his band
And he comes roaring up the land;
The King of Scots with all his power
Cannot stop Arthur of the Bower.

—Scottish nursery rhyme

Chapter Sixteen

There was little time to prepare for the wedding ceremony, as Colin did not announce their intention until after everyone had broken their fasts, and law dictated that nuptials and the bridal feast had to be performed before the sun had set on the shortening autumnal day. This suited Colin fine, as it meant everyone was kept busy with preparations and would have no time to warn the outside world of what was afoot. After the event was accomplished, he would be pleased to have events known to all who passed for society in those northern parts. But he wanted no last-moment interruption from thwarted suitors to mar the occasion, or to interfere with the Archimedes lever he meant to employ to save George and Frances Balfour.

A visibly stunned Cook, after slave-driving the sculleries in a manner worthy of any of history's great tyrants, declared herself prepared for a wedding feast just an hour before sundown. As the pale bride also agreed that she was ready, the ceremony went forth at once.

Though it caused some murmurs, they were not using the small Balfour chapel for the ceremony. The tiny room that had served her Catholic masters was decorated with a stone cross and a likeness of the Virgin Mary, which would offend their Reformist guests. Also, the small, cold room would not have comfortably held all of the Balfours and their somber visitors.

The children, free from any understanding of the whys of what was about to take place, were not so solemn as their harried elders. They were arrayed with bride laces and had sprigs of rosemary tied about their sleeves. They looked quite gay and excited to be participating in their first wedding.

Colin knew not everyone was so pleased. A swift look into the far corner of the room located a stony-faced Anne Balfour. She looked pale and frozen with disdain, her face as unforgiving as an executioner's, her eyes as cold and hard as a headsman's axe. It was probably a good thing that Angus MacBride was unlikely to ask the congregation for objections to the marriage, because Colin wouldn't put it past Anne to find one.

Colin thought about approaching Anne with a word of warning about interference, but a loud atonal wheeze from the grand staircase interrupted before he could decide what to say to this woman he suspected of betraying her kin.

The processional began. Frances appeared on the steps, her hair loose as a maiden's should be, and dressed in scarlet finery. She was led into the great hall between George and Morag, looking a bit pale and dazed, the silver and gold of her traditional bridal ornament pulling down the shoulder of her low-necked gown where it was fastened to the soft fabric. Colin had to wonder at the size and style of the brooch she wore. It had to be some ghastly Balfour heirloom, because it was far from the delicate, modern silver seal that symbolized a bride's chastity. He wondered idly if Michael Balfour had had the hypocrisy to force it on his wife before their own wedding.

Though it was an uncharitable thought on their wedding day, Colin felt rather glad that his father-in-law was no longer among the living. His own gift to the bride, a plain ring he wore for luck on the small finger of his left hand, was one that had belonged to his maternal grandmother. It was inscribed in Gaelic with the loving phrase *For the pulse of my heart.* It was much smaller and better suited to the delicate Frances, though he planned on giving her another ring—perhaps set with pearls—once they returned to Pemberton Fells. It would be his pleasure to give her many things. If she wished it, he would even clear away a part of the woods to make a meadow where she and George could play golf.

Colin, taking his place at the altar, was amused to see that Harry the hound was also in attendance, tied to the long table with a short stout rope, but allowed to share in the festivities by wearing a sprig of rosemary in his borrowed ruffed collar, Colin's second-best, lent to George for the occasion. The neck was stretched obscenely and the pleats would never be the same again, but Colin counted the loss worthwhile. Still enjoying the effects of his first bath, Harry very nearly looked like the lion he was named after. He did not behave as a lion, though. The pipes had set him to sympathetic howling, which caused those standing nearby to draw back with their ears covered. Fortunately, no one muttered anything about ill omens at the hound's howling as the bride went to the altar.

A richly if darkly clad Lucien went toward the makeshift altar before Frances, carrying a large bride cup overhead, which was filled with a goodly bundle of rosemary, hung with silken ribbons and scraps of lace dyed all colors, so the absence of flowers was not so keenly felt. A few late marigolds were also mixed in with the herbs. Colin hoped he would not be called on to eat them. He had never subscribed to the belief that eating the yellow flowers would provoke lust. In any event, the provocation of such desire was unnecessary. Frances was lure enough.

A completely dressed Tearlach came next, playing the pipes as softly as he was able, which was still entirely too loud in the enclosed space, but Colin did not complain. It was tradition and supposed to bring luck—something they all needed.

Then came the unmarried Balfour women, some bearing small bride cakes filled with seeds and grains, and others festive garlands of feathery seagrass also dyed pretty autumnal hues. It was a strange but still grand wedding party, and Colin felt something akin to genuine pleasure stir in his breast. Was it not fitting that their wedding be unconventional?

Colin was likewise finely appareled, though not in red like his bride. He knew that scarlet was a favored color by the Gaels at weddings, as it represented fertility, but he preferred the more dignified appearance of somber brown. It was also more in keeping with the preferences of their guests, who served as his groomsmen. Though not entirely wanted on this occasion, he also had a bridal escort, made up of men in hodden gray and also reluctantly wearing laces on their sleeves.

Though they sported this bit of frivolous color on their clothes, their miens were uniformly solemn, as weddings were not considered riotous occasions.

Colin, not previously a sentimental man, found himself wishing MacJannet and the smiling faces of Pemberton's servitors were with him to help celebrate. He keenly missed the joyous celebration that would have been theirs at Pemberton Fells, and vowed to plan a feast for the missing guests as soon as he and Frances returned to his home.

There was no delay of ceremony after the short procession. Angus MacBride began as soon as the last shrieking notes of Tearlach's pipes and Harry's baying died away. He wasn't a man filled with fatherly tenderness for humanity, and looked out over the sea of faces he suspected were rife with sin, then began austerely: "Greetings, all my brothers and sisters. We are gathered here to join this man and this maiden in holy wedlock, and to consider the great happiness that may flow from a full and perfect union of this kirk and kingdom, by joining of all in one and the same covenant with God."

With these words, embers of fanaticism flared and the tones of evangelical hellfire began licking at them all as he spoke.

Frances turned her head and looked at Colin, a question in her eyes. Colin wanted to groan at what was obviously to be a ceremonial mix of religion and politics, but confined himself to a small encouraging smile.

Angus went on after drawing another breath. "We are now thoroughly resolved in the truth by the word and spirit of God. And therefore we believe with our hearts, confess with our mouths, subscribe with our willing hands, and constantly affirm, before God and the entire world, that this only is the true Christian faith and religion, pleasing God, and bringing salvation to man, which now is, by the mercy of God, revealed to the world by the preaching of the blessed evangel; and is received, believed, and defended by many and sundry notable kirks and realms, but chiefly by the kirks of reborn Scotland. Let us pray."

Colin nudged a shocked and outraged Frances, winked once, and then bowed his head for a long-winded prayer. He supposed he should be happy the bishop hadn't sent John Knox.

". . . and shall defend the same, according to our vocation and power, all the days of our lives; under the pains contained in the law, and danger both of body and soul in the day of God's fearful judgment."

Colin saw a flush of anger stain his bride's cheekbones and wondered if much of the congregation looked the same. He didn't think the bishop would understand if his soldiers ended up dead, poisoned by angry Balfour women. He wondered also if evangelical MacBride noticed the hostility, and thought not. The man's eyes and voice were raised in prayer directed at the ceiling in the back of the great hall as if the Lord himself were hovering there; he noticed nothing else.

"I swear we shall be married again by a priest if you desire it," he whispered to Frances, setting lips against her ear.

"*Merci*, but I feel that I shall be quite married enough," she muttered back, her lips barely moving. "Can he not make haste? The sun is nearly set."

That was an exaggeration, but it was getting darker as clouds gathered and blotted out the waning light.

"... so that we are not moved with any worldly respect, but are persuaded only in our conscience, through the knowledge and love of God's true religion imprinted in our hearts by the Holy Spirit, as we shall answer to him in the day when the secrets of all hearts shall be disclosed. As we desire our God to be a strong and merciful defender to us in the day of our death, and coming of our Lord Jesus Christ; to whom, with the Father, and the Holy Spirit, be all honor and glory eternally, so shall we be strong and honorable. *Amen.*"

The echoed amen was heartfelt. Apparently appeased by their sincerity, MacBride at last began the ceremony of marriage. Colin mentally urged him to hasten. A feeling of nervousness had begun tickling the back of his brain. Perhaps it was the coming darkness and the castle's many ghosts that unnerved him, but he wanted to reach the moment when he pushed aside the bell of his bride's long sleeve and slipped his ring upon her hand. He'd have no peace until the deed was done.

Cook had arranged a viand royal in a very short space of time. The bridal supper had three courses, each with its own soup. The cranky goose had made the ultimate sacrifice for the occasion and appeared arrayed in a magnificent sauce, which was spiced with Tearlach's remaining surrendered ginger and sweetened with honey. There were oysters en gravey and chawettys filled with mutton, and a sotelty of the family coat of arms made out of dough. And to smooth the way for this rich feast, there was mulled wine.

Harry had been freed after the ceremony and he spent his time capering about with a sort of magnificent gallop that a pony might envy. Colin had been prepared to order George to take his pet lion away, but the sagacious hound had not committed the sin of begging at the table. Colin suspected this was because George was supplying the beast with adequate treats beneath the board, but Colin did not comment on the abuse of Cook's fine cuisine. It pleased him to see boy and dog so happy.

The bride was very quiet, and not in appetite, but Colin could hardly blame her; he felt no inclination to gluttony either. His senses, his intuition, were still actively warning him that something was amiss. It would not surprise him to learn that Frances felt the same way.

Or—he looked over at her—could it be that she was feeling shy?

Colin shook his head, wondering at his stupidity. Of course she was nervous! This was her wedding night. The fact that they had nearly made love already did not mean she didn't face this moment with trepidation. MacBride's talk of spiritual purity had probably driven all thoughts of desire from her head and had her nearer to panic than anticipation. He wondered if he should say something to her. But nothing reassuring came to him.

Very soon, it was time to retire. The Balfour women made a ring about Frances and led her away. It did not please him to see Anne Balfour among the bridal party. He hoped she would say nothing untoward.

His own somber groomsmen likewise rose from the table, intent on seeing him to his chambers and into his nightclothes, and who knew what thereafter. Among his party were the castle ghosts. They showed no understanding of what had just passed, no joy or anger.

They were probably simply attracted by the activity, or so Colin assured himself.

Glancing back at a worried-looking George, who sat alone stroking Harry and staring after his cousin, Colin decided he would permit his escort as far as his door, but no closer to the bride. Whatever the local tradition might be, he was not subjecting her to the barbaric custom of having the bride's deflowering witnessed. This wasn't a royal wedding. There was absolutely no need for it. If some proof was absolutely necessary, they could hand the sheets out in the morning.

There was another excellent reason to keep them away from the bridal bed. Their gloomy presence, condemning anything that looked even mildly pleasurable, could make a man impotent. It could even so damage a delicate girl's sensibilities that she might never enjoy the act of consummation. He would not let these creatures ruin this marital happiness for them!

Belatedly, it occurred to him that this would have been just the thing to say to put Frances's mind at ease. He would reassure her as soon as they were reunited.

I saw the new moon late yestreen,
Wi the auld moon in her arm;
And if we gang to sea, master,
I fear we'll come to harm.

—*"The Ballad of Sir Patrick Spens"*

Chapter Seventeen

The bride looked both nervous and wrathful, sitting in the middle of the nuptial bed. Colin could understand that. Thwarted desire made him wrathful, too. However, he suspected there was more to her ire than frustration at delayed gratification, and was practically certain Anne Balfour was to blame for the new chill in the bedroom air.

"You look quite cross, my love." His tone was light in spite of his anger. The Bible might be correct that a soft word could turn away wrath.

Frances said pettishly: "Those women seemed unable to conceive of me undressing myself. Do I not manage this task every evening?"

"The men had a similar conceptual problem," Colin answered soothingly, pouring out some of the wine he had ordered brought to their chamber and bringing her a glass. "But they are gone now."

All except the one ghost who hovered near the fire. Colin might have thought her to be Frances's mother, but the mode of her dress was wrong. He did his best to ignore her silent witness.

Frances took the wine but still did not meet Colin's eyes. She bowed her head slightly and the fall of her hair served as a dark curtain that draped the side of her face and hid her further from view.

"Why don't you have a little wine and then tell me what Anne Balfour said to upset you," he suggested gently.

Frances's startled gaze fluttered up briefly.

"You'd best tell me about it," he urged. "Distrust and anger grow like some horrible fungus in the dark shadows of doubt. Obviously Anne has been busy planting poisoned words. Best we clear them out before you have ugly mushrooms pouring from your ears."

Frances didn't smile at this silly sally, proving that she was actually very upset.

"Speak, my dear, or forever hold your peace. *Ce soir ou jamais*, as they say, it is tonight or never. Once this marriage is consummated, there will be no going back."

In point of fact, they were already past the point of undoing events. And even if they had not been, Colin would never permit her to throw their union away because of anger at a small misunderstanding. Still, he knew better than most how to be politic in his replies.

"Very well then! Have your truth—and so shall I. You have deceived me from the first! You almost took me as a lover—and all the while you lied about what you are! I thought this was something wonderful between us, and now you have poisoned the pleasure. I believe all men are deceivers!"

He found interesting that she objected to deceit in a lover and not in a husband. He was also very interested in where and when Anne Balfour had come by her news.

"To begin with," Colin answered calmly, "I did not lie. I said I wanted you to wife and I still do. *Cherie*, please consider the source of these rumors before you allow them to spoil your pleasure in your wedding day. Your cousin has not distinguished herself with loyalty and charity of mind or action. She is, in fact, a traitor. She knows me for an enemy of her schemes and will of course try to blacken my name to you. Doubtless she would have blamed me for your father's death and King James's, as well, had she thought you would believe it."

Frances's voice moderated, but her face remained stormy, proving that pain was often recalled by the sufferer long after an injury was inflicted. "But her traitorousness does not alter the facts that *do* exist, does it? You are not who you pretended to be." The lower lip trembled. "How can I know now if anything you say is true? I . . . I am so . . . how do you say *decevoir*?"

"Disappointed." He sighed. "I am sure you are."

"*Oui*! I had hoped that in spite of the mystery around you, I would be moving into a more honest life. One more open and free, where I did not have secret enemies. Now I discover that I have more than ever before!"

Frances tilted back her goblet and drained it. The sudden rush of spirits brought a hectic flush to her cheeks.

Colin seated himself on the edge of the bed and possessed himself of her empty hand, which he clutched tightly against himself. "Frances, look at me. I am speaking the absolute truth now. This I swear, before God and on the life of my sovereign. I am Sir Colin Mortlock, owner of Pemberton Fells. I came to Noltland to be your Master of the Gowff at my cousin MacLeod's request—just as I told you."

"But . . . but you are not *just* Sir Colin Mortlock, are you? You work for the English king against the Scots."

"I have never worked against the Scots, just against their most recent king, who was an idiot—and I am *always* Sir Colin Mortlock."

She snorted, but her hand relaxed. He preferred her scorn to the threat of tears, though he would rather have had smiles from his lady on this, their wedding night.

"That may be truth, but it is not all the truth."

"You are correct. Sometimes, when the king has need of me, I am more besides." Colin looked into those darkly troubled eyes and tried to explain what he did. "Put aside your hurt, if you can, and consider the world of the monarch. As powerful as they are, there are places where sovereigns may not go. There are things a wise ruler needs to see and know if he is to guide his country, but may not be told by his advisers—perhaps because they are pursuing their own political ends, perhaps because they are blind to everything except their own ambitions or obsessions. It is unfortunate, but still true, that these obsessed men are often the sorts who are drawn to power. Imagine how frustrating this would be for you if you were a king who actually wanted to make informed decisions."

Frances nodded once. Colin thought it was an agreement simply to consider his words, not to assent to his points.

"Sometimes that desired information is trivial, but other times it is vital. On the occasions when the information is most crucial, it nearly always happens that discretion is required while acquiring it. In these cases, I—and my father, and his father before him—have served in times of crisis as the eyes and ears of the king. This was our duty—just as your father felt it was your family's duty to lay down their lives for your king at Flodden. My presence here is dishonesty in a sense, because I have lied by omission in not announcing my sometimes occupation, but it is not deceit. It is simple survival. Everything I have done here has been for your well-being and our future happiness. It has nothing to do with my king or politics, English or Scottish. I see danger here and have moved to intercept it before it can do you or George harm."

There was a long silence as she mulled this over. The concerned ghost drew nearer. Colin made an effort to ignore her, since she didn't seem to mean any harm.

"You see it as the same thing—what you do and what my father did?" The question was, to Colin's relief, thoughtful rather than sarcastic. The tide was turning in his favor. He blessed the streak of curiosity that ran through her pragmatic mind.

"Aye, I do," he answered truthfully. "It is required that we each serve our monarchs according to our gifts. This ability to live two lives simultaneously is a peculiar talent that seems to belong to the Mortlocks.

It is decried by some men, but the power of dissembling is essential to the art of the intelligencer. Few men of morals and loyalty have the gift, for if they know truth they feel they must always speak it. And others are intent on silencing them so the truth shall not be known. These *honest* men do not survive long in the world of kings."

"But Colin!" She waved her free hand. "To live your life for politics. It is so petty."

He laughed shortly. "Petty and almost always dangerous to some degree. But I tell you that a well-thought-out stratagem wins more battles than generals and their armies. Frances, you have no concept! Petty politics sway behavior in ways that you have not ever considered." Colin set his wife's empty goblet aside and took both her hands. He drew a breath and then spoke more openly than he ever had in his life, even to MacJannet. His first truth surprised him when he heard himself say: "What a lot of virtues—like discretion—I have set aside since coming here."

Frances sniffed, apparently still unimpressed and unforgiving. "Politics. What is there to consider? It is just the maneuvering of greedy men who have no other sensible occupation."

"Perhaps, but I am quite serious about this point. Think about it, Frances. Use your wits. I know it is not your usual realm of thought, but you have seen firsthand the effects of royal maneuvering and can understand this. Consider that politics, at the very least, influences fashion—from deciding what clothes we wear to what musicians and artists will be favored in society. It even decides what sports we shall play. Look at how the bishop's men dress. Look at how your gowns are different from what ladies here wear. Think why it is that you may not go veiled into a kirk. It isn't God's revealed will that causes this. It is the whims of kings and priests that have caused this."

Surprised at his words, Frances looked down at her silken night rail, and acknowledged that this was true. No other woman in the keep would wear silk, because of religious prohibition.

"But politics does much more than this when it becomes a quest for power and influence over men's minds." Colin shook his head, searching for a way to explain how large this princely power was and how it was growing into something nearly impossible to control. "In recent years it has left the throne and climbed into the pulpits. There it has put words into the mouths of priests, and through them, political beliefs have been implanted into the hearts of otherwise godly men. It makes some into zealous reformers, and others doubt their own beliefs and become crippled by conflicting thoughts. It can be a tool for change, a weapon of destruction, even a vile usurper of princely power if perverted . . . what it *cannot* be is ignored. Not if you are a king. Not if you are a loyal subject who serves his monarch faithfully. As goes the king, so goes the country. Politics and the politicians, ugly as they often are, are about our survival."

She spoke hesitatingly. "And you are paid to do this?"

"Aye—handsomely," he answered, refusing to feel shame. He had never felt that idleness made possible by wealth made one man better than another who toiled for his bread. "But the best reward this occupation can bring is safety."

Frances's eyes widened.

"Safety?"

"Knowledge is power. Power, naked or disguised, is what keeps you safe. And if you have not enough of this strength on your own, then knowledge lets you borrow from others in times of need. But you already know this at some level. Do not forget, Frances, that you are also a dissembler."

Frances's eyes widened.

"*Qu'est-ce que*?"

Colin nodded. "Has your recent life at the castle not been all a tapestry of lies? Lying to neighbors, lying to my cousin, even lying to your own people about what we have arranged for them, weaving together an illusion—and all so that George and your family may be kept safe from the wolves at your door?"

"But that isn't the same," she protested halfheartedly.

"Of course it is. You practiced a social deceit to save your family when nothing else could. Your trickery and ingenuity is what has kept your kin safe all these months since your father died. And though I could, I would never reproach you for lying, for luring MacJannet and me here when the situation was so precarious. I honor you for your ingenuity because I understand what made you do the things you do." He added: "And I never believed in the *la vie galante* anyway. It is only a troubadour's myth. We are all sometimes moved to selfish action by necessity."

He smiled suddenly. "Just think what our children will be like! With us to guide them in the development of their wits, they shall be masters of two lands."

Frances did not smile back, though her eyes had opened wide at the mention of children. Perhaps she had been so distracted by other events that this consequence of marriage had not occurred to her before. Colin wondered if it was fortuitous that he had thought to bring up the subject in an already difficult conversation.

"So you believe that there can truly be honor without complete honesty? Deceit can be practiced without disloyalty?"

Colin nodded. "Aye, I do. As long as man is true to himself and his own morals."

"And therefore there can be some form of sensitivity to others without genuine sentiment? Can there be that, as well?" She sounded as though she were trying not to give in to some fierce inner struggle.

Colin drew in a breath and asked straightly: "Are we speaking now of our marriage? For that is a matter quite separate from politics."

"Is it?" Frances looked away. The turned cheek offended him. "Colin, is there anything else I should know about you before we . . . we consummate this bargain?"

Exasperated, and still unwilling to discuss his plans for their future, which involved removing her from Scotland, he finally ceased trying to reason with his untrusting bride. "Aye, there is." Colin took her stubborn chin in hand and turned her face to his. Whatever she saw in his countenance caused her eyes to widen. "This is a marriage, not a bargain. And I am a jealous husband. And I will guard what is mine."

He leaned forward and pressed his mouth against hers. They sank into the bedclothes. After a moment, the initial rigidity left her body and she relaxed against his harder, heavier frame. Colin lifted his head.

"If there must be struggles this night, let it be with

me and not your thoughts. There will be no more talk of duty or bargains," he said, voice low, watching as the firelight played over Frances's face. Then, more softly: "*Cherie*, your emotions see lies and deceptions where there are none. Look at me. Know the truth."

"I feel I must—*reveiller*," she whispered, a hand coming up to curl into his hair. The touch was tentative but behind it he could feel all her longing for closeness begging to be let out. "It seems that this is all a strange dream from which I cannot awake."

"You shall awaken to a new life, my sweet dreamer—and in it shall be sweetness and beauty. I swear this." He would have promised her anything on this, their wedding night, but awakening passion added to his compulsion to reassure her that she would know happiness with him.

And someday, there will be love, too, he promised silently.

"Then I shall try once more to believe," she said softly. Finally, she smiled. It was only then that Colin realized his heart was pounding, his body pulsating with a mixture of desires. His blood felt heavy and heated where it throbbed in his loins, and he realized he was about to have the answer to the question that had intrigued them from their first meeting: what would she be like?

He lowered his head and her lips parted for him, inviting him to taste. He smoothed her night rail aside and slid into the cradle of her legs, then accepted the sweet, unspoken invitation.

He touched her breasts through the sheer cloth and felt her nipples harden. They deserved kisses, too, and he eased down her body, sampling soft skin on the way. The damp of new desire dewed her skin.

Frances shivered and her legs tightened their hold. Colin was delighted. He had hoped she would be able to experience and enjoy passion. Not all women did, and union between man and woman was nothing unless both went into the fire and burned there.

Colin sat up and cast his nightshirt away. It was flattering to his esteem that her eyes went wide when she beheld him naked.

"*Etonnant*," she breathed.

"Nay, 'tis you who are amazing," Colin answered truthfully, returning to her outstretched arms.

He ran a hand along her thigh and then ghosted toward the heat of her, the last secret. A gentle touch told him she was ready. Truly, she was amazing.

"Look at me, love," he murmured. "I want to see your eyes."

He waited, poised above her, to see if there was any uncertainty, any fear. But her beautiful eyes were clear and unfrightened. Her breath came in tatters, made ragged by desire. Colin found himself shaking. It was time.

He made his possession slow, aware that, though his slide into her heat was exquisite for him, there could be pain for her. But she did not flinch or cry out. Once inside, he again waited to see if there was any shying away. But nothing marred her face.

"Colin, *mon cher*," she breathed, her hands reaching for his chest.

He moved then, and she with him. They were a bit wild in their coupling. He was made especially frantic with long-suppressed need and new emotion, and Colin suspected it was the same with his bride. It made him want to push at the boundaries of desire to see if there were actually any limits—could he actually be completely lost in the heat?—but he told himself that such desire must wait. It had to be ignored until he felt her take flight beneath him and saw her lovely eyes close at last, as ecstasy consumed her.

Frances's back arched, her fingers digging into his skin. Satisfied, Colin at last followed her into passion's sweet and all-consuming fire, and there he was reborn into his new life as a husband.

Frances dropped her face onto her knees and giggled. Bright moonlight had entered the chamber, almost overwhelming the light from the hearth.

"You laugh? At such a moment? Heartless wench! Consider my feelings."

"*Je regrette*. It is just that I have had a thing most strange revealed to me," she said, peeping at him.

"I reveal myself and it makes you laugh?" His offended tone brought another giggle.

"It is just that *it* is different."

"*It*?"

She waved a hand at his nether regions.

Truly startled, he demanded: "Different how?"

"It is different now because it is *mine*. I have never had a . . . a . . ."

"What do you mean, it's yours?" His astonishment caused her to release another peal of laughter, a sound sufficiently contagious that Colin found himself smiling. In retaliation, he grabbed her ankle and spilled her onto her back. "By your logic, then, this is mine," he said, sliding a hand up her exposed leg.

"*Oui*! But of course."

"And you are not sorry that we enjoy this from the marriage bed? I was concerned that forbidden fruit would be more enjoyable if eaten in secrecy, for it somehow seems to increase the sin and therefore the pleasure," he teased.

"*Non*! I am not so—*impudicite*?"

"Immodest? No, you are not immodest. But I have hopes of turning you into a bit of a voluptuary."

"It is possible. I am, after all, half French. We enjoy nice things."

"A fact for which I am most thankful. I don't think I could marry a woman who would not enthusiastically wear silk or perfume, or who could not enjoy a certain social exuberance. In England we are most fond of music and dancing."

"Perfume?" Frances repeated. Then, with measurable excitement: "From Santa Maria Novella, perhaps?"

Colin began to laugh, enjoying the happiness he heard in his wife's voice. He had wondered for a while if Anne and Angus MacBride had killed that joy forever.

"Aye. We'll procure some heavenly elixir from the holy brothers for your sybarite christening."

"I've never visited Sybaris, but I should like to," Frances said seriously, making Colin laugh even harder.

"Nor have I, my sweet. Perhaps we'll journey there together."

"*Ma mere* would not approve if I became *chronique scandaleuse*," she said, with sudden concern.

"Mothers rarely do approve of anything that is fun," Colin agreed, and then kissed her. He did not want her thoughts returning to the complexities and obliquities of her relationships with either her parents or him. "And in any event, I hardly think it likely. Intelligent people can almost always see the lines they should not cross, and I believe you have the will to do anything you desire."

"*Oui?*"

"*Oui.*"

Those who have arrived at any very eminent degree of excellence in the practice of an art or profession have commonly been actuated by a species of enthusiasm in their pursuit of it. They have kept one object in view amidst all the vicissitudes of time and torture.

—John Knox

Chapter Eighteen

The following day saw MacJannet's return to a still slightly unsettled Noltland. To Tearlach's credit, though he was irritated by Sine's sharp instructions to make haste with the yett and wishing to pay her back somehow for this officiousness, he did not keep the heavily cloaked traveler lingering at the gate while demanding that he identify himself or answer silly questions about his business at the castle.

Thomas MacJannet was travel-stained and a bit white about the mouth, but he smiled anyway, because he brought the happy news that the Balfour men would be returned to their home in a matter of mere days, bringing supplies and arms with them. This made him the most beautiful and welcome being Noltland had seen in many a year, and he was given a hero's reception by the grateful women.

Some of those who heard the joyous tidings that their loved ones yet lived wept and then hurried to find the others and share the news. Still others fluttered about MacJannet, patting him and offering refreshment until Colin appeared and thrust them gently aside.

"He'll tell us all more later. Come, my friend," Colin said, speaking both to MacJannet and to the bishop's men lingering uneasily nearby. "You must give me a round account of your adventures while you break your fast. You will also wish to pay your respects to my wife and young George before you rest."

"Your wife? Well! It's sorry I am to have missed the nuptials. I had hoped to return in time to see them." MacJannet was sincere.

"I wish that you might have been here." Colin was also sincere.

He and MacJannet shared a long look.

"By all means, I should indeed like to greet your lady wife. She is within?"

"Aye, she and George both are."

The two men started for the keep, talking of desultory matters until they were within the castle's walls and had a measure of privacy.

"Let us seek out my wife and do the obligatory offerings that duty claims. We mustn't violate the tenets of order unless absolutely necessary," Colin murmured. "I've already set them on their ear with this hasty marriage and having the bishop's men in their midst."

As though hearing his summons, Frances appeared at the top of the stairs and hurried down to them. To Colin's eye she looked a bit flushed and disheveled—which was how she should be after a night given to passion.

Greetings were exchanged, with MacJannet kneeling slowly to his new mistress and pledging an oddly formal oath of loyalty.

"You are hurt, MacJannet?" she asked, her concern clear as she urged him to rise.

"Nay, lady. I am just a bit stiff from sleeping upon the ground, which hasn't softened any since I last rested there. The flexibility of youth left me long ago, but the stones are as strong as ever."

"Come. I shall brew you a tisane. Or Sine shall. Mine are not so useful and taste hideous," Frances admitted confidentially. "But Sine's are very good."

"Thank you, lady, but I am perfectly well," MacJannet reassured her again, yet somehow failed to meet her eyes as he repeated his words.

"So tell me now all the news that you have held back from the others," Colin commanded, urging them toward one of the small antechambers. "I'd like it before Lucien arrives back from hunting—if that is what he is truly doing."

MacJannet glanced once at Frances and then back at Colin, clearly troubled by the intelligence he bore, and obviously reluctant to share his less happy news with Frances present.

"It is all right. Speak your mind. She has a surprising capacity for dispassionate reasoning," Colin promised. "She is strong enough to bear the truth. Especially when there is no other choice."

Frances flashed him an appreciative smile, clearly grateful for this vote of trust. There was still some tension between them from the previous night, which their lovemaking had failed to ease. Colin knew it might be a long while before she trusted him completely. He was content to wait.

She said, "I promise that sentiment shall not move me to hysteria, MacJannet. I am always most calm. And if it concerns my family, then of course I must know of it."

"As you like, lady. There is a new complication that must be assessed," MacJannet answered at last, his tone even. He turned to Colin. "It seems that the reports of Balfour obliteration were premature. Gilbert Balfour yet lives."

"My uncle is yet alive?" Frances asked.

"Aye, and the magnitude of his battlefield renown is growing."

"But this is a thing most wondrous! Gilbert shall know how to defend the keep. He is a most fearsome soldier." She turned to Colin, smiling without strain for the first time in days. "We need fear no longer. Why did you not tell everyone of this news at once?"

"The second rule of the intelligencer, my sweet, is that information loses its value when traded openly," Colin answered absently.

His reply caused MacJannet to grunt an agreement. "Aye. And though wondrous it is that he is not in his grave, we must yet ask ourselves some questions. The first being: what of young George?"

Frances blinked, as though encountering a gust of cold wind. "Oh. I suppose he cannot be the heir if Gilbert lives." She thought for a moment, dismay and gratitude at war on her face. Then she said hopefully: "But George does not like being the laird. I do not think he shall mind having my uncle here instead."

"That isn't the only difficulty," Colin said. "Consider your neighbors. What shall their reaction be when one of the bishop's men moves into their vicinity? You've avoided open political conflict until now, but it will all change if Gilbert takes up residence."

"Is he for the bishop?" Frances asked. "But how can that be? Is he not a brother to my father? Were they not allied?"

"Loyalty can be twisted by sentiment and made unreliable." Colin spread his hands. "Usually such a change of allegiance is a slow and imperceptible process. But at times it can be precipitated by one great event, or a strong personality. It is as I explained last night. A leader with enough will or charm can cause the grossest unreason in his followers. Whatever he was in the past to your father, Gilbert is the bishop's man now. And as such, your neighbors shall hardly embrace him. They are likely disturbed enough with the small party of bishop's men already here . . . I wonder if Lucien heard rumor of this?" Colin murmured, as his brow furrowed.

Frances shook her head, as though trying to clear it of the ringing the verbal buffet had caused. "Must everything be so difficult?" she whispered, scowling a bit as she sank into a chair and propped an elbow on the small table.

"There is more," MacJannet added in a sepulchral tone. "There are everywhere in higher circles whispers about Gilbert Balfour, which go unanswered except by more rumor. It is said that though he still lives he is very ill, both wounded and attacked by fever. This concern over where he resides may be a moot point if he dies. There is also talk of him forging an alliance with the English. You know what happens when rumors become large enough."

Frances looked quickly at Colin, plainly disturbed by the gossip.

He shrugged. "Then we are certainly best advised to mention this to no one until we have some facts. We don't want the tribes uniting in anticipation of deflecting the renowned warrior, Gilbert Balfour, if no army of liberation is to actually appear." Colin leaned back in his chair. "And what say the Balfour men you found? Their freedom was procured?"

"Aye, not easily or inexpensively, but their freedom they have. Unfortunately, they know nothing certain of Gilbert—or knew nothing when I last spoke to them. But the story isn't something that shall remain a secret for long, now that the army is disbanding and men are returning home. And if the bishop did not know of Gilbert's survival before, he shall shortly."

"Aye, I fear you are right." Colin sighed and turned to look at Frances. He brushed back a stray lock of her mussed hair and attempted a smile before turning again to MacJannet. "MacJannet, I hate to set you to another journey when you have only just returned, but I am afraid you must be off again tomorrow."

"The boy goes with me, too?" the other asked quietly.

"Aye, for I have still not discovered for certain who has been orchestrating events here at the castle."

"You are sending George away?" Frances asked, looking from Colin to MacJannet. "But he shall not want to go. He is much attached to me and this is his home now."

"I do not propose separating you, *cherie*. You shall go, too."

"*Qu'est-ce que?*"

"Aye, you must."

"But no! I cannot." Frances jumped to her feet. Her voice was slightly desperate. "We cannot go and leave my family here when there is danger. You are my husband—you must stay."

"*We* aren't leaving," Colin answered evenly. "You and George are. I shall stay until the men arrive and we have some definite word of Gilbert Balfour."

"You think to put me from you?" Frances demanded, dismay being replaced with wrath. "You propose that I should run away while you face danger in my stead? No! No and no and no! I shall not have it."

"I appreciate your feeling, my dear, but you are allowing emotion to entwist your reason. This is not a battle you can fight, and having you and George here as potential hostages hampers my own efforts. The traitor must be found before Gilbert returns, if he actually lives long enough to come to Noltland."

"You think I have no honor," she accused. "You are like all men who think that women cannot have courage or intelligence in troubled times."

"Hogwash!" Colin answered forcefully, as MacJannet wisely retreated from the room, closing the door softly behind him. More than ever he wished there had been time for Frances's affections to animate fully before their marriage, so there was a reciprocal bond of love between them. "I'll grant that there has been little inducement for either courage or intelligence to flourish in your sex—since both are usually suppressed from the cradle. But we both know you have honor and courage aplenty, so do stop speaking as an hysteric when I know you do not suffer from such an inveterately low intellect."

Frances stared hard at Colin. "I do not know this word *inveteratelу*. But I do know that you look very cross when you say it, so perhaps you should not use it."

"I look cross because I am cross," he answered. But already the frown was lifting from his brow. It was impossible to remain angry when staring into her flushed face. The high color all too vividly recalled him to the previous night's passions. He added feelingly: "This entire situation is bloody annoying. Here we are, married one day and already fighting."

"It *is* bloody annoying," she agreed, pleased with the expression. "But we must accommodate facts. In any event, I do not think MacJannet can leave immediately, whatever your wishes."

"No?" Colin thought about this for a moment and then asked: "Why?"

"He tried to conceal it from me, but I believe he has been wounded. Perhaps merely bruised and strained, but he did not move so stiffly before he left, nor did he favor his left leg. You cannot send George and me into danger if he is not fit. And you do not trust the bishop's men entirely, do you?"

"Well, bloody hell," Colin muttered again. "Clearly I am not at my best today. And it is you who has distracted me with your disarrayed hair. Did you not comb it after leaving our bed?"

Frances smiled triumphantly, the last of her outrage leaving her as she decided that she had indeed made her point. Reaching up a small hand, she carelessly flipped a straying tress over her shoulder.

"I'd best go speak with him and discover whom he has been brawling with," Colin muttered. "It isn't like MacJannet to engage in physical warfare."

"*Oui*. And I shall send Sine with a tisane and some food. Both shall aid him in recovery, so he may assist you in discovering the villain who has tried to kill George," she answered.

Turning about, she headed for the door. A ghost who had been eavesdropping floated to one side. Colin stared at his wife's retreating back, finally realizing that he had not just engaged in his first marital skirmish, but that he had also lost it. "Bloody hell."

The pale shade hanging in the corner stared at him sympathetically.

"If you wished to be helpful," Colin snapped to the specter, "you would show me who has been conspiring to kill the young laird."

The ghost did not answer. He merely faded into the darkness between the castle's stones. Either he didn't know, or he didn't care who would kill the young Balfour.

When the Devil would have us to sin,
he would have us to do the things which
the forlorn Witches used to do.

—*Cotton Mather,* On Witchcraft

Chapter Nineteen

Frances knew she should go about her daily routine just as if nothing had happened, but the morning—and the previous day—had brought her a series of shocks to the senses, and she had not had time for some much-needed quiet reflection.

Still, once she gained the privacy of her chamber, she found she was not thinking about Gilbert Balfour and what his presence at Noltland might mean, but rather about Colin. His advent into her life was a promontory memory, which stood tall even among the recent mountainous events that had befallen her.

And she was married!

She had been so focused on the present and what she needed to do to help her people survive that she had not been looking very far ahead. Nor had she been looking deeply, especially not inside, where everything had hurt for so long.

For ages, there had been a loneliness inside her, a feeling that was worse than any physical ache, a beast that suffered, coiled within her, starving and injured.

But unlike wounds to the body, this pain of loneliness never went entirely numb, and it never healed, and it never died. Sometimes it had hurt so much that she had almost—almost—been ready to accept some of the men who were offered as husbands. Fortunately, or perhaps not, there had also been a great deal of fear and wariness of men, left by her faithless father, to serve as a balance to such unadvised action. That fear of what a misstep could do to her family had kept her aloof. And for a time, fear had kept the painful loneliness quiescent.

But then Colin had come, and he had stirred the beast to new life. He had forced her to think and feel. She couldn't ignore it any longer.

Frances sighed. She had been alienated from herself and her needs for so long that she didn't know what she truly felt anymore, only that with Colin beside her, the beast of loneliness seemed slightly less violent. And perhaps fear and wariness were less active in their suspicions of mankind than they had been before his arrival.

Also, though it was not at all romantic, she secretly liked that he spoke to her as he might to a man, that he did not think her too stupid to understand his world. Whether she would like this world of large intrigue remained to be seen, but at least he had offered it to her. It was her choice to accept or reject it.

His world. His *whole* world? Frances shook her head. Though it might be assumed that any interest that could seduce a man into years of service would be paramount in his life, perhaps he saw politics precisely as he had explained it: an ever-changing enemy to be watched and perhaps propitiated on occasion, while it made him both powerful and wealthy. Such devotion to an occupation did not have to mean that intrigue was his real mistress and his greatest love, or that it always would be, whatever his past.

Ah love! How stupid of her to think of that. It would only remind the loneliness inside that it still starved for this, the most coveted of all emotional meats. And the most difficult to find.

"You are a greedy imbecile," she told herself. "And you have a loom that needs tending."

Frances rose and went to the narrow window. It looked out on a landscape that was even bleaker than her thoughts. The few trees near them were nearly naked now as they huddled away from the wind, and the remaining grasses and lichens had taken on the orange hues of fiery holocaust. Autumn was upon the land, and winter was coming.

Frances turned her back on the window. She was a most uncertain guide to her own feeling, but she understood that the important question facing her now was whether she had badly misjudged Colin when accusing him of having outside motives for their marriage—and whether she could trust him to keep her family safe. Lucien de Talle's overheard words had not been forgotten. Nor were they explained. It seemed as though Colin had had the intention to send her and George away even before MacJannet had brought his news. That suggested that he had some secret stratagems he had not shared with her.

"But that does not mean he does not care for us. This is how men show their protectiveness," she muttered, laying a hand to her chest and trying to soothe the phantom pain that lingered there. "It is only that he has not perfectly learned how to confide in me yet. He, too, has only just married. I must be patient."

And watchful, a small inner voice murmured.

In the meantime she had guests, and hospitality demanded that she be gracious and dignified while she saw to their wants, however tempted she was to selfishly disregard their presence and hide away with her thoughts. She would strive to be truly gracious, for it seemed to her that morning that her mother's delicate, chiding ghost was hovering nearby and watching as her daughter began her married life. The feeling was so strong that she had almost asked Colin if he felt something, too.

A part of her wanted to defend Colin, but all she could do was silently assure her mother that she had not lost her honor when she had lost her virginity to her husband, that it was stupid to think that a woman's character was tied up in her maidenhead and that by losing it to the wrong person she would forever be besmirched.

Yet there was also a part of her that seemed unable to stop listening to her father's voice, which had no high opinion of women once they lost their maiden virtue. He had lured them to his bed in great numbers, and ended up despising them all. He had believed that a woman's only honor after loss of virginity was what she could attain through her husband. He would not be happy with his daughter.

Fortunately, that angry voice was not as strident as it had once been, and Frances suspected she had Colin to thank for that. Whatever else he was, and whatever he intended by her, he had been adamant that she was capable of thinking for herself and she needn't accept someone else's judgments, or give them undue weight because they came with familial sentiments attached.

Frances smiled suddenly. It was likely his opinion would change if it were his judgment she began flouting.

"Shut the door carefully. That latch is stubborn. I must see to it tomorrow."

MacJannet grunted and took a seat near the fire. Sine's tisane was making him sleepy and his eyelids dropped lower with every blink.

"A man dies and worms eat him—that is the way of things," Lucien said as MacJannet moved his chair nearer the hearth. The Frenchman's clothes were somewhat muddied and he had returned with a hare, suggesting that he had indeed been hunting. Colin was not convinced that this had been his only occupation.

"Aye, so it is. And they tell us it is a worm that never dies."

"That may be. I do not know." Lucien shrugged. "It is the parasites who prey on the living in other ways that I find objectionable this afternoon."

"Our mastermind must be someone who is either very greedy or very vengeful," MacJannet agreed tiredly. His wrenched leg was stretched out toward the flickering hearth. He'd stopped trying to mask his injury once the women were not about.

"It would have to be revenge without bounds to seek the life of a boy who is not even a son of the old laird . . . and yet, this whole affair has been most ineptly handled. The attacks have been indirect—sending a hound that is less than fearsome, locking Frances in the dungeons. It is as though the instigator's malice is being tempered or translated into something less harmful by someone with a weaker stomach, who is not ready to do coldhearted murder."

"Anne Balfour?" Lucien asked.

"I believe so. The lady has made some telling missteps and let her malice show a time or two."

"Well, *mon ami*, I am loath to depart here at such a moment. Yet if you feel that you should have your lady wife and the boy away from the creature, I can make arrangements to take them to the bishop and return forthwith."

"I'll bear it in mind." A day ago, Colin had thought this best. Now he wasn't so eager to be parted.

"And it would be easier to question Anne if there were fewer people about to object, *oui*?"

"Perhaps. The Balfour men should begin arriving on the morrow," Colin answered. "That makes for a very short interlude for doing anything. Naturally, one doesn't like to use rough methods with a woman." Especially not in front of her family.

"*Oui*, unless all else has failed." Lucien gestured languidly, then tactfully turned the subject. "The bishop shall be most interested in hearing how the men have fared while in the South."

"I'm certain he shall be enlightened." Colin hesitated, and then returned to the previous topic. "I know it is wisest to send Frances and George away—but I am loath to do it. This is no reflection upon your skills as a guardsman, nor is it a matter of trust. It is simply that . . ."

"One does not wish to begin a marriage with discord, naturally," Lucien guessed. "And it is natural that she would wish to be here when her relatives return. George as well shall doubtless wish to see the men to whom he may be laird."

Colin shot Lucien a glance and then met MacJannet's slitted gaze. "So, you have heard the rumors of

Gilbert's survival, as well? And all while out hunting? How skillful of you."

"*Oui*, hunting takes some skill in these parts. But you wrong me, *mon ami*. This is old news—and it is in part why the bishop was so anxious for me to come to Noltland. He has also wondered, given the other tale of alliance with the English, if this might not be why you are here. King Henry's interest in these matters has him nervous. There are quite enough persons involved already."

It was not quite a question. Colin, slightly piqued at having possibly missed something strategically important and at Lucien's previous reticence, refused to answer.

"All things shall be revealed in the fullness of time. Or at the king's pleasure."

"Or at the MacLeod's?" Lucien suggested.

"Please! Acquit me of having more than one master. We may be of close kin as most people reckon it, but we are certainly not of close kind."

"As you say. And so—you do not wish me to remove your wife and young George to a safer clime on the morrow, or even tonight?"

"Not tonight, and probably not tomorrow. It would cause too much talk, especially with the men returning."

"But I shall hold myself in readiness to remove any number of people if the need should arise," Lucien answered. "Do not thank me. To be useful is what I live for."

There was a slight rustling outside the chamber door. A clumsy MacJannet and spryer Lucien jumped to their feet, but Colin beat them to the slightly open door.

Frances's stiff spine was retreating down the hall, her skirts swishing like an angry broom. Colin was relieved that it had not been Anne Balfour spying on them, but that rigid back suggested he was in for another long night of explanations.

"Bloody hell." He turned back to Lucien and MacJannet. "I truly must see to this latch."

Lucien laughed softly. "That may not be the only thing requiring repair."

"I know that well." Colin frowned at Lucien. "You are not her favorite person anymore. This is the second time she has heard you offering to part us."

"Alas! Yet I shall endure."

"As shall I."

"Just less cheerfully," Lucien suggested.

"You are heartless, even for a Frenchman."

MacJannet chuckled.

Annoyed at both companions, Colin left the room to seek out the smithy and the tools stored there. He would fix the bloody latch himself. And then he would sit down to write Frances a poem. It would not be a very good one, but mayhap it would apologize better than he could, since he wasn't able to ask for forgiveness for arranging the things he needed to do to keep her safe. He regretted her anger—but not what he might well be required to do to protect her.

Or have we eaten on the insane root
That takes the reason prisoner?

—William Shakespeare, Macbeth

Chapter Twenty

The room was very nearly dark when Colin came to bed, and Frances was feigning sleep. She had managed not to have any private discussion with him the whole of the day, even at the evening meal. And Colin was not alone in his expulsion from grace. February blizzards were now more welcome than Lucien de Talle. Only MacJannet was spared, and that was probably because Frances didn't know he had been in the room when the discussion took place.

Colin eyed the angry bundle huddled on her side of the bed and decided to let sleeping Frances lie. A night's rest might well improve her temper, he thought hopefully.

However, Colin was unable to test his theory, for when he awoke the next morning, Frances was already gone from their chamber.

He was not a habitually heavy sleeper and therefore concluded that she must have been practicing great stealth when she stole away from him. He had not heard the bolt being drawn back or the creaking of the door. It occurred to him that she had probably dressed herself in some other chamber, since it was unlikely she had donned clothing in the common passage.

That thought truly annoyed him, and for the first time he considered bridling his strong-willed wife and bringing her to heel. It was time she reordered her loyalties. Her first allegiance was to her husband, and her first duty was helping to present the world with a united front.

But before he set about redirecting his erring wife, it seemed wisest to check up on George. Whither Frances went, George was likely to follow—and the boy hadn't her strength or wiliness when it came to dealing with unexpected problems. Frances was likely to cave in the skull of anyone who threatened her bodily. Colin was not certain that George was made of such ruthless material.

Colin presently discovered George in the courtyard, engaged in the laudable goal of attempting to teach Harry some of the fundamentals of obedience, a thankless task to which Colin was content to leave the boy while he finally sought out his wife.

Frances was likewise soon discovered in a storeroom, directing MacJannet in the mounting of shelves. The inconvenience of her reduced height had finally driven her to undoing her father's work in the pantry and stillroom, and ordering the rude wooden shelves reworked so the women could more easily reach the things stored upon them. It was perhaps an unnecessary task, with the men returning to the castle. But it was a harmless one, and Colin felt safe leaving her in MacJannet's care while he went out into the drizzle to explore the eastern beaches.

His seemingly undirected rambles took him in this new direction, previously unexplored because of the ruggedness of the coastline, but now made attractive because of this very discouraging geographical unpleasantness. The path soon disappeared and he was obliged to carry on, using both hands and feet to find his way over the slimy stone intrusions while water drooled down upon him from the sullen sky.

It seemed ridiculous to persist in this quest with the weather worsening overhead, but an inner sense, honed through years of watchfulness, told him there was still some means of egress into the castle that he had not discovered. Many ocean-side fortifications had secret passages leading to sea caves where boats could be stored, in the event that sudden and clandestine evacuation was necessary. He would not be content until he had ruled out the existence of such an architectural vulnerability at Noltland.

After a short distance, something that remotely resembled a path again appeared, and Colin was able to resume his standard bipedal stance. A few careful steps around a particularly large boulder and he came across the place Tearlach had once mentioned. It was a *drochaid*, a causeway leading to a tiny deserted islet, Eilean am Meadhan. Mostly buried under rusty seaweed and still in the grip of the fearsome white tidal waters, churned to new heights by the oncoming storm, it was slowly coming exposed as the tide reluctantly retreated the last few hand widths from the ancient gray and red stones.

Colin grunted in satisfaction: where there were causeways, there were often moorings.

He turned and examined the rocks about him. The high-water mark, barely visible with the rain coming down, told him that at the tide's zenith there would be plenty of room for a boat with an average draft to navigate to the shore, if it remained tucked up to the mainland until it reached the naturally occurring jetty jutting out from the cliff face.

A soft inhuman moan behind him drew Colin's attention. Mostly invisible from the shore, and completely invisible from the sea because of overlapping boulders, was an entrance to a cave. The violent tidal retreat was causing it to exhale in an eerie manner.

"Aha!"

Hair rising along his neck, Colin followed the line of tattered seaweed up to the cavern's dark mouth. There he paused and cursed himself for not having had the foresight to bring a lantern.

Not long deterred by this oversight, he soon recovered his temper and began thinking sensibly. He had a quick hunt around the entrance, seeking out high ledges where a lantern might be stored, and presently was rewarded with the discovery of an oilskin bag that rendered up both a lantern and flint. The lantern's shallow well seemed nearly empty, suggesting either that the last visitor had been careless about refilling it before he came ashore, or else the passage from the castle was a long and possibly complicated one, which had consumed most of the unpleasant-smelling oil in the reservoir.

It took some doing, because the sea and wet wind were both set against cooperation, but Colin finally managed to set the wick alight. By then the ocean had surrendered as much land as it cared to and was beginning to double back on its treacherous course.

Colin muttered several more bad words but made haste into the cave's interior. The walls were wet to just past his head, but barren of tidal life, something he found curious. The tide must run too quickly to permit any of the usual crustaceans and limpets to make their homes there. A quick touch of the glassy smooth wall confirmed his theory and also argued for extreme caution. Any tide that could polish the walls of a stone cave smooth to the height of a man was not something to be navigated frivolously. Still, he had a few minutes yet . . .

He walked quickly to the back of the cave and discovered three channels opening off of the main chamber, all adequately large to serve as a passage for a man or even a pony. He began an exploration of the passage on the right, but halted when he discovered that it also branched. Both forks headed downward, putting them below the level of the cave. Water would pour through them at a breakneck rate when the sea arrived at the cavern mouth. Anything caught in the wrong passage at the incorrect time would be forced into the bowels of the cliff and drowned in the darkness. It was quite likely that no body would ever be found.

It was also more than possible that the passage had been laid with traps. Usually the Scots did not bother with such subtleties, but Noltland's builder had obviously not been the usual, straightforward variety of man. Those horrible gibbets positioned right outside the bedchamber windows proved that. Who could guess what subtle tortures he might have indulged in while building the castle?

Colin muttered again, this time combining curses into a new and unusual pattern and adding some particularly rude Flemish phrases. He wanted to go on, but he had nothing with which he could mark the walls to ensure his safe return if he grew disoriented underground, not even a rope to lay down a short trail. His lantern was also feeling very light now, and its flame was fading.

He couldn't risk exploring, not with the greedy sea already on the turn and being driven by the weather. He and Lucien would have to come back at low tide tomorrow. Colin would have preferred to have MacJannet with him, but with the man's bad leg, such rough exploration was out of the question.

The day was not a complete loss, however. Colin was certain now that there was yet some other secret entrance to the castle that he had been unable to find from the castle's side. He could do nothing else about it today, but he would find it on the morrow and see that it was finally sealed. After that, Frances and George would be fairly safe from outside attack.

MacJannet had been correct in his prediction that the men would begin their return that day. More than a dozen arrived before the storm loosed itself on the land, and a handful more before the day ended. They came heavily laden with packs and some even with loaded ponies. They were, on the whole, rather thin, and many bore new scars, but were happy in spite of their defeat by the English, the king's death, and a minor skirmish with a band of overbold Gunns who were hunting in the area.

There was fresh rejoicing at Noltland, but also order as Frances oversaw the tearful preparation for yet another feast. Colin watched her with pride as he greeted the returning Balfours.

The men did not know what to think. They were not inclined to welcome into their midst a man who was half English and half MacLeod, and who had also had the temerity to marry their late laird's daughter without asking anyone's permission. On the other hand, they knew that they had Colin Mortlock to thank for their liberation and for looking after Noltland while they were locked in futile battles in the South.

Which wasn't actually the case. Frances had managed the deed quite nicely on her own for many months, but Colin didn't correct their misconceptions and neither did George. He hadn't instructed the lad in what to say, but the boy was canny enough to sense that a united male front was what was needed to carry the day in the face of so much skepticism and, in some cases, outright hostility.

George did his part well, but it was plain that the men were dismayed at the small and rather unhealthy boy who was the new laird. They looked from Colin to George to the bishop's men and then back again, their minds plainly busy with uneasy thoughts that would have to be sorted out once the celebration of homecoming was over. They did not make formal declarations of allegiance, and neither Colin nor George pressed for one.

Colin had explained to the boy before they went downstairs that it was possible his uncle still lived, and therefore he might not actually be the rightful heir to the title of laird. George had digested this news in thoughtful silence, not volunteering his thoughts on the matter. So sober and reflective had he been that Colin had felt moved to hastily reassure the boy that whatever happened, he—and Harry—would always have a place with Frances and him.

George had looked up and smiled fleetingly, but made no comment other than a soft-voiced thank-you. Colin found himself agreeing with Frances's sometime comment that the boy was too much within himself and needed more recreation. If he were left too long in his own somber company, his personality might be permanently overshadowed by gloom. It made Colin more determined than ever to rid the land of their would-be assassin, so they could safely depart from Noltland before the winter stranded them in the North.

MacJannet circulated easily among the men, as did Lucien de Talle, but the weary soldiers said, to a man, that they knew nothing of Gilbert Balfour's whereabouts, or whether he even lived.

This was disappointing, but in other respects Colin was pleased with what he saw. The men were obviously taken aback by George's age, and therefore it was highly unlikely that they had known anything about him. That in turn decreased the odds that any of them had had a hand in trying to eliminate him. It was something Colin had to consider carefully, for any of them made a great suspect in this piece of villainy. Anne Balfour would likely aid a family member, and they could very well know about secret passages into the castle.

Colin was used to pretense and feigning untrue emotion, but he was fairly certain that this new and inconvenient feeling of love and protectiveness would have forbidden him from breaking bread with any man he suspected of harboring lethal ill will for either George or Frances. It would probably have also forbidden him from letting any suspected villain live. And that would probably upset Frances. Most ladies did not care for bloodshed at the table.

Nothing in his life
Became him like the leaving it; he died
As one that had been studied in his death,
To throw away the dearest thing he ow'd,
As 'twere a careless trifle.

—*William Shakespeare,* Macbeth

Chapter Twenty-one

Colin and Frances finally had time for a private discussion after the castle's inhabitants retired to bed. While the Balfour men were being reunited with their loving wives and going to their rest in welcoming arms, Colin and Frances were still arguing about future plans, matters of trust, and eavesdropping.

The latest words of accusation and disappointment still hung in the air between them, waiting for something—perhaps words of forgiveness—to dissipate them when the moon began to set.

At last breaking off from the battle of gazes, Frances glanced over at the pillow beside her, the bolster on which Colin—*her husband, lord, and master*, she reminded herself—was supposed to rest, and saw a small sheet of parchment tucked beneath it.

"Frances," he said softly. "Perhaps this is not the moment—"

Hands suddenly trembling, she lifted the paper and read:

To Frances
It is a short time since I kissed you,
And from that morn lov'd you true;
Your graceful form and raven hair,
May with a fabl'd Diana compare;
Your voice, so honey sweet,
Still on my heart does seem to beat;
And 'twas the first wish of my life,
To win thee for my wife;
Deign, ma belle, a sign to send,
And may your heart my plea defend.

She looked up at Colin, her eyes wide. It was a bad poem, but the sentiment behind it was lovely beyond expectation and a gift she had not expected. Her hurt and anger began to drain away.

Her lips parted, but before she could speak there came an urgent knocking upon their door. Three short knocks, a pause, and then two more.

Colin went immediately to the chamber door and drew back the bolt. MacJannet, carrying a lantern and his sword, slipped inside.

"The boy's gone and there's blood on the chamber floor. A few drops only, but—"

"And the hound? Where is Harry?" Colin reached for his own sword, donning it along with some cloak of purpose that made him look suddenly hard and tall, and showed Frances clearly the difference between annoyance and true rage in her husband. She would never mistake one for the other again.

Suddenly the Colin in her chamber was a stranger to her.

"He's been locked up below with a bone. Probably

lured there by our traitor. I suppose we are a bit late in bricking up the last passage."

MacJannet's words struck fear into Frances's heart, driving away all other emotions. "George is gone?" she whispered. "He has been taken?"

"Roust the household and free the hound." Colin's voice was harsh. "See that everyone is armed. We go to hunt."

"Anne Balfour?" MacJannet asked.

"I'll deal with her."

As MacJannet slipped from the room, Colin turned and gave his wife a short look, which she could not interpret in the dim light. It was cold enough to chill her, yet she knew none of the anger was directed at her. "Bolt the door behind me and do not leave the chamber."

"But," Frances began, pushing the covers from her trembling legs. "I must come. It is George—"

"This may be a trick!" Colin answered. "We can't know how many are in the castle. We may soon be overrun. They have one prisoner. Let us not be generous and give them two."

It seemed for an instant that he would leave on those words. But then he took the three steps to her side, and pulling her close, he kissed her briefly.

"Don't let our possible last words be angry ones," he murmured. Then: "Say you love me—and then bolt the door behind me."

"I love you," she answered, not thinking whether this reply was true or not, only knowing that she needed to answer him at once.

"And I you, Frances."

It wasn't until he was gone that the full import of

what he said entered Frances's mind. But once there, the seed rooted quickly.

Last words . . . We may be overrun.

I love you.

And I you.

"*Mon Dieu*!"

Frances stood for a moment, trembling with fear and cold, and also the beginnings of rage. Then she made her decision. Instead of reaching for the bolt, she turned toward her pannier, reaching for her heaviest club. She tarried only long enough to thrust her feet into her shoes and then she was out the door.

No one was going to take George and Colin from her, not while she had breath left in her body! She had waited too long for happiness!

Colin stood over a weeping Anne Balfour. Her lips were bloodless and he had seen overboiled tripe with better color.

"I did not know he would take the boy! I thought the plot at an end when I left the note telling him of your marriage."

"How many of our enemy have you let inside, and which clan are they? The Gunns?"

"Nay, I cannot—"

Colin raised his sword, his face and voice as cold as the iron in his hands. "You'll name them now or go to Hell with your soul dyed in sin."

"'Tis Iain Dubh of the MacDonnells," she choked out, stricken eyes on the sword above her. Knowing the MacLeod's history with this man, she clearly expected to be struck down for naming him to the laird's cousin.

"Why, Anne? Tell me why," Frances whispered, coming into the room. The fingers that held her club were as white as her night rail. "George never did you any harm. He is just a boy."

"I did it because I loved him," Anne wept, dropping her face into her hands. Clearly, she did not mean George. "And he said he would not marry me if I did not let him in . . . But it is only Iain Dubh and his brother, I swear. No other was with them. He promised. He said he would not hurt the boy—just take him away."

"No other was with him then," Colin answered. "But who knows how many may have followed once the tunnel was opened. And you are a stupid woman if you believed that George's life would be spared. Why should it be?"

Anne Balfour wept harder.

Colin raised his sword again, prepared to strike, but then paused.

Lucien de Talle entered the room, his sword also drawn. "Finish it," he said harshly.

"Nay, we may need her. It is possible that she may have some useful knowledge. I'll question her later."

Lucien digested this and then finally nodded. He turned on his heel and left the chamber. His voice called back: "They went to the dungeons. There is a trail of blood on the stairs."

"I know," Colin answered. "Start looking for a passage in the east wall."

"Make haste! Or we shall go without you."

"I'm coming! Frances, stay with her," Colin said, turning to Frances as he lowered his voice. "Do not get close enough for her to grab you. I'd not put it past her to stick a dagger in you if she can. Bolt the door behind me—and this time do as I say! If she tries to leave the chamber, kill her. If we don't find the passage I shall return to fetch her. Be here."

Frances swallowed once but she did not flinch at the commands. She managed a nod.

"I'll find George, Frances. I swear it. You must have faith, *cherie*."

The door closed sharply behind Colin, and this time Frances did throw the bolt. "It is not about faith," she whispered, listening to the many footsteps hurrying by in the passage. "It is about love—and duty."

"He promised! He promised! He said we should escape together," Anne wept, still huddled on the floor. "We would go away tonight."

"Be still!" Frances ordered, swinging her club hard and making the air whistle with menace. Rage made her voice shake. "Weeping solves nothing. He has abandoned you. You are lost. But George may not yet be dead. So you will tell me now: what was this plan you made? Where might they have taken George? Where is this secret passage you opened for them?"

A shocked Anne looked up. Whatever she saw in her kinswoman's face frightened her into tearlessness.

"I do not need to wait for Colin to question you," Frances warned softly, again swinging her club.

"It's in the cellar—in the cave maze." Anne's voice quavered.

"Get up!" Frances ordered. "You will show me where this passage is. Does it lead to the sea as Colin suspects?"

Anne climbed clumsily to her feet. Her eyes, tattooed with purple circles about the lids, were glued to the thick stick in Frances's hands. "Aye, he has a boat there."

"Then we shall go to the cellars. Do not tempt me, Anne, unless you are eager to die, for I shall strike you dead if you try to escape." And in that moment, Frances absolutely meant those words. "Light that lantern and hold it before you as we go."

Frances pulled back the bolt from the door and opened it wide. Once the lantern was lit, she gestured for Anne to go ahead of her. The keep was eerily quiet. Everyone, except perhaps the children, had been roused and sent out to seek George and his kidnappers. She and Anne might as well have been the only two people left in the world.

They went down the stairs as quickly as Anne's trembling legs would take her. The keep was not in total darkness, but most of the torches had been snapped up by searchers, and those that remained cast wholly inadequate light, which had a tendency to waver alarmingly in the eddies caused by the women's passage.

Frances had hoped to find someone still in the cellars, but all had gone on into the dungeon. She and Anne were still on their own. She wanted to call out to Colin, but knew the acoustics might betray her quavering voice and her position to an enemy hiding in the cellar or the secret passage.

Anne found the door behind the empty whisky barrels still open, but hesitated on the threshold, with her lantern held high.

"Go on," Frances said.

"I have never been inside," Anne answered fearfully. "I do not know the way from here. We might get lost."

This gave Frances pause. She knew about sea caves' evil reputation. She looked about consideringly until she saw the end of a badly charred torch wedged between two casks. Keeping an eye on Anne, she quickly retrieved it.

"We shall use soot to mark the walls if we come to a divide," she suggested. "Go on. We are wasting time. We must hasten if we are to stop this tragedy."

Anne nodded reluctantly and then stepped into the dark passage. Frances, though very determined to go on, found that she also had to pause at the doorway and gather her courage before journeying on.

The sea passage was narrow—so narrow that she would be unable to swing her club. It sloped downward steeply and was very dark and damp. It was also filled with unpleasant rustlings and whispers, which caused much churning in her imagination.

A sudden rush of dizziness hit her as she stared into the black, traveling from ankles to heart and then on to her head. Frances wanted to blame the terrible feeling on bad air, but she knew it was fear. Fear for George, fear of whoever waited in the darkness, fear of the dark itself.

"Colin," she whispered, invoking his name like a talisman. It did not help her nerves when a low moaning filled the passage and washed over them, making Anne catch her breath and momentarily freeze. "That was only the ocean or the wind. For George you must be courageous," she encouraged herself, stepping after Anne. She called softly: "Hurry. We must hurry!"

She did not admit to herself that the moan might have come from George, but the unspoken fear forced her onward when her timid mind called to her to go back to the safety of the light and other people.

When shall we three meet again?
In thunder, lightning, or in rain?

—William Shakespeare, Macbeth

Chapter Twenty-two

Frances and Anne had just entered the dripping sea cave and started toward the two struggling figures they found there when Frances felt a presence behind her. Before she could do more than half spin around, an arm in a saffron sark snaked out and wrapped itself about her throat, pulling her tightly against a barrel chest. The man smelled of sweat and whisky. Frances opened her mouth to scream but only managed a short cry before her air was blocked off by the brutal living clamp at her neck.

She struggled, but the man was fantastically strong, and one look at Anne's shocked face and shrinking posture told Frances that she could expect no help from that quarter.

"Gi'e us a hand here, Iain!" the man puffed as he tried to subdue her.

As the villain began to drag her toward the front of the cave where a large lantern glowed, Frances tightened her hands about her club, preparing to defend herself. Her assailant's most vulnerable parts were his naked shins. She prayed for a true aim and the strength to deliver a crippling blow. She knew she was unlikely to have another chance once the second man finished with the frantically struggling George and added his efforts to restraining her.

A familiar ghost, the sad lady who had been in his chamber on his wedding night, appeared before Colin and pointed back the way they had come. He spun about abruptly.

"The cellar!" he exclaimed. "The passage has to be there! This is too far belowground anyway."

Lucien looked skeptical, but MacJannet never questioned Colin's judgment. He could not see spirits as Colin did, but he did not doubt that one was near. Colin's nerves were on the jump that night, but those nerves had an uncanny ability to know trouble when it was near. As Colin hurried back toward the cellars, MacJannet followed, hobbling as quickly as he could.

Harry was heard woo-wooing frantically as he, too, took up the hunt.

"Damnation!" Colin swore, his voice echoing in the long stone room. "We went right past this stack of overturned barrels! The door is bloody obvious."

"What?" MacJannet demanded, taken aback. He refrained from cursing, but felt blasphemous every time his leg twinged. "I am certain it was not thus when we passed before. Something has overturned these barrels. Maybe the hound has found a scent?"

"They dragged George down to the dungeon. He hasn't been in here. Who then?"

The worried ghost floated nearby, still pointing. Colin nodded and pulled the old door wide. A faint noise crawled up from the dank blackness. Colin stopped breathing and listened intently. "Bloody hell!"

"What?"

"That was Frances!" He was certain of this even without the ghost's admonition. "The MacDonnells have her, too!"

Without hesitation Francis swung her club downward at her assailant's legs. At her attacker's sharp cry and stumble, she threw herself against his strangling arm. To her surprise, the ploy worked.

Once free of her human noose, she spun about, raising her arms high. Frances next delivered a mighty swing, connecting with the side of the man's tammed head, with her full strength behind the blow. There was a horrible cracking noise as his tam flew into the air. The man grunted and then dropped like a stone onto the cave's wet floor.

Hearing a shout behind her, Frances spun about, raising her club again. "George, beware!" she screamed as she began another mighty swing.

Colin rushed recklessly down the rough passage that led toward the sea cave, following the spirit. He couldn't hear much beyond the echoes of his feet, his ragged breathing, and the moaning of the sea. The lantern shed sufficient light so that he could see when to duck, but the leather soles of his shoes were confoundedly slippery and much of his time was spent recovering his balance after near-accidents.

Suddenly there came the sound of something large and wet hitting stone. Colin had heard enough cracking skulls to recognize the sound of a head hitting something solid. A heavy thud followed.

"Frances got one!" he called back to MacJannet, pride at her courage battling with terror in his heart.

There came a high thin scream of someone either facing Hell or slipping over the edge of sanity. It didn't sound like either Frances or George, but with the distortion of noise in the cavern, it wasn't possible to identify the noise enough to know that it was even human.

Forgetting all caution, Colin threw himself toward the dim glimmer at the end of the tunnel. He threw his lantern aside as soon as the passage broadened, and he drew his sword as he leapt into the chamber.

He took in the scene at a glance. Anne Balfour, keening like a banshee, was huddled over a man's body. Frances, with her club raised, was prepared to do further harm to the remaining kidnapper if she could get around his human shield—George.

Colin took a flanking position, but he also hesitated at the sight of the naked blade pressed into George's bare throat. The boy's eyes were wide with fear, but he wasn't screaming.

A livid MacJannet erupted into the chamber behind Colin, followed by an even more enraged Harry, who howled his anger at the man who had taken his beloved George and locked him in the dungeon. More footsteps and cursing voices echoed down the passage.

"Let the lad go, man," Colin said. Harry crouched beside Colin, clearly furious but also uncharacteristically cautious.

"You can take your boat and go. We'll not stop you," Colin said. "But hurt that boy and I'll spit you where you stand."

"I'm takin' the boat—and the laddie." The voice was laced with equal parts of hate and fear.

"*Non*. This you shall not do!" Frances took a step forward. The sad ghost also darted in, trying but unable to affect events on the human plane.

"Frances!" Colin warned. He didn't want her placing herself between the man and his own sword.

"He shall not take George!" she answered furiously. "I'll kill George first." Her threat was fierce and Colin almost believed her. He hoped the would-be kidnapper believed her, too.

The ghost suddenly tipped back her head and let out a silent scream. Instantly a keening, higher and more piercing than Anne's and Harry's combined, filled the chamber. Frances froze at the sound.

"*Mon Dieu*!"

The echo had barely died away when Tearlach and Lucien hurtled into the room.

"Can you not silence that beast, *mon ami*?" Lucien demanded. "He is curdling my blood."

A second and even louder howling reverberated in the cavern. Frances flinched away from the sound and the man holding George began to tremble.

"What manner of beast is that?" Lucien demanded.

"'Tis the hellhound! A creature frae the night side." Tearlach's voice was barely heard over the unnatural echoes that lingered longer they should have. "Someone is about tae die."

"Get it away!" the kidnapper screamed. "Get it away or I'll kill the laddie!"

With a third eerie howling that nearly stopped the blood with dams of icy terror, the true hellhound of the Balfours appeared. One moment there was nothing, and then a black shape stalked out of the shadows. Colin had seen many spirits in his life, but none like this beast.

The kidnapper's eyes widened at the sight of the infernal hound, and a tiny mewl of terror escaped his lips. The knife that had been at George's throat was turned toward the black beast that stalked either him or the boy: none could tell for sure who was the target.

"Get away! Get away!" the MacDonnell screamed.

With a sudden wrench that left his torn shirt behind, the agile George was able to break away from his captor. If the intruder had hoped that the hound would follow George, his wishes were dashed in the instant before he died. The Bokey hound was apparently still loyal to his Balfour masters. He had died once to protect his laird and would again. The ghost pointed at the kidnapper in silent command, and the beast leapt.

The man ran for the sea in a desperate bid for freedom, perhaps recalling the legend that said ghosts could not travel over water. There was a clatter of toenails on hard stone, and a second voice rose in canine anguish as Harry also launched himself at the intruder's fleeing form. Frances jumped back toward the mouth of the cave and the figures rushing down on her, and then vanished in the blackness as the panicked man fled toward what he hoped would be salvation.

Harry and the Bokey hound both launched themselves into the air. For an instant, the two beasts were joined, one sandy brown and the other a black shadow. Both bodies flew at the trespasser, teeth showing.

The man screamed once and fell to the cave floor under the weight of the hounds, half of his body outside the cave. It was difficult for anyone to see what happened then, as the lantern near the man's feet was tipped over and the shutter fell half closed, but there could be no denying that when Harry jumped back from the man's body a moment later, his prey was dead. The man's head rested at an unnatural angle that only occurred when a neck was broken.

The ghost remained for a moment longer, then wavered like a candle flame caught in a wind and went out.

For a long moment no one moved, then Tearlach threw off his paralysis and went to stand over the body while George knelt to embrace the trembling Harry.

"You are an excellent hound! So brave and smart. Oh Harry!" the boy said, burying his face in the dog's ruffed neck.

Harry licked the boy's neck and ear, comforting him as best he could. The dog himself seemed bewildered, and Colin wondered if he had been in control at the time of the attack or if the spectral hound had somehow possessed him.

"Frances!" Colin called, putting up his sword. "Where are you?"

Frances came stumbling out of gloom at the front of the cave and then, regaining her balance, she hurled herself into Colin's arms. Her hands and hem were wet from where she had stumbled in the surf. Colin didn't complain about the wet and cold.

"Colin, it was the *real* hound," she cried into his shirt as he ran his hands over her, assuring himself that she had met with no injury.

"Aye, I saw it."

"We all did and I pray I never witness such a thing again," MacJannet said amazedly, coming forward awkwardly and putting an arm around George and urging him to his feet. "Lad, are you hurt?"

"Nay, just a bloodied nose. Frances arrived in time. She cracked that man's head open." This was said with joy rather than horror. Colin was relieved that it was so.

"*Mon Dieu, mon Dieu, mon Dieu*," Lucien muttered, still stunned by what they had witnessed. His previous life had never prepared him for an encounter with anything of a spectral nature.

"My sentiments precisely," Colin answered. He had encountered many spirits but still found himself shaken by what he had witnessed. He could only imagine what this meant to the others in the cave, who had never seen an apparition. "Yet I think we had best decide what we are going to tell the others about this night. It would be best if we presented a united tale."

"We tell them nothing of this," Lucien answered swiftly, waving a hand at the man with the broken neck. "Their beliefs make no allowance for . . . for . . . things of this nature. They must believe it was the work of earthly agents or it could go ill for all of us. There can be no talk of demon dogs or a Balfour curse or anything from the night side."

"That's all well and good, but there is one here who may not hold her tongue," Tearlach answered, finally backing away from the corpse. "Have ye all forgotten the traitor?"

They all turned then and looked at the cowering Anne Balfour. She had stopped screaming and crying, and was staring off into space, her eyes blank as an empty mirror. Her complexion was bloodless. For one moment, Colin wondered if she was in fact dead.

"I don't believe this woman will be saying anything for a long while," MacJannet answered. "She may never speak again."

"She's a woman," Tearlach retorted. "Ye ken that she'll speak again. And once she does, there'll be nae shutting her up again. I say we silence her now."

I dare do all that may become a man;
Who dares do more, is none.

—William Shakespeare, Macbeth

Chapter Twenty-three

The conspirators agreed on the story that Colin had killed one of the intruders and Harry the other, sparing the belatedly emotional Frances of accusations of unfemininity for taking part in George's rescue, from the likely hidebound Balfour males. Why this should suddenly be the cause of mental mortification escaped Tearlach, who was very proud of Frances's unfeminine calm in the face of disaster, but even he agreed to hold fast to this story when she entreated him for silence.

This stratagem also conveniently spared those who had not clearly seen the Bokey hound themselves from admitting that the beast existed, or else suspecting that several of their party had run mad while breathing bad cavern air. Any howling would be blamed on Harry and the cave's unusual acoustics, which did play tricks with voices.

Privately, Colin assured Frances that he thought she was magnificently brave—and that if she ever blatantly disregarded his commands again, he'd lock her in a dungeon for the rest of her life. This was an empty threat, as Pemberton Fells didn't have one, but Frances promised faithfully to always be dutiful in immediately attending to his wishes.

Colin didn't believe her, but he supposed the chances of their ever being in a similar situation were so remote that he would not dwell on all the hideous possibilities of what might have happened, had she not had her golf club and a good deal of luck.

Though there was unanimity on the subject of the hound, they had disagreement over the matter of what to do with Anne Balfour. Lucien wanted her dead, as did Tearlach. MacJannet reserved his opinion, but Colin was sure he also agreed that this was the best solution for the traitor.

George would not voice an opinion either, and Colin did not press him. The boy was spending a lot of time practicing archery and talking to his hound. Colin was certain that George would recover his spirits once they were away from Noltland, but the boy's emotional withdrawal was another reason to make haste away from the haunted and unhappy place.

"At the very least, she should have her thumbs branded, to mark her for the traitor she is," Colin had argued with his stubborn bride.

But, for once, his lady did not call for blood: "She shall return to her people when she is well enough to travel. Her lover is dead and she is half mad. That is punishment enough."

"You are too forgiving." But Colin did not argue further for Anne Balfour's punishment. The woman looked so frail that it seemed the breath of heaven itself might be too much for her to withstand if it blew upon her. Also, it was as he had explained to Lucien: he had no stomach for warring on women.

Frances shrugged at this observation and then said: "I have learned that love can make a woman do all sorts of foolish things."

Colin couldn't refute that. Love made men do foolish things, too.

They had an hour's warning the following day before Gilbert Balfour's retinue arrived, and therefore there was time for the much-practiced Balfour women to arrange one more feast. It would have to be the last, though, for they were running out of wine and there were no more birds to give their lives for the glory of the groaning board.

The true heir to the Balfours arrived at the castle looking pale but otherwise sound, and was very relieved to discover that he was both expected and welcomed by the occupants, even though his politics differed drastically from his brother's. Colin was certain his own presence was a bit of shock to the true laird, but knew that having an Englishman about was only a small part of what bemused the wounded soldier. Gilbert was pleased at the unexpected presence of the bishop's men at the keep, and predisposed to like Colin for bringing them. His qualified approval became almost total approbation when he discovered it was Colin who had arranged, at his own expense, to have the Balfour men paid their wages and returned to Noltland, and that later Colin and Frances had been married by Angus MacBride. Apparently the two Protestant men were much in each other's confidences, and Colin and Frances's union's blessing by this man could only be seen as a sign of grace.

Gilbert was stunned but again pleased when his young cousin, rather than being upset at discovering Gilbert was actually alive, and therefore the heir to

Noltland and the title, instead announced plainly that he was relieved to find this the case because he wanted to go to England with Colin and Frances, and eventually attend university.

Frances, too, was a bit of a surprise to the hardened soldier, who had no daughters of his own. Gilbert had hardly known what to answer when his pretty niece looked up at him and asked: "*Mon oncle*, do you perhaps like to play gowff? *Non*? But do not despair. Colin shall teach you. We are all quite fond of the game here."

Neither Colin nor Gilbert rushed to act on this suggestion.

In spite of Gilbert's assurance that he would love to have his niece and her husband remain for the winter, plans for the bridal couple's departure were made forthwith. Winters in the North tended to be an assault on the senses, molesting them constantly until the season turned again to spring. They waited only for MacJannet's leg to heal. They would travel overland rather than by boat—and they would not be halting at Dunnvegan to visit the MacLeod.

The party had also grown a bit because, in addition to George and Harry, Tearlach had decided to journey south with them. Frances was at first inclined to object to his presence, but the piper had seemingly been reformed. Apparently after consuming an indecent amount of whisky, the late laird's ghost had reappeared to him and announced that he was lifting the curse of impotency and that Tearlach should go to England to look after the laird's grandchildren-to-be. Tearlach's behavior became exemplary after this.

Colin suspected the dream had conveniently appeared because Gilbert had his own piper—and a very skilled one at that—but after the plain appearance of the spectral hound, Colin didn't feel qualified to absolutely rule out the possibility that the late laird's ghost *had* given Tearlach specific instructions about their children-to-be. It seemed safer to take the piper along than risk a haunting by an irate father-in-law. Ghosts might not travel over open water, but they had no problem journeying over land.

Colin debated for a time, but finally decided to write a letter to his cousin MacLeod before leaving the North, explaining the situation at Noltland. He could only hope that the half loaf of not having the keep in the hands of the MacDonnells or Gunns was enough to stay his cousin from foolhardy actions, but knowing Alasdair, Colin did not entirely discount the possibility of some stubborn gesture against Gilbert Balfour.

His cousin's stubbornness aside, life was good and Colin felt beforehand with the world. The only thing that vaguely troubled Colin was his bride. Or, more specifically, her failure to repeat her words of love to him in the days since their deadly adventure.

Colin was aware that he had coaxed the words of devotion from her at a moment of great stress and that it was possible she had not truly meant them. On the other hand, she gave a very convincing performance as a loving wife . . .

He was not at all certain how to discover what her feelings actually were. There had been little private time for them since Gilbert had arrived, because a great deal needed to be accomplished before they could leave Noltland, and Frances came to bed at night already half asleep. That didn't seem the moment to inaugurate a serious discussion.

Finally there came an afternoon when the weather was pleasant and no urgent tasks demanded their attention, and Colin was able to persuade Frances to take a long ramble out on the shore to test a few more of the MacLeod's clubs.

At first Frances was hesitant to take up a club again after the killing, but as always her courage came to the fore. After looking Colin in the eye and nodding her head, she took up the long weighted stick, and was soon enjoying brutalizing her leather ball and chatting happily about the upcoming luxury of having a shorn meadow in which to play gowff.

Colin watched Frances play. The autumnal sun spun a halo about Frances and the gentle breeze fluttered her cloak behind her like angel's wings. In spite of nature's attempts to keep Colin's thoughts elevated, his vision failed to see his wife as an ethereal being. She was of the earth, a being of passions and thoughts, who hungered for earthly things. And so was he.

"You are looking forward with pleasure to seeing Pemberton Fells?" he asked, tucking her hand into his arm as they chased down her ball, so she would not stumble over the flotsam the storm had washed up on the beach.

"*Oui*. It sounds most wonderfully appointed. And I have not forgotten your promise," she added, smiling mischievously.

"Which promise is that?" Colin asked, staring down at the upcurved lips and suddenly having trouble following the conversation.

"That I am to be made into a creature of pleasure—a voluptuary who wears perfume and silk."

"Ah! That promise," he answered lightly. "We shall see to it at once."

"Before the gowffing green?"

"They shall both be seen to immediately," he promised, then added casually: "I was wondering if perhaps you were thinking of some other promises."

"Which ones?"

"Perhaps the ones about love and honor?"

"And obedience?"

"That one, too," he answered promptly. "Did you mean those promises, Frances?"

Frances looked down at her ruffling hem and considered the question seriously. "I have promised twice to obey—and I shall *try.*"

"Aye."

She continued to look down, but Colin saw the beginnings of a smile. "And I have always honored you. There can be no doubt of this."

"In your own fashion," he agreed politely. "And?"

"And I wish to know if you meant *your* vows?" Frances looked up, her eyes twinkling, and Colin knew he was being teased.

"I offered my protection and my purse—and I've given you both."

"*Oui.*"

"And I've promised you a meadow to play gowff on and perfume from Santa Maria Novella."

"And silk dresses," she reminded him.

"And silk dresses," he agreed.

"Then what else could there be?" she asked, eyes shining.

"Love perhaps?"

"Oh, love. Well, if you must—" Frances squeaked as Colin put his hands about her waist and lifted her into the air. Her golf club dangled from her hand as he brought them nose to nose.

"Aye—*love*. What of that, my wife?"

"If you must have it so plainly expressed—"

"I find that I must."

"Then have the words. I love you." Frances leaned forward and set her lips to Colin's.

They kissed until his arms tired and only then did he return her to the ground.

"And have you nothing to say to me in return?" she asked, pouting.

Colin kept his face serious. "Let me think. You promised to love, honor, and obey." Colin turned and began to stroll up the beach. "And I promised you perfume and silk—and a gowffing green. No, I don't believe there could be anything—"

Frances reached out with her club and snagged Colin's ankle, tumbling him into the sand. Before he could do more than roll over, his wife pounced upon him.

"You must think over matters more carefully," she said, flattening herself on his body and wiggling as she felt him stirring to life beneath her. "There is something else, I believe. You must cast about in your mind until you recall it."

"There is?" he asked, clearing his throat. "Give me a moment. This sand is confoundedly wet and cold, but I believe that I am beginning to recall . . ."

Frances wiggled again. "*Oui*?"

"Let's see . . . Could it be love?"

"*Could* it be?" she asked, her expression sobering slightly. "I know you said it was, but . . ."

"Oh it most definitely could be," he answered, taking her in his arms and rolling her away from the encroaching tide. He looked down at her, happiness filling his soul. “Aye, I am quite sure ’tis love.”

“You swear it?”

“I swear it.”

And then he sealed his vow with a kiss.

AUTHOR'S NOTE

As with my first novel, *Iona*, I have taken great liberties with history in this story, particularly with the Balfours, who have had four hundred years of family lore compressed and embellished to fit into the less than three hundred pages of *The Night Side*. Chief among the inaccuracies, Gilbert Balfour (who makes a late appearance in the story) did not actually inherit Noltland until 1546, but lucky Gilbert: in this book he gets the castle two years earlier.

Other sundry characters are composites of historic figures that have been compressed into single beings. The large historic personages such as Henry VIII and Mary of Guise, regent and mother of Mary Queen of Scots, are portrayed as accurately as possible, but the hero, heroine, and supporting cast of Noltland Castle are all made up out of my head and therefore won't be found in any history books. Especially Tearlach, who is patterned after a relation of mine—but which relative I shall not say, since I must face my family at Thanksgiving. The sins of omission in this book are endless. I did not take the space to explain in detail all the combatants in the religious war because that would be tedious. As it is, there were Catholics, English Protestants, and Scottish Reformers all running amok as they struggled for political power, and that seemed complicated enough for a romance. The true nastiness of the warfare of this era has also been glossed over, because I found no way to deal realistically with the zealous John Knox and the murder of Cardinal Beaton and keep things light and romantic. Please forgive the very abridged history of an important time in Scotland. Unfortunately, there are no great lessons, historic or religious, to be learned from this tale, except that gowff could be a dangerous game when played with the gout-ridden Henry VIII. For more information about the early game of golf as played in Scotland, see *A Swing Through Time: Golf in Scotland 1457–1744* by Olive M. Geddes.

Also, lovers of Shakespeare will think they see a misquote from *As You Like It* in chapter 19 (men have died from time to time and worms have eaten them—but not for love). But as Shakespeare had yet to pen this play at the time of the story, I ask you to believe that the worm my characters speak of is the one in Hell that eats and never dies. This is more applicable, as at that moment they are discussing murder and not romance.

Please drop me a line and let me know how you enjoyed the story. E-mail can be directed to melaniejaxn@hotmail.com or my Web site at http://www.melaniejackson.com.

Welcome to my imaginary Scotland. Happy reading and *slan leat* (health upon you).

Melanie Jackson

Keep reading to meet Ms. Percy Parker, an albino beauty who has come to London and must learn not only to deal with the ghosts that she can see, but her own part in the puzzling prophecy that threatens the world . . .

The Strangely Beautiful Tale of Miss Percy Parker

by Leanna Renee Hieber

Prologue

London, England, 1867

The air in London was grey. This was no surprise; but the common eye could not see the particular heaviness of the atmosphere, nor the unusual weight of this special day's charcoal clouds. In a remote place, far from England, one by one six candles had guttered out in windows and released smoke birthed from the death of their flames. Six souls had passed on. The sky was now pregnant with a potent wind, for The Guard was searching for their new mortal hosts.

On to London they'd come, and that wind full of spirits began now to course through the streets of the city; merciless, searching. Around corners, elbowing aside London's commoners and high society alike, nudging their way through market crowds and tearing down dirty alleys, The Guard sought their intended.

A candle burst into flame in the window of an earl's house. The tiny cry of a young boy summoned his mother into the drawing room. Similar sounds went up in other parts of the city, confused gasps growing into amazed giggles before being subdued into solemnity. One by one the intended targets were seized.

Six. Five . . .

Where is Four? Ah . . . Four.

Now, Three.

Alone and unaccompanied, these children left their respective houses and began to walk.

And, Two.

Searching for the final piece, the greatest of the possessors paused, a hesitating hunter. Deliberate. And, finally . . . the brightest, boldest, most promising catch of the day.

One, and done!

A sigh of relief. The city's infamous fog thinned.

Only a bird above espied the six drawing toward London's center; weaving through a maze of clattering carriages, stepping cautiously over putrid puddles, a sextet of children looked about the cluttered merchant streets and sober business avenues with new eyes and saw strange sights. There were ghosts everywhere: floating through walls and windows, they rose up through streets and strolled beside quiet couples. One by one, each transparent form turned to the children, who could only stare in wonder and apprehension. In ethereal rags, spirits of every century bowed in deference, as if they were passing royalty.

Drawn in a pattern from all corners of London, the children gathered in a knot at the crest of Westminster Bridge. Nodding a silent greeting to one another, or curtseying, the youths found each other's faces unsettlingly mature. Childish excitement tempered only by confusion crept into their expressions as they evaluated their new peers, in garb ranging from fine clothing to simple frocks, their social statuses clearly as varied as their looks.

A spindly girl whose brown hair was pinned tightly to her head kept turning, looking for something, clutching the folds of her linen frock and shifting on the heels of her buttoned boots. It was her tentative voice that at last broke the silence.

"Hello. I'm Rebecca. Where is our leader, then?"

A sturdy, ruddy-cheeked boy in a vest and cap, cuffs rolled to his elbows, gestured to the end of the street. "Hello, Rebecca, I'm Michael. Is that him?"

Approaching the cluster was a tall, well dressed, unmistakable young man. A mop of dark hair held parley with the wind, blowing about the sharp features of his face, while timeless, even darker eyes burned in their sockets. His fine black suit gave the impression of a boy already a man. He reached the group and bowed, his presence magnetic, confident . . . and somewhat foreboding.

In a rich, velvet voice deep as the water of the Thames, he spoke. "Good day. My name is Alexi, and this has turned into the strangest day of my life." He glanced at the spindly brunette next to him, who blushed.

"Hello, Alexi, I'm Rebecca, and I feel the same."

Alexi firmly met every child's gaze in turn, prompting introductions.

"Elijah," a thin blond boy said, his features sharp and his eyes a startling blue. He was garbed in striped satin finery that seemed rakish if not foppish for such a young man, and he was clearly the wealthiest of the lot.

"Josephine," added a soft, French accent belonging

to a beautiful brunette, olive skinned and sporting the latest in youthful fashions. Two shocks of white hair framed her face.

"Michael," chimed in the sturdy boy with a brilliant, contagious smile.

"Lucretia Marie O'Shannon Connor," replied an Irish accent, shyly, and its owner stared at the cobblestones, dark blonde hair falling to veil her frightened face. Her plain calico dress bespoke modest means.

"Pardon?" Elijah's already drawn and angular face became more pinched.

"I suppose you could call me Jane if that's easier," the girl murmured with a shrug, still staring at the street.

"I'll say," Elijah retorted.

Alexi's lips twitched in disdain, and his eyes flashed with an unfocused anger. "And here I thought all my life I'd be a scientist. It seems the forces inside us have other plans. I don't suppose any of you have the slightest idea what we're supposed to *do*?"

Everyone shook their heads, just as surprised with their new destinies as he.

"Then, let me ask a mad question," Alexi said. His tone was cautious. "Does anyone, all of a sudden . . . see ghosts?"

"Yes!" everyone chorused, relieved that if it was madness, they weren't alone in it.

"Can you hear them speak?" he asked.

"No," they replied.

"Neither can I, thank God, or we'd never have another moment's peace." Alexi sighed. "Well, I suppose we'd better get to the bottom of this. I . . . saw a chapel. But I've never been there and don't know where it is."

Rebecca, still blushing, pointed. "I-I think that raven can show us."

Above, a hovering black bird was waiting for them. The new Guard looked up and nodded, then followed through the bustling heart of the city to where the crow stopped at an impressive edifice labeled Athens Academy. The red sandstone building had appeared of a sudden, nestled impossibly among several less interesting lots. The multistoried construction was shuttered, clearly unoccupied by staff or students. It was, however, occupied by ghosts. And as the wide wooden doors opened for the six, these ghosts pointed the way toward an interior chapel, as if everything here had been waiting.

While the others walked ahead, Alexi lingered behind, studying what seemed to be a normal school, normal halls and stately foyers, hoping to find further clues. When he at last reached the chapel doors, the candles at the altar burst into flame. The ladies in the group gasped.

Alexi furrowed his brow. He was a young man of methods and proofs; such recent happenings defied the knowledge he'd already gleaned from a more definite world. He lifted his palm, and the candles extinguished. Seeing ghosts? Fire at his command? His frown deepened.

The bright white chapel was of simple décor, with a painted dove high above a plain altar. A hole formed in the air before them, first as a black point but growing into a rectangle. This dark portal opened with a sound like a piece of paper being torn, surely leading to a place more foreign than the children had ever seen. The group approached it in silence.

"This must be a sacred space for us alone," Michael

said quietly, peering into the void, seeing a staircase that led to a beckoning light below.

Alexi set his jaw, strode forward and descended the staircase. The others followed.

The room below was circular, lined with Corinthian pillars but blurred in the shadows, as if this were a place at the edge of time, a dream. There was a different bird depicted in stained glass over their heads, not a dove but something great and fiery. A feather was engraved in the stone below the glass, with an inscription.

Alexi read aloud: "'In darkness, a door. In bound souls, a circle of fire. Immortal force in mortal hearts. Six to calm the restless dead. Six to shield the restless living.'"

Immediately, a circle of blue-coloured fire leapt up around them. Everyone gasped except Alexi, who was looking curiously at the cerulean flame, wondering how on earth such a thing was possible. The fire remained in a perfect circle, at a height of a few inches, and gave off no heat.

"Alexi, look," Rebecca cried, pointing to his hands. He'd been contemplating the possible chemical compounds inherent to the fire, not noticing the licking tendrils of that same blue conflagration emanating from his own palms and trickling down to the circle.

Another ripping sound tore through the room, this one far greater, and at a new portal threshold there suddenly stood an indescribable woman. Alexi forgot the fire, and the fact that it was coming from his hands. He forgot his troubled, logical concerns. He could only stare at her, overtaken. His mind, body and heart exploded with new sensations.

She was tall and lithe, glowing with a light of power

and love, with features as perfect as a statue and hair that was golden. No; it was lustrous brown . . . no, rich red . . . She shifted from one hue to the next, maintaining her breathtaking beauty but seeming to be many colors at once. Diaphanous material wrapped her perfect body, sweeping layers and transitioning hues like the rest of her. Her eyes were crystalline lamps, sparkling and magnetic. There was no other answer than that she was a divine creature.

She spoke. Her voice held echoes of every element; an orchestra of stars.

"My beloveds. I've not much time, but I must inaugurate you, as I have done since your circle began the greatest of Work in ancient times. You won't remember those who came before. What's now inside has not overtaken you. It *heightens* you. You are heroes of your Age. The Guard picked you six because your mortal hearts are bold and strong.

"There has never been a more crucial time than in this century, in this city. Your mortal world is filled with new ideas, new science, new ideas on God, the body . . . and most importantly, spirits. There's never been such talk of spirits. And you are the ones who must respond."

She turned to Alexi, and he felt himself stop breathing. Her gemlike eyes filled with tears that became rubies, then emeralds, then sapphires as they coursed down her perfect cheeks and tinkled to the stone floor before vanishing. Unconsciously, Alexi reached out a hand to dry those tears, though she remained beyond his reach within her portal.

"Alexi, you are the leader here. Inside of you alone lives what's left of my true love, a winged being of power and light—the first Phoenix of ancient times.

Murdered by jealous Darkness, he was burned alive. His great power was splintered but not destroyed. This fire from your hands is your tool. It was the weapon used against you long ago, but now you control the element and are born again within it. My love lives on in you, worthy Alexi, and you will fight Darkness, bear the eternal flame of our vendetta."

She turned to the others, and breath stole back into Alexi's lungs.

"The power that inhabits the rest of you comes from great beings in those days—Muses, forces of Beauty that chose to follow the broken Phoenix as votaries, to keep chaotic Darkness from infiltrating this world. Together you are the new Guard, and this task is yours."

"The Guard?" Rebecca piped up nervously.

"That is what you will do: guard the living from the dead, whom you now see if cannot hear, wandering the earth. Your Grand Work is to maintain the balance between this world and the one beyond, beside. Darkness would like to run rampant over your great city and beyond, and will unless you silence his emissaries wherever they threaten. Hold fast, for the struggle will worsen. Darkness will seek to destroy the barrier pins between worlds for good. And to fight this, a Prophecy must be fulfilled. A seventh member will join you. She will come as your peer to create a new dawn."

Suddenly, she winced as if struck. Alexi rushed forward to protect or comfort the divine apparition, but she put out a hand that stopped him dead. She continued. "But you must understand that once the Seventh joins you, it will mean war."

The group couldn't help but shiver, even if they didn't understand.

"Who *are* you?" Alexi asked softly, unable to hide the yearning in his voice.

She smiled sadly. "I hope you will know her when she comes, Alexi, my love. And I hope she will know you, too. Await her, but beware. She will not come with answers but be lost, confused. I have put some protections in place, but she will be threatened and seeking refuge. There shall be tricks, betrayals and many second guesses. Caution, beloved. Mortal hearts make many mistakes. Choose your seventh carefully, for if you draw a false prophet to your bosom, the end of your world shall follow."

"A sign then—surely there will be a sign when she has come!" The boy named Michael couldn't hold back a string of desperate questions. "And when will she come? And how will we know how, and what, to fight?"

"You'll know how to fight the machinations of evil and the minions of Darkness by instincts within you. Nor will you always be fighting. You are *also* as you were; your mortal lives and thoughts remain unchanged, though they are augmented by the spirits of the past. Each of you has a specific talent you will bring."

She looked to Josephine, "The Artist," turned to Jane, "the Healer;" then to Rebecca, "the Intuition." Michael she named "the Heart," and Elijah, "the Memory." Then, finally, Alexi: "The Power."

"As for a sign when she has come—your seventh—look for a door." The divine beauty gestured to the portal in which she stood. "A door like this should be your gauge. But don't go in," she cautioned, glancing around her woefully. "You wouldn't want to come inside this place. And you'll see this threshold together, all of you, I'm sure, when it is time. As for when she will come, I cannot say. I'm powerful, but only the great Cosmos is omnipotent. Time is different here than in your world. And we are in uncharted waters. But she *will* be placed in your path. And once she is, you won't have much time—perhaps only two of your months. Then, a most terrible storm."

There was a disturbing sound from deep within the darkness behind the divine woman. She glanced back fearfully before turning again to the group.

"What is your name?" Alexi insisted, desperate to know more.

The apparition smiled sadly, and her glimmering eyes changed hue. "It hardly matters. We've had so many names over the years—all of us." She surveyed the group, and then her eyes rested once more on Alexi. "Please be careful. Especially you, my love. Caution. Listen to your instincts and stay together. A war is coming, and it isn't what you think. Hell isn't down, it's around us, pressing inward. And it will come for you. But *she* will be there when it does, or she will have died in vain."

"Died?" Alexi cried sharply.

The divine beauty smiled again; wisely, sadly. "One must die to live again." Then, after blowing a kiss to Alexi, she disappeared.

Their sacred space faded, returning the dazed group to the empty chapel. In overwhelmed silence, they filed out the back into a quiet London alley. The group looked at one another in alarm and wonder.

Wracked with emotions his person could not decipher, unable to face his new friends for the shame of his confusion, Alexi stalked off. Rebecca started off after him, even called his name, but he was gone. He went his separate way even though instinct urged him to remain with the company; there was something bitter in the air indicating their work must begin immediately. His temple throbbed. He wished to lock himself away and simply go back to his plans of pillaging the secrets of science.

And yet, a goddess had given him a task, told him he was a leader, and he couldn't deny her anything.

The new power coursing through him could not calm his inner tumult, and Alexi, so-called leader, retreated home alone. His first mistake. His head spinning and his heart pounding with a fierce desire he'd never experienced, transformed in one afternoon from boy to a powerful man craving an otherworldly woman, he returned to his family's grand estate.

He returned to chaos. It looked as if an angry hand had swept down and smote the entrance foyer and staircase. At the foot of the stair lay his elder sister, Alexandra, crumpled in a heap of taffeta skirts, her body twisted unnaturally. His grandmother, clutching her heart, all fine lace and severe looks, was bent over the girl.

He rushed forward. "Alexandra!" he murmured, scared to touch her body lest he somehow break it further. His sister was whimpering, staring from her grandmother to him alternately, helpless from the waist down, paralyzed.

"What happened?" he cried.

"Something terrible," his grandmother wheezed, in

a heavy Russian accent. "A force . . . Oh, I cannot describe. *Evil* swept through." And suddenly his grandmother's eyes grew bright. She had always had a frightening way of knowing things. "There's something different about you," she said softly, and then began speaking quickly in Russian: "The Firebird. That's it. There is a darkness coming, my boy. And you must light the darkness with your fire." Taking a shuddering breath, her head eased back against the wall. She did not breathe again.

Young Alexi Rychman felt the color drain from his face. Could he, with his new powers, have prevented this? Did failure mark the beginning of this new burden with which he'd been saddled?

It was all far too much for one day, too much for one young man who'd only ever sought scientific explanation, never the inexplicable. The first of many times to come, the terror of failing not only those he loved but the very world itself froze his heart. And, *he* was the leader? How could he lead when he couldn't even believe what he'd seen and heard?

Clearly he was yet a frail mortal, as were those left to him. The fight they had been promised would not be easy. He would need the help of that powerful stranger, that strange seventh—and then maybe his goddess would return.

Chapter One

London, England, 1888

A young woman, the likes of which London had never seen, alighted from a carriage near Bloomsbury and gazed at the grand facade before her. Breathless at the sight of the Romanesque fortress of red sandstone that was to be her new home, Miss Percy Parker ascended the front steps beneath the portico with a carpetbag in tow. One slender, gloved hand heaved open the great arched door of Athens Academy, and in the foyer beyond milled a few young men, papers and books in hand. Percy stepped into the diffuse light cast by a single chandelier, and hesitated.

The jaws of passing students fell in turn. What they saw as a petite, unmistakable apparition stood in the doorway. Most of her snow-white skin was hidden from view by a scarf draped around her head and bosom. Dark blue glasses kept eerie, ice blue eyes from unsettling every stare she nervously returned. Her trappings aside, only a mask could have hidden the ghostly pallor of Miss Parker's fine-featured face.

The sudden tinkling of a chandelier crystal broke the thick silence. Percy's gaze flickered up to behold a young man, equally pale as herself, floating amidst the gas flames. The transparent spirit wafted down to meet her. It was clear from the stares of the young men of solid mass, rudely focused on Percy, that they were oblivious to the ghost. She acknowledged the spirit only subtly, lest she be thought distract as well as deformed.

The schoolboy from another age spoke in a soft Scots brogue. "You'd best give up your pretensions, miss. You'll never be one of them. And you're certainly not one of us. What the devil are you, then?"

Percy met the spirit's hollow gaze. Behind her glasses, her opalescent eyes flared with defiance and she asked the room, her voice sweet and timid, "Could someone be so kind as to direct me towards the Headmistress's office?" When a gaping, living individual pointed to a hallway on her left, she offered him a, "Thank you, sir."

Eager to retreat from the curiosity, she burned with embarrassment. The only sounds that followed were the rustling layers of Miss Parker's sky blue taffeta skirts and the hurried echoes of her booted footfalls down the hall.

HEADMISTRESS THOMPSON was announced boldly in script across a large wooden door. Percy took a moment to catch her breath before knocking and holding it again.

She soon found herself in a small office filled to overflowing with books and files. A sharp voice bade her sit, and she was promptly engulfed in a leather armchair. Across the desk sat a severe woman dressed primly and buttoned tight in grey wool. Middle-aged and thin, she had a pinched nose and high cheekbones that gave her a birdlike quality. Tight lips twisted in a half frown. Brown hair was piled atop her head, save one misbehaving lock at her temple. Blue-grey eyes pierced Percy's obscuring glasses.

The woman wasted no time. "Miss Parker, we've received word that you're an uncommonly bright girl. I'm sure you're well aware that your previous governance, unsure what to do with you, supposed you'd best be sent somewhere else. Becoming a sister did not suit you, Miss Parker?"

Percy had no time to wonder if she was sardonic or understanding, for the Headmistress continued: "Your Reverend Mother made many inquiries before stumbling across our quiet little bastion. Considering your particular circumstances, I accepted you despite your age of eighteen. You're older than many who attend here. I'm sure I needn't tell you, Miss Parker, that at your age most women do not think it advantageous to remain *academic*. I hope you know enough of the world outside convent walls to understand this." Headmistress Thompson's sharp eyes suddenly softened and something mysterious twinkled there. "We must acknowledge the limitations of our world, Miss Parker. I, of course, chose to run an institution rather than a household," she stated, conspiratorial.

Percy couldn't help but smile, drawn in by the Headmistress's more amiable turn, as if she considered herself unique by lifestyle inasmuch as Percy was unique by fate. But the twinkle soon vanished. "We expect academic excellence in all subjects, Miss Parker. Your Reverend Mother proclaimed you quite proficient in several languages, with particularly keen knowledge of Latin, Hebrew and Greek. Would you consider yourself proficient?"

"I have no wish to flatter myself—"

"Honesty will suffice."

"I'm f-fluent in several tongues," Percy stammered. "I'm fondest of Greek. I know French, German, Spanish and Italian well. I dabble in Russian, Arabic, Gaelic . . . as well as a few ancient and obscure dialects."

"Interesting." The Headmistress absently tapped the desk with her pen. "Do you attribute your affinity for foreign tongues to mere interest and diligence?"

Percy thought a moment. "This may sound very strange . . ."

"It may shock you how little I find strange, Miss Parker," the Headmistress replied. "Go on."

The unexpected response emboldened Percy to continue. "Since childhood, certain things were innate. The moment I could read, I read in several languages as if they were native to me." She bit her lip. "I suppose that sounds rather mad."

There was a pause, yet to Percy's relief the Headmistress appeared unmoved. "Should you indeed prove such a linguist, and a well-rounded student, Athens may have ongoing work for you next year as an apprentice, Miss Parker."

"Oh!" Percy's face lit like a sunbeam. "I'd relish the opportunity! Thank you for your generous consideration, Headmistress."

"You were raised in the abbey, correct?"

"Yes, Headmistress."

"No immediate family?"

"None, Headmistress."

"Do you know anything of them? Is there a reason . . . ?"

Percy knew it was her skin that gave the woman pause. "I wish I could offer you an answer regarding my colour, Headmistress. It's always been a mystery. I know nothing of my father. I was told my mother was Irish."

"That is all you know?"

Percy shifted in her seat. "She died within the hour she brought me to the Sisters. Perhaps I was a traumatic birth. She told Reverend Mother that she brought me to the Institute of the Blessed Virgin Mary because the Blessed Virgin herself had come proclaiming the child she bore must be an educated woman. And so she left them with that dying wish." Percy looked away, surprised to find herself still willing to speak, despite the pain. "My mother said her purpose had been fulfilled, and, as if she were simply used up, she died."

"I see." Miss Thompson made a few notes. It was well that Percy did not expect pity or sentiment, for she was given neither. "Miss Parker, Athens is unique in that we recognize all qualities in our students. We've a Quaker model here at Athens. We champion the equality of the sexes and I happen to believe that learning is not bound in books alone. It is my personal practicc to ask our students if they believe they possess a gift. Other than your multiple languages, do you have any other particular talents?"

Percy swallowed hard. She was unprepared for this question. For anyone else it may have been a perfectly normal inquiry without giving the slightest cause for discomfort. But Percy knew she was far from average. "I have a rather strange manner of dreams."

The Headmistress blinked slowly. "We all dream, Miss Parker. That is nothing extraordinary."

"No. Of course not, Headmistress."

"Unless these dreams come more in the manner of visions?"

Percy hoped the flash of panic in her eyes remained hidden behind her tinted glasses. Years ago, when Reverend Mother found out about the visions and ghosts, she'd put aside her shock to caution Percy about speaking of such things. Neither was something the science-mad, rational world would celebrate. Percy knew her appearance was odd enough, let alone seeing the dead or having visions.

It was lonely to be so strange, and Percy wanted to confess everything she felt was wrong with her and have the Headmistress accept her. But she also recalled the horrible day when unburdening her soul had caused a priest to try to exorcise her best friend, a ghost named Gregory, from the convent courtyard. She'd never find anyone who could truly understand. Thus, she would not associate herself with the word "vision" and she would most certainly never again admit to seeing ghosts.

She cleared her throat. "Those who claim to have visions are either holy or madmen," she pronounced.

The Headmistress was clearly taken aback—as much as her patrician façade might indicate. She raised an eyebrow. "As a girl raised in a convent, do you not consider yourself a woman of religion?"

Percy shifted again. Miss Thompson had unwittingly touched upon a troubling topic. Percy could not help but wonder about her faith. Those in her abbey's order, the oldest of its kind existing in England, had withstood innumerable trials under the Empire.

Every novice and sister took fierce pride in their resilience and that of their elders. But Percy, a girl who kept to herself and was left to herself, felt out of place, the colorless curiosity of her skin notwithstanding; her restless disposition had difficulty acquiescing to the rigours of the cloth. Only the presence of a spirit out of its time—such as her Elizabethan-era Gregory—had made her feel at home. Doctrine could not explain the world as Percy knew it. An unsettling sense of fate made her ache in ways prayer could not wholly relieve. Here, outside the convent, she hoped for answers. The scientific bent of the era, in addition to the general English mistrust of Catholicism, was advantageous to her religious vagaries.

But as none of this was appropriate to discuss in present circumstances, Percy debated a proper reply. "I am a woman of . . . *spirit*, Headmistress. By no means would I commend myself holy. And I'd like to think I'm not mad."

The raucous shriek of a bird came close to Miss Thompson's window. The sound made Percy jump. A raven settled on the ledge outside. Percy couldn't help but notice an oddly coloured patch on the large black bird's breast. Percy didn't stare further, lest she seem easily distracted. She waited for Headmistress Thompson's gaze to pin her again, which it soon did.

"Dreams then, Miss Parker?"

"Yes, Headmistress. Just dreams."

The Headmistress scribbled a note and frowned curiously at an unopened envelope in Percy's file before placing it carefully at the back of the folder. Before Percy could wonder about it, the Headmistress continued. "We have no dream study, Miss Parker. A girl like you doesn't have many options, and so I would advise you to make the most of your time here. It seems fitting your focus should be Languages, however you must maintain high marks in all courses in order to continue at the Academy. Do you have other interests, Miss Parker?"

"Art has always been a great love of mine," Percy stated eagerly. "I used to paint watercolors for the parish. I also adore Shakespeare."

A scrawl into her file. "Dislikes?"

"I'm afraid the sciences and mathematics are beyond me. Neither were subjects the convent felt necessary for young ladies."

The Headmistress loosed a dry chuckle that made Percy uneasy. "There is no escaping at least one mathematics or science sequence. I am placing you in our Mathematics and Alchemical Study."

Percy held back a grimace. The class sounded terrifying. "Certainly, Headmistress."

Miss Thompson cleared her throat and leveled a stern gaze at her. "And now, Miss Parker, I must warn you of the dangers of our unique, coeducational institution. There is to be no—and I repeat, *no*—contact between members of the opposite sex. Not of your peer group, and most certainly not with your teachers! The least infraction, however innocent it may seem—the holding of a hand, the kiss on a cheek—will cause immediate dismissal. You must understand our position. Any word of fraternization or scandal will doom our revolutionary program. And while I hardly think any of this would become an issue for you in particular, Miss Parker, I must say it nonetheless."

Percy nodded, at first proud that the Headmistress should think so highly of her virtue; then came the sting as she realized the Headmistress meant her looks would garner no such furtive conduct. Worse, Percy was sure she was right.

"Classes begin Monday. Here is a schedule and key for Athene Hall, room seven."

As Percy took the papers and key, she was gripped by a thrill. "Thank you so very much, Miss Thompson! I cannot thank you enough for the opportunity to be here."

The Headmistress maintained a blank, severe stare. "Do not thank me. Do not fail."

"I promise to do my best, Headmistress!"

"If it may be of any interest to you, a meditative Quaker service is held Sundays. You'll find none of your Catholic frills here. But indeed, Miss Parker, the school keeps quiet about all of that, as I am sure you may well do yourself, living in intolerant times."

"Yes, Headmistress."

"Good day, Miss Parker—and welcome to Athens."

"Thank you, Headmistress. Good day!" Percy beamed, and she darted out the door to explore her new home.

Inside the office, Headmistress Rebecca Thompson stared at the door, feeling the strange murmur in her veins that was part of her intuitive gift. Her instincts were never clarion, but they alerted her when something was of import. Miss Parker, her gentle nature evident in the sweet timbre of her voice, had set off a signal. Rebecca now thought about the envelope in her file, "Please open upon Miss Parker's graduation—or when she has been provided for," the envelope read.

"I daresay a girl like you won't find yourself 'provided for,' Miss Parker," she muttered, turning to the window.

She opened the casement, and the raven outside hopped in and began strutting over the wooden file cabinets, occasionally stopping to preen his one bright blue breast feather that indicated his service to The Guard.

"It's odd, Frederic," she remarked to the bird. "I can't imagine that awkward, unfortunate girl could have something to do with us; it doesn't follow. It *shouldn't* follow."

As youths, when The Guard made choices about their mortal professions, it was agreed that a few of them should remain near the chapel and portal of The Grand Work on the fortresslike grounds of Athens. Rebecca and Alexi were the perfect candidates for academia, and for twenty years now had been set upon that path. But the two agreed to never bring The Grand Work upon their students. The chapel aside, Athens was a place where Alexi and Rebecca were known by their students as nothing other than upstanding Victorian citizens providing for the intellectual improvement of the young men and women of London. Athens was the one place where it seemed they controlled destiny, rather than destiny controlling them. And they had fought to keep it that way.

Yes, the secrets of The Grand Work were matters for the world *beyond* the school walls. Their prophetic seventh had been named a peer, and that meant these students were not subjects of scrutiny. No, while Miss Parker did not appear a "normal" girl, and though she happened to spark interest, she was likely nothing more than a child deserving a solid, Academy education.

The Headmistress sighed, easing into her chair as Frederic hopped up on her shoulder. She thought about asking Alexi to come for tea, but she sadly assumed he was steeped, as usual, in solitude, frowning over texts of scholarship, his favorite companions. As predicted, their personalities and desires had not changed when the six great spirits entered her and her friends. Still, their lives revolved around their duty, a reality that Rebecca resented more with each passing year. Privately she wished those spirits *had* taken her heart when they arrived, for it was a terribly lonely destiny, and even their Grand Work couldn't change that.

ELISSA WILDS

". . . Fun, fascinating and unforgettable."
—*New York Times* and *USA Today*
Bestselling Author Julie Leto

He is a god, and he embodies everything the word implies. Everything. That makes Aurora a very lucky woman. Because Mobius wants *her*—not for her ability to neutralize the dark forces of the Umbrae, or for her kick-butt approach to the Finders wreaking havoc all over Earth. No, he wants to protect her, to harmonize their separate energies, to show her exactly what it means to be perfectly attuned to another being.

In a realm where creating a sexy little red dress is as simple as thinking it, the mind is the most powerful tool of all. And Aurora will use hers to tantalize her lover, outwit their enemies and defeat the . . .

DARKNESS RISING

"A winning and creative story that fans of the magical will not want to miss."
—Romance Reviews Today on *Between Light and Dark*

ISBN 13: 978-0-505-52792-9

Leanna Renee Hieber

What fortune awaited sweet, timid Percy Parker at Athens Academy? Hidden in the dark heart of Victorian London, the Romanesque school was dreadfully imposing, a veritable fortress, and little could Percy guess what lay inside. She had never met its powerful and mysterious Professor Alexi Rychman, knew nothing of the growing shadows, of the Ripper and other supernatural terrors against which his coterie stood guard. She saw simply that she was different, haunted, with her snow white hair, pearlescent skin and uncanny gift. This arched stone doorway was a portal to a new life, to an education far from what could be had at a convent—and it was an invitation to an intimate yet dangerous dance at the threshold of life and death . . . .

The Strangely Beautiful Tale of Miss Percy Parker

"Tender, poignant, exquisitely written."
—C. L. Wilson, *New York Times* Bestselling Author

ISBN 13: 978-0-8439-6296-3

Marjorie Liu

Long ago, shape-shifters were plentiful, soaring through the sky as crows, racing across African veldts as cheetahs, raging furious as dragons atop the Himalayas. Like gods, they reigned supreme. But even gods have laws, and those laws, when broken, destroy.

Zoufalství. Epätoivo. Asa. Three words in three very different languages, and yet Soria understands. Like all members of Dirk & Steele, she has a gift, and hers is communication: That was why she was chosen to address the stranger. Strong as a lion, quick as a serpent, Karr is his name, and in his day he was king. But he is a son of strife, a creature of tragedy. As fire consumed all he loved, so an icy sleep has been his atonement. Now, against his will, he has awoken. *Zoufalství. Epätoivo. Asa.* In English, the word is despair. But Soria knows the words for love.

ISBN 13: 978-0-8439-5940-6

NINA BANGS

"No one combines humor and sex in quite the way Nina Bangs does."

—*RT Book Reviews*

The Castle of Dark Dreams is just part of an adult theme park, right? The most decadent attraction in a place where people go to play out their wildest erotic fantasies. Holgarth isn't really a wacky wizard, and Sparkle Stardust doesn't actually create cosmic chaos by hooking up completely mismatched couples. And that naked guy chained up in the dungeon? No way he's a *vampire.*

Wrong . . . dead wrong, as botanist Cinn Airmid is about to find out. It's up to her to save the night feeder's sanity, but to do that she'll have to get close to the most dangerously sexy male she's ever encountered. And one look in Dacian's haunted black eyes tells her close will take on a whole new meaning with someone who's had 600 years to practice his technique. Even a girl with a name that conjures up images of forbidden pleasure has a few tricks to learn from . . .

My Wicked Vampire

ISBN 13: 978-0-8439-5955-0